The Thief's Journal

OTHER WORKS BY JEAN GENET
Published by Grove Weidenfeld

The Balcony
The Blacks
Funeral Rites
The Maids *and* Deathwatch
The Miracle of the Rose
Our Lady of the Flowers
Querelle
The Screens

The Thief's Journal
by Jean Genet

FOREWORD BY JEAN-PAUL SARTRE

TRANSLATED FROM THE FRENCH BY
BERNARD FRECHTMAN

GROVE WEIDENFELD
NEW YORK

Published by Grove Weidenfeld
A division of Grove Press, Inc.
841 Broadway
New York, NY 10003-4793

Originally published by *Librairie Gallimard* in Paris,
France, under the title *Journal du Voleur*, copyright © 1949
by *Librairie Gallimard*.

Library of Congress Cataloging-in-Publication Data

    Genet, Jean, 1910–
    The thief's journal.

    Translation of: Journal du voleur.
    I. Title
PQ2613.E53J613   1987   843'.912   87-12095
ISBN 0-8021-3014-3

Manufactured in the United States of America

Printed on acid-free paper

First Grove Press Edition 1964
First Black Cat Edition 1973
First Evergreen Edition 1987

10 9 8 7 6 5 4 3 2

à SARTRE
au CASTOR

FOREWORD

Not all who would be are Narcissus. Many who lean over the water see only a vague human figure. Genet sees himself everywhere; the dullest surfaces reflect his image; even in others he perceives himself, thereby bringing to light their deepest secrets. The disturbing theme of the double, the image, the counterpart, the enemy brother, is found in all his works.

Each of them has the strange property of being both itself and the reflection of itself. Genet brings before us a dense and teeming throng which intrigues us, transports us and changes into Genet beneath Genet's gaze. Hitler appears, talks, lives; he removes his mask: it was Genet. But the little servant girl with the swollen feet who meanwhile was burying her child—that was Genet too. In *The Thief's Journal* the myth of the double has assumed its most reassuring, most common, most *natural* form. Here Genet speaks of Genet without intermediary. He talks of his life, of his wretchedness and glory, of his loves; he tells the story of his thoughts. One might think that, like Montaigne, he is going to draw a good-humored and familiar self portrait. But Genet is never familiar, even with himself. He does, to be sure, tell us everything. The whole truth, nothing but the truth, but is it the sacred truth. He opens up one of his myths; he tells us: "You're going to see what stuff it's made of," and we find another myth. He reassures us only to disturb us further. His autobiography is *not* an autobiography; it merely seems like one; it is a sacred cosmogony. His stories *are not* stories. They excite you and fascinate you; you think he is relating *facts* and suddenly you realize he is describing rites. If he talks of the wretched beggars of the Barrio Chino, it is only to debate, in lordly style, questions of precedence and etiquette; he is the Saint-Simon of this Court of Miracles. His memories *are not* memories; they are exact but sacred; he speaks about his life like an evangelist, as a wonder-struck witness. When Edouard, the novelist in Gide's *The Counterfeiters,* writes the journal of his novel, he is no longer fictitious. But Genet the novelist, speaking of Genet the thief, is more of a thief than the thief; the thief and his double are alike sacred. Thus there comes into being that new object: a mythology of the myth (like the blues song that was called *The Birth of the Blues*); behind the first-degree myths—The Thief, Murder, the Beggar, the Homosexual—we discover the reflective myths: the Poet, the Saint, the Double, Art. Nothing but myths, then; a Genet with a Genet stuffing, like the prunes of Tours. If, however, you are able to see at the seam the thin line separating the enveloping myth from the enveloped myth, you will discover the truth, which is terrifying. That is why I do not fear to call this book, the most beautiful that Genet has written, the *Dichtung und Wahrheit* of homosexuality.

Jean-Paul Sartre

Convicts' garb is striped pink and white. Though it was at my heart's bidding that I chose the universe wherein I delight, I at least have the power of finding therein the many meanings I wish to find: *there is a close relationship between flowers and convicts.* The fragility and delicacy of the former are of the same nature as the brutal insensitivity of the latter.[1] Should I have to portray a convict—or a criminal—I shall so bedeck him with flowers that, as he disappears beneath them, he will himself become a flower, a gigantic and new one. Toward what is known as evil, I lovingly pursued an adventure which led me to prison. Though they may not always be handsome, men doomed to evil possess the manly virtues. Of their own volition, or owing to an accident which has been chosen for them, they plunge lucidly and without complaining into a reproachful, ignominious element, like that into which love, if it is profound, hurls human beings. Erotic play discloses a nameless world which is revealed by the nocturnal language of lovers. Such language is not written down. It is whispered into the ear at night in a hoarse voice. At dawn it is forgotten. Repudiating the virtues of your world, criminals hopelessly

---

[1] My excitement is the oscillation from one to the other.

agree to organize a forbidden universe. They agree to
live in it. The air there is nauseating: they can breathe
it. But—criminals are remote from you—as in love, they
turn away and turn me away from the world and its
laws. Theirs smells of sweat, sperm, and blood. In short,
to my body and my thirsty soul it offers devotion. It was
because their world contains these erotic conditions that
I was bent on evil. My adventure, never governed by
rebellion or a feeling of injustice, will be merely one
long mating, burdened and complicated by a heavy,
strange, erotic ceremonial (figurative ceremonies leading
to jail and anticipating it). Though it be the sanction,
in my eyes the justification too, of the foulest crime, it
will be the sign of the most utter degradation. That
ultimate point to which the censure of men leads was
to appear to me the ideal place for the purest, that is,
the most turbid amatory harmony, where illustrious ash-
weddings are celebrated. Desiring to hymn them, I use
what is offered me by the form of the most exquisite
natural sensibility, which is already aroused by the garb
of convicts. The material evokes, both by its colors and
roughness, certain flowers whose petals are slightly fuzzy,
which detail is sufficient for me to associate the idea of
strength and shame with what is most naturally precious
and fragile. This association, which tells me things about
myself, would not suggest itself to another mind; mine
cannot avoid it. Thus I offered my tenderness to the
convicts; I wanted to call them by charming names, to
designate their crimes with, for modesty's sake, the
subtlest metaphor (beneath which veil I would not have
been unaware of the murderer's rich muscularity, of the
violence of his sexual organ). Is it not by the following
image that I prefer to imagine them in Guiana: the
strongest, with a horn, the "hardest," veiled by mosquito
netting? And each flower within me leaves behind so

solemn a sadness that all of them must signify sorrow,
death. Thus I sought love as it pertained to the penal
colony. Each of my passions led me to hope for it, gave
me a glimpse of it, offers me criminals, offers me to
them or impels me to crime. As I write this book, the
last convicts are returning to France. The newspapers
have been reporting the matter. The heir of kings feels
a like emptiness if the republic deprives him of his
anointment. The end of the penal colony prevents us
from attaining with our living minds the mythical underground regions. Our most dramatic movement has been
clipped away: our exodus, the embarkation, the procession on the sea, which was performed with bowed head.
The return, this same procession in reverse, is without
meaning. Within me, the destruction of the colony corresponds to a kind of punishment of punishment: I am
castrated, I am shorn of my infamy. Unconcerned about
beheading our dreams of their glories, they awaken us
prematurely. The home prisons have their power: it is
not the same. It is minor. It has none of that elegant,
slightly bowed grace. The atmosphere there is so heavy
that you have to drag yourself about. You creep along.
The home prisons are more stiffly erect, more darkly and
severely; the slow, solemn agony of the penal colony was
a more perfect blossoming of abjection.[1] So that now the
home jails, bloated with evil males, are black with them,
as with blood that has been shot through with carbonic
gas. (I have written "black." The outfit of the convicts—
captives, captivity, even prisoners, words too noble to
name us—forces the word upon me: the outfit is made of

---

[1] Its abolition is so great a loss to me that I secretly recompose,
within me and for myself alone, a colony more vicious than that of
Guiana. I add that the home prisons can be said to be "in the
shade." The colony is in the sun. Everything transpires there in a
cruel light which I cannot refrain from choosing as a sign of lucidity.

brown homespun.) It is toward them that my desire will turn. I am aware that there is often a semblance of the burlesque in the colony or in prison. On the bulky, resonant base of their wooden shoes, the frame of the condemned men is always somewhat shaky. In front of a wheelbarrow, it suddenly breaks up stupidly. In the presence of a guard they bow their heads and hold in their hands the big straw sun bonnet—which the younger ones decorate (I should prefer it so) with a stolen rose granted by the guard—or a brown homespun beret. They strike poses of wretched humility. If they are beaten, something within them must nevertheless stiffen: the coward, the sneak, cowardice, sneakiness are—when kept in a state of the hardest, purest cowardice and sneakiness—hardened by a "dousing," as soft iron is hardened by dousing. They persist in servility, despite everything. Though I do not neglect the deformed and misshapen, it is the handsomest criminals whom my tenderness adorns.

Crime, I said to myself, had a long wait before producing such perfect successes as Pilorge and Angel Sun. In order to finish them off (the term is a cruel one!) it was necessary for a host of coincidences to concur: to the beauty of their faces, to the strength and elegance of their bodies there had to be added their taste for crime, the circumstances which make the criminal, the moral vigor capable of accepting such a destiny, and, finally, punishment, its cruelty, the intrinsic quality which enables a criminal to glory in it, and, over all of this, areas of darkness. If the hero join combat with night and conquer it, may shreds of it remain upon him! The same hesitation, the same crystallization of happy circumstances governs the success of a pure sleuth. I cherish them both. But if I love their crime, it is for the punishment it involves, "the penalty" (for I cannot suppose that they have not anticipated it. One of them, the former boxer Ledoux, answered the inspectors smilingly: "My crimes? It's before committing them that I might have regretted them") in which I want to accompany them so that, come what may, my love may be filled to overflowing.

I do not want to conceal in this journal the other reasons which made me a thief, the simplest being the need to eat, though revolt, bitterness, anger or any similar sentiment never entered into my choice. With fanatical care, "jealous care," I prepared for my adventure as one arranges a couch or a room for love; I was *hot* for crime.

I give the name violence to a boldness lying idle and enamoured of danger. It can be seen in a look, a walk, a smile, and it is in you that it creates an eddying. It unnerves you. This violence is a calm that disturbs you. One sometimes says: "A guy with class!" Pilorge's delicate features were of an extreme violence. Their delicacy in particular was violent. Violence of the design of Stilitano's only hand, simply lying on the table, still, rendering the repose disturbing and dangerous. I have worked with thieves and pimps whose authority bent me to their will, but few proved to be really bold, whereas the one who was most so—Guy—was without violence. Stilitano, Pilorge and Michaelis were cowards. Java too. Even when at rest, motionless and smiling, there escaped from them through the eyes, the nostrils, the mouth, the palm of the hand, the bulging basket, through that brutal hillock of the calf under the wool or denim, a radiant and somber anger, visible as a haze.

But, almost always, there is nothing to indicate it, save the absence of the usual signs. René's face is charming at first. The downward curve of his nose gives him a roguish look, though the somewhat leaden paleness of his anxious face makes you uneasy. His eyes are hard, his movements calm and sure. In the cans he calmly beats up the queers; he frisks them, robs them, sometimes, as a finishing touch, he kicks them in the kisser with his heel. I don't like him, but his calmness masters me. He operates, in the dead of night, around the urinals, the lawns, the shrubbery, under the trees on the Champs-Elysées, near the stations, at the Porte Maillot, in the Bois de Boulogne (always at night) with a seriousness from which romanticism is excluded. When he comes in, at two or three in the morning, I feel him stocked with adventures. Every part of his body, which is nocturnal, has been involved: his hands, his arms, his legs, the back of his neck. But he, unaware of these marvels, tells me about them in forthright language. From his pockets he takes rings, wedding bands, watches, the evening's loot. He puts them in a big glass which will soon be full. He is not surprised by queers or their ways, which merely facilitate his jobs. When he sits on my bed, my ear snatches at scraps of adventure: An officer in underwear whose wallet[1] he steals and who, pointing with his forefinger, orders: "Get out!" René-the-wise-guy's answer: "You think you're in the army?" Too hard a punch on an old man's skull. The one who fainted when René, who was all excited, opened a drawer in which there was a supply of phials of morphine. The queer who was broke and whom he made get down on his knees before him. I am attentive to these accounts. My Antwerp life grows stronger, carrying on in a firmer body, in accordance with manly methods. I encourage René, I give him advice, he listens to me. I tell him never to talk first. "Let the guy come up to you, keep him dangling. Act a little surprised when he suggests that you do it. Figure out who to act dumb with."

Every night I get a few scraps of information. My imagination does not get lost in them. My excitement seems to be due to my assuming within me the role of

---

[1] He says: "I did his wallet."

both victim and criminal. Indeed, as a matter of fact, I emit, I project at night the victim and criminal born of me; I bring them together somewhere, and toward morning I am thrilled to learn that the victim came very close to getting the death penalty and the criminal to being sent to the colony or guillotined. Thus my excitement extends as far as that region of myself, which is Guiana.

Without their wishing it, the gestures and destinies of these men are stormy. Their soul endures a violence which it had not desired and which it has domesticated. Those whose usual climate is violence are simple in relation to themselves. Each of the movements which make up this swift and devastating life is simple and straight, as clean as the stroke of a great draftsman—but when these strokes are encountered in movement, then the storm breaks, the lightning that kills them or me. Yet, what is their violence compared to mine, which was to accept theirs, to make it mine, to wish it for myself, to intercept it, to utilize it, to force it upon myself, to know it, to premeditate it, to discern and assume its perils? But what was mine, willed and necessary for my defense, my toughness, my rigor, compared to the violence they underwent like a malediction, risen from an inner fire simultaneously with an outer light which sets them ablaze and illuminates us? We know that their adventures are childish. They themselves are fools. They are ready to kill or be killed over a card game in which an opponent— or they themselves—was cheating. Yet, thanks to such guys, tragedies are possible.

This kind of definition—by so many opposing examples —of violence shows you that I shall not make use of words the better to depict an event or its hero, but so that they may tell you something about myself. In order to understand me, the reader's complicity will be necessary. Nevertheless, I shall warn him whenever my lyricism makes me lose my footing.

Stilitano was big and strong. His gait was both supple and heavy, brisk and slow, sinuous; he was nimble. A large part of his power over me—and over the whores of the Barrio Chino—lay in the spittle he passed from one cheek to the other and which he would sometimes draw out in front of his mouth like a veil. "But where does he get that spit," I would ask myself, "where does he bring it up from? Mine will never have the unctuousness or color of his. It will merely be spun glassware, transparent and fragile." It was therefore natural for me to imagine what his penis would be if he smeared it for my benefit with so fine a substance, with that precious cobweb, a tissue which I secretly called the veil of the palace. He wore an old gray cap with a broken visor. When he tossed it on the floor of our room, it suddenly became the carcass of a poor partridge with a clipped wing, but when he put it on, pulling it down a bit over the ear, the opposite edge of the visor rose up to reveal the most glorious of blond locks. Shall I speak of his lovely bright eyes, modestly lowered—yet it could be said of Stilitano: "His bearing is immodest"—over which there closed eyelids and lashes so blond, so luminous and thick, that they brought in not the shade of evening but the shade of evil. After all, what meaning would there be in the sight that staggers me when, in a harbor, I see a sail, little by little, by fits and starts, spreading out and with difficulty rising on the mast of a ship, hesitantly at first, then resolutely, if these movements were not the very symbol of the movements of my love for Stilitano? I met him in Barcelona. He was living among beggars, thieves, fairies and whores. He was handsome, but it remains to be seen whether he owed all that beauty to my fallen state. My clothes were dirty and shabby. I was hungry and cold. This was the most miserable period of my life.

1932.   Spain at the time was covered with vermin, its beggars. They went from village to village, to Andalusia because it is warm, to Catalonia because it is rich, but the whole country was favorable to us. I was thus a louse, and conscious of being one. In Barcelona we hung around the Calle Mediodia and the Calle Carmen. We sometimes slept six in a bed without sheets, and at dawn we would go begging in the markets. We would leave the Barrio Chino in a group and scatter over the Parallelo, carrying shopping baskets, for the housewives would give us a leek or turnip rather than a coin. At noon we would return, and with the gleanings we would make our soup. It is the life of vermin that I am going to describe. In Barcelona I saw male couples in which the more loving of the two would say to the other:

"I'll take the basket this morning."

He would take it and leave. One day Salvador gently pulled the basket from my hands and said, "I'm going to beg for you."

It was snowing. He went out into the freezing street, wearing a torn and tattered jacket—the pockets were ripped and hung down—and a shirt stiff with dirt. His face was poor and unhappy, shifty, pale, and filthy, for we dared not wash since it was so cold. Around noon, he returned with the vegetables and a bit of fat. Here I draw attention to one of those lacerations—horrible, for I shall provoke them despite the danger—by which beauty was revealed to me. An immense—and brotherly—love swelled my body and bore me toward Salvador. Leaving the hotel shortly after him, I would see him a way off beseeching the women. I knew the formula, as I had already begged for others and myself: it mixes Christian religion with charity; it merges the poor person with God; it is so humble an emanation from the heart that I think it scents with violet the straight, light breath of the beggar who utters it. All over Spain at the time they were saying:

"Por Dios."

Without hearing him, I would imagine Salvador murmuring it at all the stalls, to all the housewives. I would keep an eye on him as the pimp keeps an eye on his whore, but with such tenderness in my heart! Thus, Spain and my life as a beggar familiarized me with the stateliness of abjection, for it took a great deal of pride (that is, of love) to embellish those filthy, despised creatures. It took a great deal of talent, which came to me little by little. Though I may be unable to describe its mechanism to you, at least I can say that I slowly forced myself to consider that wretched life as a deliberate necessity. Never did I try to make of it something other than what it was, I did not try to adorn it, to mask it, but, on the contrary, I wanted to affirm it in its exact sordidness, and the most sordid signs became for me signs of grandeur.

I was dismayed when, one evening, while searching me after a raid—I am speaking of a scene which preceded the one with which this book begins—the astonished detective took from my pocket, among other things, a tube of vaseline. We dared joke about it since it contained mentholated vaseline. The whole record office, and I too, though painfully, writhed with laughter at the following:

"You take it in the nose?"

"Watch out you don't catch cold. You'd give your guy whooping cough."

I translate but lamely, in the language of a Paris hustler, the malicious irony of the vivid and venomous Spanish phrases. It concerned a tube of vaseline, one of whose ends was partially rolled up. Which amounts to saying

that it had been put to use. Amidst the elegant objects
taken from the pockets of the men who had been picked
up in the raid, it was the very sign of abjection, of that
which is concealed with the greatest of care, but yet the
sign of a secret grace which was soon to save me from
contempt. When I was locked up in a cell, and as soon as
I had sufficiently regained my spirits to rise above the
misfortune of my arrest, the image of the tube of vaseline never left me. The policemen had shown it to me
victoriously, since they could thereby flourish their revenge, their hatred, their contempt. But lo and behold!
that dirty, wretched object whose purpose seemed to the
world—to that concentrated delegation of the world which
is the police and, above all, that particular gathering of
Spanish police, smelling of garlic, sweat and oil, but sub-
stantial looking, stout of muscle and strong in their moral
assurance—utterly vile, became extremely precious to me.
Unlike many objects which my tenderness singles out,
this one was not at all haloed; it remained on the table
a little gray leaden tube of vaseline, broken and livid,
whose astonishing discreteness, and its essential corre-
spondence with all the commonplace things in the record
office of a prison (the bench, the inkwell, the regulations,
the scales, the odor), would, through the general indifference, have distressed me, had not the very content of
the tube made me think, by bringing to mind an oil lamp
(perhaps because of its unctuous character), of a night
light beside a coffin.

In describing it, I recreate the little object, but the
following image cuts in: beneath a lamppost, in a street
of the city where I am writing, the pallid face of a little
old woman, a round, flat little face, like the moon, very
pale; I cannot tell whether it was sad or hypocritical. She
approached me, told me she was very poor and asked for

a little money. The gentleness of that moon-fish face told me at once: the old woman had just got out of prison.

"She's a thief," I said to myself. As I walked away from her, a kind of intense reverie, living deep within me and not at the edge of my mind, led me to think that it was perhaps my mother whom I had just met. I know nothing of her who abandoned me in the cradle, but I hoped it was that old thief who begged at night.

"What if it were she?" I thought as I walked away from the old woman. Oh! if it were, I would cover her with flowers, with gladioluses and roses, and with kisses! I would weep with tenderness over those moon-fish eyes, over that round, foolish face! "And why," I went on, "why weep over it?" It did not take my mind long to replace these customary marks of tenderness by some other gesture, even the vilest and most contemptible, which I empowered to mean as much as the kisses, or the tears, or the flowers.

"I'd be glad to slobber over her," I thought, overflowing with love. (Does the word *glaïeul* [gladiolus] mentioned above bring into play the word *glaviaux* [gobs of spit]?) To slobber over her hair or vomit into her hands. But I would adore that thief who is my mother.

The tube of vaseline, which was intended to grease my prick and those of my lovers, summoned up the face of her who, during a reverie that moved through the dark alleys of the city, was the most cherished of mothers. It had served me in the preparation of so many secret joys, in places worthy of its discrete banality, that it had become the condition of my happiness, as my sperm-spotted handkerchief testified. Lying on the table, it was a banner telling the invisible legions of my triumph over the police. I was in a cell. I knew that all night long my tube of vaseline would be exposed to the scorn—the contrary of a Perpetual Adoration—of a group of strong, handsome, husky policemen. So strong that if the weakest of them barely squeezed his fingers together, there would shoot forth, first with a slight fart, brief and dirty, a ribbon of gum which would continue to emerge in a ridiculous silence. Nevertheless, I was sure that this puny and most humble object would hold its own against them; by its mere presence it would be able to exasperate all the police in the world; it would draw down upon itself contempt, hatred, white and dumb rages. It would perhaps be slightly bantering—like a tragic hero amused at stirring up the wrath of the gods—indestructible, like him, faithful to my happiness, and proud. I would like to hymn it with the newest words in the French language. But I would have also liked to fight for it, to organize massacres in its honor and bedeck a countryside at twilight with red bunting.[1]

The beauty of a moral act depends on the beauty of its expression. To say that it is beautiful is to decide that it will be so. It remains to be proven so. This is the task of images, that is, of the correspondences with the splendors of the physical world. The act is beautiful if it provokes, and in our throat reveals, song. Sometimes the consciousness with which we have pondered a reputedly vile act, the power of expression which must signify it, impel us to song. This means that treachery is beautiful if it makes us sing. To betray thieves would be not only to find myself again in the moral world, I thought, but also to find myself once more in homosexuality. As I grow strong, I am my own god. I dictate. Applied to men, the word beauty indicates to me the harmonious quality of a face and body to which is sometimes added manly grace. Beauty is then accompanied by magnificent, mas-

---

[1] I would indeed rather have shed blood than repudiate that silly object.

terly, sovereign gestures. We imagine that they are determined by very special moral attitudes, and by the
cultivation of such virtues in ourselves we hope to endow
our poor faces and sick bodies with the vigor that our
lovers possess naturally. Alas, these virtues, which they
themselves never possess, are our weakness.

Now as I write, I muse on my lovers. I would like them
to be smeared with my vaseline, with that soft, slightly
mentholated substance; I would like their muscles to
bathe in that delicate transparence without which the
tool of the handsomest is less lovely.

When a limb has been removed, the remaining one is
said to grow stronger. I had hoped that the vigor of the
arm which Stilitano had lost might be concentrated in
his penis. For a long time I imagined a solid member,
like a blackjack, capable of the most outrageous impudence, though what first intrigued me was what Stilitano
allowed me to know of it: the mere crease, though curi-
ously precise in the left leg, of his blue denim trousers.
This detail might have haunted my dreams less had
Stilitano not, at odd moments, put his left hand on it,
and had he not, like ladies making a curtsey, indicated
the crease by delicately pinching the cloth with his nails.
I do not think he ever lost his self-possession, but with
me he was particularly calm. With a slightly impertinent
smile, though quite nonchalantly, he would watch me
adore him. I know that he will love me.

Before Salvador, basket in hand, crossed the threshold
of our hotel, I was so excited that I kissed him in the
street, but he pushed me aside:
"You're crazy! People'll take us for mariconas!"
He spoke French fairly well, having learned it in the
region around Perpignan where he used to go for the
grape harvesting. Deeply wounded, I turned away. His

face was purple. His complexion was that of winter cab-
bage. Salvador did not smile. He was shocked. "That's
what I get," he must have thought, "for getting up so
early to go begging in the snow. He doesn't know how
to behave." His hair was wet and shaggy. Behind the
window, faces were staring at us, for the lower part of
the hotel was occupied by a café that opened on the
street and through which you had to pass in order to go
up to the rooms. Salvador wiped his face with his sleeve
and went in. I hesitated. Then I followed. I was twenty
years old. If the drop that hesitates at the edge of a
nostril has the limpidity of a tear, why shouldn't I drink
it with the same eagerness? I was already sufficiently involved in the rehabilitation of the ignoble. Were it not
for fear of revolting Salvador, I would have done it in
the café. He, however, sniffled, and I gathered that he
was swallowing his snot. Basket in arm, passing the beggars and the guttersnipes, he moved toward the kitchen.
He preceded me.

"What's the matter with you?" I said.

"You're attracting attention."

"What's wrong?"

"People don't kiss that way on the sidewalk. Tonight,
if you like . . ."

He said it all with a charmless pout and the same disdain. I had simply wanted to show my gratitude, to warm
him with my poor tenderness.

"But what were you thinking?"

Someone bumped into him without apologizing, separating him from me. I did not follow him to the kitchen.
I went over to a bench where there was a vacant seat
near the stove. Though I adored vigorous beauty, I didn't
bother my head much about how I would bring myself
to love this homely, squalid beggar who was bullied by
the less bold, how I would come to care for his angular

buttocks . . . and what if, unfortunately, he were to have a magnificent tool?

The Barrio Chino was, at the time, a kind of haunt thronged less with Spaniards than with foreigners, all of them down-and-out bums. We were sometimes dressed in almond-green or jonquil-yellow silk shirts and shabby sneakers, and our hair was so plastered down that it looked as if it would crack. We did not have leaders but rather directors. I am unable to explain how they became what they were. Probably it was as a result of profitable operations in the sale of our meager booty. They attended to our affairs and let us know about jobs, for which they took a reasonable commission. We did not form loosely organized bands, but amidst that vast, filthy disorder, in a neighborhood stinking of oil, piss and shit, a few waifs and strays relied on others more clever than themselves. The squalor sparkled with the youth of many of our number and with the more mysterious brilliance of a few who really scintillated, youngsters whose bodies, gazes and gestures were charged with a magnetism which made of us their object. That is how I was staggered by one of them. In order to do justice to the one-armed Stilitano I shall wait a few pages. Let it be known from the start that he was devoid of any Christian virtue. All his brilliance, all his power, had their source between his legs. His penis, and that which completes it, the whole apparatus, was so beautiful that the only thing I can call it is a generative organ. One might have thought he was dead, for he rarely, and slowly, got excited: he watched. He generated in the darkness of a well-buttoned fly, though buttoned by only one hand, the luminosity with which its bearer will be aglow.

My relations with Salvador lasted for six months. It was not the most intoxicating but rather the most fecund of loves. I had managed to love that sickly body, gray

face, and ridiculously sparse beard. Salvador took care
of me, but at night, by candlelight, I hunted for lice, our
pets, in the seams of his trousers. The lice inhabited us.
They imparted to our clothes an animation, a presence,
which, when they had gone, left our garments lifeless.
We liked to know—and feel—that the translucent bugs
were swarming; though not tamed, they were so much a
part of us that a third person's louse disgusted us. We
chased them away but with the hope that during the day
the nits would have hatched. We crushed them with our
nails, without disgust and without hatred. We did not
throw their corpses—or remains—into the garbage; we let
them fall, bleeding with our blood, into our untidy under-
clothes. The lice were the only sign of our prosperity, of
the very underside of prosperity, but it was logical that
by making our state perform an operation which justified
it, we were, by the same token, justifying the sign of
this state. Having become as useful for the knowledge
of our decline as jewels for the knowledge of what is
called triumph, the lice were precious. They were both
our shame and our glory. I lived for a long time in a
room without windows, except a transom on the corridor,
where, in the evening, five little faces, cruel and tender,
smiling or screwed up with the cramp of a difficult position, dripping with sweat, would hunt for those insects
of whose virtue we partook. It was good that, in the
depths of such wretchedness, I was the lover of the poor-
est and homeliest. I thereby had a rare privilege. I had
difficulty, but every victory I achieved—my filthy hands,
proudly exposed, helped me proudly expose my beard
and long hair—gave me strength—or weakness, and here
it amounts to the same thing—for the following victory,
which in your language would naturally be called a come-
down. Yet, light and brilliance being necessary to our
lives, a sunbeam did cross the pane and its filth and pene-

trate the dimness; we had the hoarfrost, the silver thaw,
for these elements, though they may spell calamity, evoke
joys whose sign, detached in our room, was adequate for
us: all we knew of Christmas and New Year's festivities
was what always accompanies them and what makes them
dearer to merrymakers: frost.

The cultivation of sores by beggars is also their means
of getting a little money—on which to live—but though
they may be led to this out of a certain inertia in their
state of poverty, the pride required for holding one's
head up, above contempt, is a manly virtue. Like a rock
in a river, pride breaks through and divides contempt,
bursts it. Entering further into abjection, pride will be
stronger (if the beggar is myself) when I have the knowledge—strength or weakness—to take advantage of such
a fate. It is essential, as this leprosy gains on me, that I
gain on it and that, in the end, I win out. Shall I therefore become increasingly vile, more and more an object
of disgust, up to that final point which is something still
unknown but which must be governed by an aesthetic
as well as moral inquiry? It is said that leprosy, to which
I compare our state, causes an irritation of the tissues;
the sick person scratches himself; he gets an erection.
Masturbation becomes frequent. In his solitary eroticism
the leper consoles himself and hymns his disease. Poverty
made us erect. All across Spain we carried a secret, veiled
magnificence unmixed with arrogance. Our gestures grew
humbler and humbler, fainter and fainter, as the embers
of humility which kept us alive glowed more intensely.
Thus developed my talent for giving a sublime meaning
to so beggarly an appearance. (I am not yet speaking of
literary talent.) It proved to have been a very useful
discipline for me and still enables me to smile tenderly
at the humblest among the dregs, whether human or material, including vomit, including the saliva I let drool on

my mother's face, including your excrement. I shall preserve within me the idea of myself as beggar.

I wanted to be like that woman who, at home, hidden
away from people, sheltered her daughter, a kind of hideous, misshapen monster, stupid and white, who grunted
and walked on all fours. When the mother gave birth,
her despair was probably such that it became the very
essence of her life. She decided to love this monster, to
love the ugliness that had come out of her belly in which
it had been elaborated, and to erect it devotedly. Within
herself she ordained an altar where she preserved the
idea of Monster. With devoted care, with hands gentle
despite the calluses of her daily toil, with the willful zeal
of the hopeless, she set herself up against the world, and
against the world she set up the monster, which took on
the proportions of the world and its power. It was on the
basis of the monster that new principles were ordained,
principles constantly combated by the forces of the world
which came charging into her but which stopped at the
walls of her dwelling where her daughter was confined.[1]

But, for it was sometimes necessary to steal, we also
knew the clear, earthly beauties of boldness. Before we
went to sleep, the chief, the liege lord, would give us
advice. For example, we would go with fake papers to
various consulates in order to be repatriated. The consul,
moved or annoyed by our woes and wretchedness, and
our filth, would give us a train ticket to a border post.
Our chief would resell it at the Barcelona station. He

---

[1] I learned from the newspapers that, after forty years of devotion, this mother sprayed her sleeping daughter, and then the whole
house, with gasoline—or petroleum—and set fire to the house. The
monster (the daughter) died. The old woman (age seventy-five)
was rescued from the flames and was saved, that is, she was brought
to trial.

also let us know of thefts to commit in churches—which Spaniards would not dare do—or in elegant villas; and it was he himself who brought us the Dutch and English sailors to whom we had to prostitute ourselves for a few pesetas.

Thus we sometimes stole, and each burglary allowed us to breathe for a moment at the surface. A vigil of arms precedes each nocturnal expedition. The nervousness provoked by fear, and sometimes by anxiety, makes for a state akin to religious moods. At such times I tend to see omens in the slightest accidents. Things become signs of chance. I want to charm the unknown powers upon which the success of the adventure seems to me to depend. I try to charm them by moral acts, chiefly by charity. I give more readily and more freely to beggars, I give my seat to old people, I stand aside to let them pass, I help blind men cross the street, and so on. In this way, I seem to recognize that over the act of stealing rules a god to whom moral actions are agreeable. These attempts to throw out a net, on the chance that this god of whom I know nothing will be caught in it, exhaust me, disturb me and also favor the religious state. To the act of stealing they communicate the gravity of a ritual act. It will really be performed in the heart of darkness, to which is added that it may be rather at night, while people are asleep, in a place that is closed and perhaps itself masked in black. The walking on tiptoe, the silence, the invisibility which we need even in broad daylight, the groping hands organizing in the darkness gestures of an unwonted complexity and wariness. Merely to turn a doorknob requires a host of movements, each as brilliant as the facet of a jewel. When I discover gold, it seems to me that I have unearthed it; I have ransacked continents, south-sea islands; I am surrounded by negroes; they threaten my defenseless body with their poisoned spears, but then the virtue of the gold acts, and a great vigor crushes or exalts me, the spears are lowered, the negroes recognize me and I am one of the tribe. The perfect act: inadvertently putting my hand into the pocket of a handsome sleeping negro, feeling his prick stiffen beneath my fingers and withdrawing my hand closed over a gold coin discovered in and stolen from his pocket—the prudence, the whispering voice, the alert ear, the invisible, nervous presence of the accomplice and the understanding of his slightest sign, all concentrate our being within us, compress us, make of us a very ball of presence, which so well explains Guy's remark:

"You feel yourself living."

But within myself, this total presence, which is transformed into a bomb of what seems to me terrific power imparts to the act a gravity, a terminal oneness—the burglary, while being performed, is always the last, not that you think you are not going to perform another after that one—you don't think—but because such a gathering of self cannot take place (not in life, for to push it further would be to pass out of life); and this oneness of an act which develops (as the rose puts forth its corolla) into conscious gestures, sure of their efficacy, of their fragility and yet of the violence which they give to the act, here too confers upon it the value of a religious rite. Often I even dedicate it to someone. The first time, it was Stilitano who had the benefit of such homage. I think it was by him that I was initiated, that is, my obsession with his body kept me from flinching. To his beauty, to his tranquil immodesty, I dedicated my first thefts. To the singularity too of that splendid cripple whose hand, cut off at the wrist, was rotting away somewhere, under a chestnut tree, so he told me, in a forest of Central Europe. During the theft, my body is exposed. I know that it is

sparkling with all my gestures. The world is attentive to
all my movements, if it wants me to trip up. I shall pay
dearly for a mistake, but if there is a mistake and I catch
it in time, it seems to me that there will be joy in our
Father's dwelling. Or, I fall, and there is woe upon woe
and then prison. But as for the savages, the convict who
risked "the Getaway" will then meet them by means of
the procedure briefly described above in my inner adventure. If, going through the virgin forest, he comes upon
a placer guarded by ancient tribes, he will either be killed
by them or be saved. It is by a long, long road that I
choose to go back to primitive life. What I need first is
condemnation by my race.

Salvador was not a source of pride to me. When he did
steal, he merely filched trifles from stands in front of
shop windows. At night, in the cafés where we huddled
together, he would sadly worm himself in among the
most handsome. That kind of life exhausted him. When
I entered, I would be ashamed to find him hunched over,
squatting on a bench, his shoulders huddled up in the
green and yellow cotton blanket with which he would
go out begging on wintry days. He would also be wearing an old, black woolen shawl which I refused to put on.
Indeed, though my mind endured, even desired, humility,
my violent young body rejected it. Salvador would speak
in a sad, reticent voice:

"Would you like us to go back to France? We'll work
in the country."

I said no. He did not understand my loathing—no, my
hatred—of France, nor that my adventure, if it stopped
in Barcelona, was bound to continue deeply, more and
more deeply, in the remotest regions of myself.

"But I'll do all the work. You'll take it easy."

"No."

I would leave him on his bench to his cheerless poverty.

I would go over to the stove or the bar and smoke the butts I had gleaned during the day, with a scornful young Andalusian whose dirty white woolen sweater exaggerated his torso and muscles. After rubbing his hands together, the way old men do, Salvador would leave his bench and go to the community kitchen to prepare a soup and put a fish on the grill. Once he suggested that we go down to Huelva for the orange picking. It was an evening when he had received so many humiliations, so many rebuffs while begging for me that he dared reproach me for my poor success at the Criolla.

"Really, when you pick up a client, it's *you* who ought to pay *him*."

We quarreled in front of the proprietor of the hotel, who wanted to put us out. Salvador and I therefore decided to steal two blankets the following day and hide in a south-bound freight train. But I was so clever that that very evening I brought back the cape of a customs officer. As I passed the docks where they mount guard, one of the officers called me. I did what he required, in the sentry box. After coming (perhaps, without daring to tell me so, he wanted to wash at a little fountain), he left me alone for a moment and I ran off with his big black woolen cape. I wrapped myself up in it in order to return to the hotel, and I knew the happiness of the equivocal, not yet the joy of betrayal, though the insidious confusion which would make me deny fundamental oppositions was already forming. As I opened the door of the café, I saw Salvador. He was the saddest-looking of beggars. His face had the quality, and almost the texture, of the sawdust that covered the floor of the café. Immediately I recognized Stilitano standing in the midst of the ronda players. Our eyes met. His gaze lingered on me, who blushed. I took off the black cape, and at once they started haggling over it. Without yet taking part, Stilitano watched the wretched bargaining.

"Make it snappy, if you want it," I said. "Make up your minds. The customs man is sure to come looking for me."

The players got a little more active. They were used to such reasons. When the general shuffle brought me to his side, Stilitano said to me in French:

"You from Paris?"

"Yes. Why?"

"For no reason."

Although it was he who had made the first advance, I knew, as I answered, the almost desperate nature of the gesture the invert dares when he approaches a young man. To mask my confusion, I had the pretext of being breathless, I had the bustle of the moment. He said, "You did pretty well for yourself."

I knew that this praise was cleverly calculated, but how handsome Stilitano was amidst the beggars (I didn't know his name yet)! One of his arms, at the extremity of which was an enormous bandage, was folded on his chest as if in a sling, but I knew that the hand was missing. Stilitano was an habitué of neither the café nor even the street.

"What'll the cape cost me?"

"Will you pay me for it?"

"Why not?"

"With what?"

"Are you scared?"

"Where are you from?"

"Serbia. I'm back from the Foreign Legion. I'm a deserter."

I was relieved. Destroyed. The emotion created within me a void which was at once filled by the memory of a nuptial scene. In a dance hall where soldiers were danc-

ing among themselves, I watched their waltz. It seemed
to me at the time that the invisibility of two legionnaires
became total. They were charmed away by emotion.
Though their dance was chaste at the beginning of
"Ramona," would it remain so when, in our presence,
they wedded by exchanging a smile, as lovers exchange
rings? To all the injunctions of an invisible clergy the
Legion answered, "I do." Each one of them was the
couple wearing both a net veil and a dress uniform (white
leather, scarlet and green shoulder braid). They haltingly
exchanged their manly tenderness and wifely modesty.
To maintain the emotion at a high pitch, they slowed up
and slackened their dance, while their pricks, numbed by
the fatigue of a long march, recklessly threatened and
challenged each other behind a barricade of rough denim.
The patent-leather vizors of their képis kept striking together. I knew I was being mastered by Stilitano. I
wanted to play sly:
"That doesn't prove you can pay."
"Trust me."
Such a hard-looking face, such a strapping body, were
asking me to trust them. Salvador was watching us. He
was aware of our understanding and realized that we had
already decided upon his ruin, his loneliness. Fierce and
pure, I was the theater of a fairyland restored to life.
When the waltz ended, the two soldiers disengaged themselves. And each of those two halves of a solemn and
dizzy block hesitated, and, happy to be escaping from
invisibility, went off, downcast, toward some girl for the
next waltz.
"I'll give you two days to pay me," I said. "I need
dough. I was in the Legion too. And I deserted. Like
you."
"You'll get it."
I handed him the cape. He took it with his only hand

and gave it back to me. He smiled, though imperiously, and said, "Roll it up." And joshingly added, "While waiting to roll me one."

Everyone knows the expression: "to roll a skate."[1] Without batting an eyelash, I did as he said. The cape immediately disappeared into one of the hotel proprietor's hiding places. Perhaps this simple theft brightened my face, or Stilitano simply wanted to act nice; he added: "You going to treat an ex-Bel-Abbès boy to a drink?"

A glass of wine cost two sous. I had four in my pocket, but I owed them to Salvador, who was watching us.

"I'm broke," Stilitano said proudly.

The card players were forming new groups which for a moment separated us from Salvador. I muttered between my teeth, "I've got four sous and I'm going to slip them to you, but you're the one who'll pay."

Stilitano smiled. I was lost. We sat down at a table. He had already begun to talk about the Legion when, staring hard at me, he suddenly broke off.

"I've got a feeling I've seen you somewhere before."

As for me, I had retained the memory.

I had to grab hold of invisible tackle. I could have cooed. Words, or the tone of my voice, would have not merely expressed my ardor, I would not have merely sung, my throat would have uttered the call of indeed the most amorous of wild game. Perhaps my neck would have bristled with white feathers. A catastrophe is always possible. Metamorphosis lies in wait for us. Panic protected me.

I have lived in the fear of metamorphoses. It is in order to make the reader fully conscious, as he sees love swooping down on me—it is not mere rhetoric which requires the comparison—like a falcon—of the most exquisite of

---

[1] *Rouler un patin* (to roll a skate) is French slang meaning to kiss with the tongue.—Translator's note.

frights that I employ the idea of a turtle dove. I do not know what I felt at the moment, but today all I need do is summon up the vision of Stilitano for my distress to appear at once in the relationship of a cruel bird to its victim. (Were it not that I felt my neck swell out with a gentle cooing, I would have spoken rather of a robin redbreast.)

A curious creature would appear if each of my emotions became the animal it evokes: anger rumbles within my cobra neck; the same cobra swells up my prick; my steeds and merry-go-rounds are born of my insolence. . . . Of a turtle dove I retained only a hoarseness, which Stilitano noticed. I coughed.

Behind the Parallelo was an empty lot where the hoodlums played cards. (The Parallelo is an avenue in Barcelona parallel to the famous Ramblas. Between these two wide thoroughfares, a multitude of dark, dirty, narrow streets make up the Barrio Chino.) Squatting on the ground, they would organize games; they would lay out the cards on a square piece of cloth or in the dust. A young gypsy was running one of the games, and I came to risk the few sous I had in my pocket. I am not a gambler. Rich casinos do not attract me. The atmosphere of electric chandeliers bores me. The affected casualness of the elegant gambler nauseates me. And the impossibility of acting upon the balls, roulettes and little horses discourages me, but I loved the dust, filth and haste of the hoodlums. When I bugger . . . ,[1] as I bend farther forward I get a profile view of his face crushed against the pillow, of his pain. I see the wincing of his features, but also their radiant anguish. I often watched this on the grimy faces of the squatting urchins. This whole popula-

---

[1] Since the hero, whom at first I called by his real name, is my current lover (1948), prudence advises me to leave a blank in place of his name.

tion was keyed up for winning or losing. Every thigh was quivering with fatigue or anxiety. The weather that day was threatening. I was caught up in the youthful impatience of the young Spaniards. I played and I won. I won every hand. I didn't say a word during the game. Besides, the gypsy was a stranger to me. Custom permitted me to pocket my money and leave. The boy was so good looking that by leaving him in that way I felt I was lacking in respect for the beauty, suddenly become sad, of his face, which was drooping with heat and boredom. I kindly gave him back his money. Slightly astonished, he took it and simply thanked me.

"Hello, Pépé," a kinky, swarthy-looking cripple called out as he limped by.

"Pépé," I said to myself, "his name is Pépé." And I left, for I had just noticed his delicate, almost feminine little hand. But hardly had I gone a few steps in that crowd of thieves, whores, beggars and queers than I felt someone touching me on the shoulder. It was Pépé. He had just left the game. He spoke to me in Spanish:

"My name is Pépé."

"Mine is Juan."

"Come, let's have a drink."

He was no taller than I. His face, which I had seen from above when he was squatting, looked less flattened. The features were finer.

"He's a girl," I thought, summoning up the image of his slender hand, and I felt that his company would bore me. He had just decided that we would drink the money I had won. We made the round of the bars, and all the while we were together he was quite charming. He wore a very low-necked blue jersey instead of a shirt. From the opening emerged a solid neck, as broad as his head. When he turned it without moving his chest, an enormous tendon stood out. I tried to imagine his body, and, despite

the almost frail hands, I imagined it to be solid, for his
thighs filled out the light cloth of his trousers. The
weather was warm. The storm did not break. The nervousness of the players around us heightened. The whores
seemed heavier. The dust and sun were oppressive. We
drank hardly any liquor, but rather lemonade. We sat
near the peddlers and exchanged an occasional word. He
kept smiling, with a slight weariness. He seemed to be
indulging me. Did he suspect that I liked his cute face?
I don't know, but he didn't let on. Besides, I had the
same sly sort of look as he; I seemed a threat to the well-
dressed passer-by; I had his youth and his filth, and I was
French. Toward evening he wanted to gamble, but it was
too late to start a game as all the places were taken. We
strolled about a bit among the players. When he brushed
by the whores, Pépé would kid them. Sometimes he would
pinch them. The heat grew more oppressive. The sky was
flush with the ground. The nervousness of the crowd became irritating. Impatience prevailed over the gypsy who
had not decided which game to join. He was fingering
the money in his pocket. Suddenly he took me by the arm.

"Venga!"

He led me a few steps away to the one comfort station
on the Parallelo. It was run by an old woman. Surprised
by the suddenness of his decision, I questioned him:

"What are you going to do?"

"Wait for me."

"Why?"

He answered with a Spanish word which I did not
understand. I told him so and, in front of the old woman
who was waiting for her two sous, he burst out laughing
and made the gesture of jerking off. When he came out,
his face had a bit of color. He was still smiling.

"It's all right now. I'm ready."

That was how I learned that, on big occasions, players

went there to jerk off in order to be calmer and more
sure of themselves. We went back to the lot. Pépé chose
a group. He lost. He lost all he had. I tried to restrain
him; it was too late. As authorized by custom, he asked
the man running the bank to give him a stake from the
kitty for the next game. The man refused. It seemed to
me then that the very thing that constituted the gypsy's
gentleness turned sour, as milk turns, and became the
most ferocious rage I have ever seen. He whisked away
the bank. The man bounded up and tried to kick him.
Pépé dodged. He handed me the money, but hardly had
I pocketed it than his knife was open. He planted it in
the heart of the Spaniard, a tall, bronzed fellow, who fell
to the ground and who, despite his tan, turned pale, contracted, writhed and expired in the dust. For the first
time I saw someone give up the ghost. Pépé had disappeared, but when, turning my eyes away from the corpse,
I looked up, there, gazing at it with a faint smile, was
Stilitano. The sun was about to set. The dead man and
the handsomest of humans seemed to me merged in the
same golden dust amidst a throng of sailors, soldiers,
hoodlums and thieves from all parts of the world. The
Earth did not revolve: carrying Stilitano, it trembled
about the sun. At the same moment I came to know death
and love. This vision, however, was very brief, for I could
not stay there because I was afraid I might have been
spotted with Pépé and lest a friend of the dead man
snatch away the money which I kept in my pocket, but as
I moved off, my memory kept alive and commented upon
the following scene, which seemed to me grandiose: "The
murder, by a charming child, of a grown man whose tan
could turn pale, take on the hue of death, the whole
ironically observed by a tall blond youngster to whom
I had just become secretly engaged." Rapid as my glance
at him was, I had time to take in Stilitano's superb mus-

cularity and to see, between his lips, rolling in his half-open mouth, a white, heavy blob of spit, thick as a white worm, which he shifted about, stretching it from top to bottom until it veiled his mouth. He stood barefoot in the dust. His legs were contained in a pair of worn and shabby faded blue denim trousers. The sleeves of his green shirt were rolled up, one of them above an amputated hand; the wrist, where the resewn skin still revealed a pale, pink scar, was slightly shrunken.

Beneath a tragic sky, I was to cross the loveliest landscapes in the world when Stilitano took my hand at night. What was the nature of that fluid which passed with a shock from him to me? I walked along dangerous shores, emerged into dismal plains, heard the sea. Hardly had I touched him, when the stairway changed: he was master of the world. With the memory of those brief moments, I could describe to you walks, breathless flights, pursuits, in countries of the world where I shall never go.

*

*　*

Stilitano smiled and laughed at me.

"Are you stringing me along?"

"A little," he said.

"Go right ahead."

He smiled again and raised his eyebrows.

"Why?"

"You know that you're a good-looking kid. And you think you don't have to give a damn about anyone."

"I've got a right to. I'm a nice guy."

"You're sure?"

He burst out laughing.

"Sure. No mistake. I'm so likable that sometimes I can't

get rid of people. In order to shake them off I sometimes have to do them dirt."

"What kind of dirt?"

"You want to know? Just wait, you'll see me on the job. You'll have time to see what it's like. Where are you staying?"

"Here."

"Don't. The police'll be around. They'll look here first. Come with me."

I told Salvador that I couldn't stay at the hotel that night and that a former member of the Legion was offering me his room. He turned pale. The humility of his pain made me feel ashamed. In order to leave him without remorse I insulted him. I was able to since he loved me to the point of devotion. He gave me a woebegone look, but it was charged with a poor wretch's hatred. I replied with the word: "Fruit." I joined Stilitano, who was waiting for me outside. His hotel was in the darkest alley in the neighborhood. He had been living there for some days. A stairway from the corridor which opened out to the sidewalk led to the rooms. As we were going up, he said to me, "D'you want us to shack up together?"

"If we feel like it."

"You're right. We'll stay out of trouble easier."

In front of the door of the corridor he said to me, "Hand me the box."

We had only one box of matches between us.

"It's empty," I said.

He swore. Stilitano took me by the hand, putting his own behind his back, for I was at his right.

"Follow me," he said. "And stop talking. The staircase has ears."

Gently he led me from step to step. I no longer knew where we were going. A wondrously supple athlete was leading me about in the night. A more ancient and more Greek Antigone was making me scale a dark, steep Calvary. My hand was confident, and I was ashamed to stumble at times against a rock or root, or to lose my footing. My ravisher was carrying me off.

"He's going to think I'm clumsy."

However, he thoughtfully and patiently helped me, and the silence he enjoined upon me, the secrecy with which he surrounded the evening, our first night, made me for a moment believe in his love for me. The house smelled neither better nor worse than the others in the Barrio Chino, but the horrible odor of this one will always remain for me the very odor not only of love but of tenderness and confidence. After making love, the animal odor of my lover lingers in my nostrils a long time. Probably some particles remain clinging to the hairs which line the interior, and it is a bit of his body that I encounter and recreate in me when I sniff. When my sense of smell remembers Stilitano's odor, the odor of his armpits, of his mouth, though it may suddenly come upon them with a disquieting veracity, I believe them capable of inspiring me with the wildest rashness. (Sometimes at night I meet a youngster and go with him to his room. At the foot of the stairs, for my trade lives in shady hotels, he takes me by the hand. He guides me as skillfully as did Stilitano.)

"Watch out."

He mumbled these words, which were too sweet for me. Because of the position of our arms I was pressed against his body. For a moment I felt the movement of his mobile buttocks. Out of respect, I moved a little to the side. We mounted, narrowly limited by a fragile wall which must have contained the sleep of the whores, thieves, pimps and beggars of the hotel. I was a child being carefully led by his father. (Today I am a father led to love by his child.)

At the fourth landing, I entered his grubby little room. My whole respiratory rhythm was upset. I was in the throes of love. In the Parallelo bars Stilitano introduced me to his cronies. There were so many mariconas among the people of the Barrio Chino that no one seemed to notice that I liked men. Together, he and I pulled off a few easy jobs which provided us with what we needed. I lived with him, I slept in his bed, but this big fellow was so exquisitely modest that never did I see him entirely. Had I obtained what I so keenly wanted from him, Stilitano would have remained in my eyes the firm and charming master, though neither his strength nor his charm would have gratified my desire for all the manly types: the soldier, the sailor, the adventurer, the thief, the criminal. By remaining inaccessible, he became the epitome of those whom I have named and who stagger me. I was therefore chaste. At times, he was so cruel as to require that I button the waistband of his trousers, and my hand would tremble. He pretended not to see anything and was amused. (I shall speak later of the character of my hands and of the meaning of this trembling. It is not without reason that in India sacred or disgusting persons and objects are said to be Untouchable.) Unable to see it, I invented the biggest and loveliest prick in the world. I endowed it with qualities: heavy, strong and nervous, sober, with a tendency toward pride and yet serene. Beneath my fingers, I felt, sculpted in oak, its full veins, its palpitations, its heat, its pinkness, and at times the racing pulsation of the sperm. It occupied less my nights than my days. Behind Stilitano's fly it was the sacred Black Stone to which Heliogabalus offered up his imperial wealth. Stilitano was happy to have me at his beck and call and he introduced me to his friends as his right arm. Now, it was his right hand that had been amputated. I would repeat to myself delightedly that I certainly was his right arm; I was the one who took the place of the strongest limb. If he had a girl friend among the whores of the Calle Carmen, I was unaware of it. He exaggerated his contempt for fairies. We lived together in this way for a few days. One evening when I was at the Criolla, one of the whores told me to leave. She said that a customs officer had been around looking for me. It must have been the one I had first satisfied and then robbed. I went back to the hotel and told Stilitano about it. He said he would attend to the matter and then left.

I was born in Paris on December 19, 1910. As a ward of the *Assistance Publique*,[1] it was impossible for me to know anything about my background. When I was twenty-one, I obtained a birth certificate. My mother's name was Gabrielle Genet. My father remains unknown. I came into the world at 22 Rue d'Assas.

"I'll find out something about my origin," I said to myself, and went to the Rue d'Assas. Number 22 was occupied by the Maternity Hospital. They refused to give me any information. I was brought up in Le Morvan by peasants. Whenever I come across *genêt* (broom) blossoms on the heaths—especially at twilight on my way back from a visit to the ruins of Tiffauges where Gilles de Rais lived—I feel a deep sense of kinship with them. I regard them solemnly, with tenderness. My emotion seems ordained by all nature. I am alone in the world, and I am not sure that I am not the king—perhaps the sprite—of these flowers. They render homage as I pass, bow without bowing, but recognize me. They know that I am their living, moving, agile representative, conqueror of the wind. They are my natural emblem, but through them I have roots in that French soil which is fed by the

---

[1] The French national agency in charge of the care of foundlings. —Translator's note.

powdered bones of the children and youths buggered, massacred and burned by Gilles de Rais.

Through that thorny plant of the Cevennes,[1] I take part in the criminal adventures of Vacher. Thus, through her whose name I bear, the vegetable kingdom is my familiar. I can regard all flowers without pity; they are members of my family. If, through them, I rejoin the nether realms—though it is to the bracken and their marshes, to the algae, that I should like to descend—I withdraw further from men.[2]

The atmosphere of the planet Uranus appears to be so heavy that the ferns there are creepers; the animals drag along, crushed by the weight of the gases. I want to mingle with these humiliated creatures which are always on their bellies. If metempsychosis should grant me a new dwelling place, I choose that forlorn planet, I inhabit it with the convicts of my race. Amidst hideous reptiles, I pursue an eternal, miserable death in a darkness where the leaves will be black, the waters of the marshes thick and cold. Sleep will be denied me. On the contrary, I recognize, with increasing lucidity, the unclean fraternity of the smiling alligators.

It was not at any precise period of my life that I decided to be a thief. My laziness and daydreaming having led me to the Mettray Reformatory, where I was supposed to remain until "the age of twenty-one," I ran away and enlisted for five years so as to collect a bonus for voluntary enlistment. After a few days I deserted, taking with me some valises belonging to negro officers.

For a time I lived by theft, but prostitution was better suited to my indolence. I was twenty years old. I had

---

[1] The very day he met me, Jean Cocteau called me "his Spanish *genêt*" (*genêt d'Espagne*—rush-leaved broom). He did not know what that country had made of me.

[2] Botanists know a variety of *genêt* which they call winged-broom (*genêt ailé*).

therefore known the army when I came to Spain. The dignity conferred by the uniform, the isolation from the world which it imposes, and the soldier's trade itself afforded me a certain peace—though the army is on the *fringe* of society—and self-confidence. My situation as a naturally humiliated child was, for some months, tempered. I knew at last the sweetness of being welcomed by men. My life of poverty in Spain was a kind of degradation, a fall involving shame. I was fallen. Not that during my stay in the army I would have been a pure soldier, governed by the rigorous virtues which create castes (my homosexuality would have been enough for me to incur disapproval), but there was still going on within my mind a secret labor which one day came to light. It is perhaps their moral solitude—to which I aspire —that makes me admire traitors and love them—this taste for solitude being the sign of my pride, and pride the manifestation of my strength, the employment and proof of this strength. For I shall have broken the stoutest of bonds, the bonds of love. And I so need love from which to draw vigor enough to destroy it! It was in the army that I witnessed for the first time (at least I think it was) the despair of one of my robbed victims. To rob soldiers was to betray, for I was breaking the bonds of love uniting me with the soldier who had been robbed.

Plaustener was good looking, strong and confident. He got up on his bed in order to look in his pack. He tried to find in it the hundred-franc note which I had taken a quarter of an hour earlier. His gestures were those of a clown. He was on the wrong track. He imagined the most unlikely hiding places: the mess kit from which he had nevertheless just eaten, the brush bag, the grease can. He was ridiculous. He kept saying, "I'm not crazy. I wouldn't have put it there."

Not knowing whether he was crazy, he checked; he found nothing. Hoping to counter the evidence, he resigned himself and stretched out on his bed only to get up again and search in places where he had already looked. I saw his certainty, the certainty of a man four-square on his thighs and sure of muscle, crumble, pulverize, powder him with a softness he had never had, chip away his sharp angles. I was present at this silent transformation. I feigned indifference. However, this self-confident young soldier seemed to me so pitiful in his ignorance that his fear, almost his wonderment, with respect to a malignity of which he had been unaware—not thinking it would dare reveal itself to him for the first time by actually taking him for victim—his shame too, almost softened me so far as to make me want to give him back the hundred-franc note which I had hidden, folded up into sixteen parts, in a crack of the barracks wall, near the clothes drier. The head of a robbed man is hideous. The robbed men's heads which frame him give the thief an arrogant solitude. I dared say, in a curt tone, "You're funny to watch. You look as if you've got the runs. Go to the can and pull the chain."

This reflection saved me from myself.

I felt a curious sweetness; a kind of freedom lightened me, gave my body as it lay on the bed an extraordinary agility. Was that what betrayal was? I had just violently detached myself from an unclean comradeship to which my affectionate nature had been leading me, and I was astonished at thereby feeling great strength. I had just broken with the army, had just shattered the bonds of friendship.

The tapestry known as "Lady with the Unicorn" excited me for reasons which I shall not attempt to go into here. But when I crossed the border from Czechoslovakia into Poland, it was a summer afternoon. The border ran through a field of ripe rye, the blondness of which was as blond as the hair of young Poles; it had the somewhat buttery softness of Poland, about which I knew that in the course of history it was more sinned against than sinning. I was with another fellow who, like me, had been expelled by the Czech police, but I very soon lost sight of him; perhaps he had strayed off behind a bush or wanted to get rid of me. He disappeared. The rye field was bounded on the Polish side by a wood at whose edge was nothing but motionless birches; on the Czech side, by another wood, but of fir trees. I remained a long time squatting at the edge, intently wondering what lay hidden in the field. What if I crossed it? Were customs officers hidden in the rye? Invisible hares must have been running through it. I was uneasy. At noon, beneath a pure sky, all nature was offering me a puzzle, and offering it to me blandly.

"If something happens," I said to myself, "it will be the appearance of a unicorn. Such a moment and such a place can only produce a unicorn."

Fear, and the kind of emotion I always feel when I cross a border, conjured up at noon, beneath a leaden sun, the first fairyland. I ventured forth into that golden sea as one enters the water. I went through the rye standing up. I advanced slowly, surely, with the certainty of being the heraldic character for whom a natural blazon has been formed: azure, field of gold, sun, forests. This imagery, of which I was a part, was complicated by the Polish imagery.

"In this noonday sky the white eagle should soar invisible!"

When I got to the birches, I was in Poland. An enchantment of another order was about to be offered me. The "Lady with the Unicorn" is to me the lofty expression of this crossing the line at noontide. I had just experienced, as a result of fear, an uneasiness in the presence of the mystery of diurnal nature, at a time when the French countryside where I wandered about, chiefly at night, was peopled all over with the ghost of Vacher, the killer of shepherds. As I walked through it, I would listen within me to the accordion tunes he must have played there, and I would mentally invite the children to come and offer themselves to the cutthroat's hands. However, I have just referred to this in order to try to tell you at what period of my life nature disturbed me, giving rise within me to the spontaneous creation of a fabulous fauna, or of situations and accidents whose fearful and enchanted prisoner I was.[1]

The crossing of borders and the excitement it arouses in me were to enable me to apprehend directly the essence of the nation I was entering. I would penetrate less into a country than to the interior of an image. Naturally, I wished to possess it, but also by acting upon it. Military attire being that which best denotes it, this was what I hoped to tamper with. For the foreigner, there are no other means than espionage. Mixed in with it, perhaps, was the concern about polluting, through treason, an institution which regards integrity—or loyalty—as its essential quality. Perhaps I also wanted to alienate myself further from my own country. (The explanations I am giving occur to me spontaneously. They seem valid for my case. They are to be accepted for mine alone.) In any event, I mean that as a result of a certain frame of mind which is natural to enchantment (being further exalted by my emotion in the presence of nature, endowed with a power recognized by men) I was ready to act, not in

---

[1] The first line of verse which to my amazement I found myself composing was the following: "Harvester of stolen breath." I am reminded of it by what I have written above.

accordance with the rules of morality but in accordance
with certain laws of a fictional aesthetic which makes the
spy out to be a restless, invisible, though powerful character. In short, a preoccupation of this kind gave, in
certain cases, a practical justification to my entering a
country to which nothing obliged me to go, except, however, expulsion from a neighboring country.

It is with regard to my feeling in the presence of nature
that I speak of espionage, but when I was deserted by
Stilitano, the thought of it was to occur to me as a con-
solation, as if to anchor me to your soil where loneliness
and poverty made me not walk but fly. For I am so poor,
and I have already been accused of so many thefts, that
when I leave a room too quietly on tiptoe, holding my
breath, I am not sure, even now, that I am not carrying
off with me the holes in the curtains or hangings. I do not
know how informed Stilitano was about military secrets
or what he might have learned in the Legion, in a
colonel's office. But he was thinking of turning spy.
Neither the profit to be derived from the operation nor
even the danger appealed to me. Only the idea of treason
already had that power which was taking greater and
greater hold of me.

"Who'll we sell them to?"

"Germany."

But after a few moments' reflection he decided:

"Italy."

"But you're Serbian. They're your enemies."

"So what?"

Had we gone through with this adventure, it would
have drawn me out to some extent from the abjection in
which I was caught. Espionage is a practice of which
states are so ashamed that they ennoble it for its being
shameful. We would have profited from this nobleness.
Except that in our case it was a matter of treason. Later

on, when I was arrested in Italy and the officers questioned me about the protection of our frontiers, I was
able to discover a dialectic capable of justifying my dis-
closures. In the present case I would have been backed
up by Stilitano. I could not but wish, through these revelations, to be the abettor of a terrible catastrophe. Stilitano might have betrayed his country and I mine out of
love for Stilitano. When I speak to you later about Java,
you will find the same characteristics, indeed almost the
same face as Stilitano's; and as the two sides of a triangle
meet at the apex which is in the sky, Stilitano and Java
go off to meet a star forever extinguished: Marc Aubert.[1]

Though the blue woolen cape I had stolen from the
customs officer had already afforded me a kind of presen-
timent of a conclusion wherein law and outlaw merge,
one lurking beneath the other but feeling, with a touch
of nostalgia, the virtue of its opposite, to Stilitano it would
offer an adventure less spiritual or subtle but more deeply
involved in daily life, better utilized. It will not yet be a
question of treason. Stilitano was a power. His egotism
sharply marked out his natural frontiers. (Stilitano was a
power to *me*.)

When he entered late at night, he told me that the

---

[1] This face also merges with that of Rasseneur, a crook with whom
I worked around 1936. I recently read in the weekly *Detective
Magazine* that he has been given a life sentence, whereas that very
same week a petition of writers asked, for the very same punishment, that the President of the Republic grant me a reprieve. The
photo of Rasseneur in court was on the second page. The journalist
stated ironically that he seemed quite pleased about being shipped
off. That doesn't surprise me. At the Santé Prison he was a little
king. He'll be a big shot at Riom or Clairvaux. Rasseneur is, I think,
from Nantes. He also robbed homosexuals. I learned from a friend
that a car, driven by one of his victims, looked all over Paris for him
for a long time in order to run him over "accidentally." There is a
terrible fairy vengeance.

whole matter was settled. He had met the customs officer.

"He won't bother you. It's all over. You can go out without worrying."

"But what about the cape?"

"I'm keeping it."

Feeling that a strange mingling of baseness and charm from which I was naturally excluded had just taken place that night, I dared not ask for further details.

"Get started!"

With a gesture of his vivid hand, he motioned to me that he wanted to undress. As on other evenings, I got down on my knees to unhook the bunch of grapes. Inside his trousers was pinned one of those imitation bunches of thin cellulose grapes stuffed with cotton wool. (They are as big as greengage plums; elegant Spanish women of the period wore them on their loose-brimmed, straw sun bonnets.) Whenever some queer at the Criolla, excited by the swelling, put his hand on Stilitano's basket, his horrified fingers would encounter this object, which he feared might be actual balls.

The Criolla was not only a fairy joint. Some boys in dresses danced there, but women did too. Whores brought their pimps and their clients. Stilitano would have made a lot of money were it not that he spat on queers. He despised them. He was amused at their annoyance about his grapes. The game lasted a few days. So I unhooked the bunch, which was fastened to his blue trousers by a safety pin, but, instead of putting it on the mantelpiece as usual and laughing (for we would burst out laughing and joke during the operation), I could not restrain myself from keeping it in my cupped hands and laying my cheek against it. Stilitano's face above me turned hideous.

"Drop it, you bitch!"

In order to open the fly, I had squatted on my haunches, but Stilitano's rage, had my usual fervor been insufficient, made me fall to my knees. That was the position

I used to take mentally in spite of myself. I stopped moving. Stilitano struck me with his two feet and his one fist. I could have got away. I stayed there.

"The key's in the door," I thought. Through the fork of the feet that were kicking me furiously I saw it sticking out of the keyhole, and I would have liked to turn it with a double turn so as to be locked in alone with my executioner. I made no attempt to understand the reason for his anger, which was so disproportionate to its cause, for my mind was unconcerned with psychological motives. As for Stilitano, from that day on he stopped wearing the bunch of grapes. Toward morning, having entered the room earlier than he, I waited for him. In the silence, I heard the mysterious rustling of the sheet of yellow newspaper that replaced the missing windowpane.

"That's subtle," I said to myself.

I was discovering a lot of new words. In the silence of the room and of my heart, in the waiting for Stilitano, this slight noise disturbed me, for before I came to understand its meaning there elapsed a brief period of anxiety. Who—or what—is calling such fleeting attention to itself in a poor man's room?

"It's a newspaper printed in Spanish," I said to myself again. "It's only natural that I don't understand the sound it's making."

Then I really felt I was in exile, and my nervousness was going to make me permeable to what—for want of other words—I shall call poetry.

The bunch of grapes on the mantelpiece nauseated me. One night Stilitano got up to throw it into the toilet. During the time he had worn it, it had not marred his beauty. On the contrary, in the evening, slightly encumbering his legs, it had given them a slight bend and his step a slightly rounded and gentle constraint, and when he walked near me, in front or behind, I felt a delicious agitation because my hands had prepared it. I still think it was by virtue of the insidious power of these grapes that I grew attached to Stilitano. I did not detach myself until the day when, in a dance hall, while dancing with a sailor, I happened to slip my hand under his collar. This seemingly most innocent of gestures was to reveal a fatal virtue. My hand, lying flat on the young man's back, knew that it was gently and piously hidden by the sign of the candor of sailors. It felt as if something were flapping against it, and my hand could not keep from thinking that Java was flapping his wing. It is still too soon to talk about him.

I shall prudently refrain from comment upon this mysterious wearing of the bunch of grapes; yet it pleases me to see in Stilitano a queer who hates himself.

"He wants to baffle and hurt, to disgust the very people who desire him," I say to myself when I think of him. As I ponder it more carefully, I am more disturbed by the idea—which I find pregnant with meaning—that Stilitano had bought a fake wound for that most noble spot (I know that he was magnificently hung) in order to save his lopped-off hand from scorn. Thus, by means of a very crude subterfuge here I am talking again about beggars and their misfortunes. Behind a real or sham physical ailment which draws attention to itself and is thereby forgotten is hidden a more secret malady of the soul. I list the secret wounds:

> decayed teeth,
> foul breath,
> a hand cut off,
> smelly feet, etc. . . .

to conceal them and to kindle our pride we had

> a gouged eye,
> a peg leg, etc.

We are fallen during the time we bear the marks of the fall, and to be aware of the imposture is of little avail. Using only the pride imposed by poverty, we aroused pity by cultivating the most repulsive wounds. We became a reproach to your happiness.

I aggravated this foul adventure by an attitude that became an actual disposition. One day, just for the fun of it, Stilitano said to me, "I'm going to have to stick my prick up your ass."

"It would hurt," I said with a laugh.

"Not a bit. I'll put trees in it."

"Trees" are put into shoes. I pretended to myself that he would put "trees" into his cock so that it would get even bigger, until it became a monstrous, unnamable organ, cultivated specially for my loathing, and not for my pleasure. I accepted this make-believe explanation without disgust.

Meanwhile, Stilitano and I were having a hard time. When, thanks to a few queers, I brought in a little money, he showed such pride that I sometimes wonder whether he is not great, in my memory, because of the bragging of which I was the pretext and chief confidant. The quality of my love required that he prove his virility. If he was the splendid beast gleaming in the darkness of his ferocity, let him devote himself to sport worthy of it. I incited him to theft.

We decided to rob a store together. In order to cut the telephone wire, which, most imprudently, was near the door, a pair of pliers was needed. We entered one of the many Barcelona bazaars where there were hardware departments.

"Manage not to move if you see me swipe something."

"What'll I do?"

"Nothing. Just look."

Stilitano was wearing white sneakers, his blue trousers, and a khaki shirt. At first I noticed nothing, but when we left, I was amazed to see, at the flap of his shirt-pocket, a kind of small lizard, both restless and still, hanging by the teeth. It was the steel pliers that we needed and that Stilitano had just stolen.

"That he charms monkeys, men and women," I said to myself, "is comprehensible, but what can be the nature of the magnetism, born of his glib muscles and his curls, of that blond amber, that can enthral objects?"

However, there was no doubt about the fact that objects were obedient to him. Which amounts to saying that he understood them. So well did he know the nature of steel, and the nature of that particular fragment of polished steel called pliers, that it remained, to the point of fatigue, docile, loving, clinging to his shirt to which he had known, with precision, how to hook it, biting desperately into the cloth with its thin jaws so as not to fall. At times, however, these objects, which are irritated by a clumsy movement, would hurt him. Stilitano used to cut himself, his fingertips were finely gashed, his nail was black and crushed, but this heightened his beauty. (The purple of sunsets, according to physicists, is the result of a greater thickness of air which is crossed only by short waves. At midday, when nothing is happening in the sky, an apparition of this kind would disturb us less; the wonder is that it occurs in the evening, at the most poignant time of day, when the sun *sets*, when it disappears to pursue a mysterious destiny, when perhaps it dies. The physical phenomenon that fills the sky with such pomp is possible only at the moment that most exalts the imagination: at the setting of the most brilliant of the heavenly bodies.) Ordinary objects, those used every day, will adorn Stilitano. His very acts of cowardice melt my rigor. I liked his taste for laziness. He was leaky, as one says of a vessel. When we had the pliers, he slipped out.

"There may be a dog around."

We thought of putting it out of the way with a piece of poisoned meat.

"Rich people's dogs don't eat just any old thing."

Suddenly Stilitano thought of the legendary gypsy trick: the thief was said to wear a pair of trousers smeared with lion's fat. Stilitano knew that this was unobtainable, but the idea excited him. He stopped talking. He was probably imagining himself in a thicket, at night, stalking his prey, wearing a pair of trousers stiff with fat. He was strong with the lion's strength, savage as a consequence of being thus prepared for war, the stake, the spit and the grave. In his armor of grease and imagination he was resplendent. I do not know whether he was aware of the beauty of adorning himself with the strength and boldness of a gypsy, nor whether he was thrilled at the idea of thus penetrating the secrets of the tribe.

"Would you like to be a gypsy?" I once asked him.

"Me?"

"Yes, you."

"I wouldn't mind. Only I wouldn't want to stay in a caravan."

Thus he did dream occasionally. I thought I had discovered the flaw in his petrified shell through which a bit of my tenderness might slip in. Stilitano was too little excited by nocturnal adventures for me to feel any real exhilaration in his company when we slunk along walls, lanes and gardens, when we scaled fences, when we robbed. I have no significant memory of any such excitement. It was with Guy, in France, that I was to have the profound revelation of what burglary was.

(*When we were locked in the little storeroom, waiting for night and the moment to enter the empty offices of the Municipal Pawnshop in B., Guy suddenly seemed to me secret, inscrutable. He was no longer the ordinary guy you happen upon somewhere or other; he was a kind*

*of destroying angel. He tried to smile. He even broke out
into a silent laugh, but his eyebrows were knitted. From
within this little fairy where a hoodlum was confined
there sprang forth a determined and terrifying fellow,
ready for anything—and primarily for murder if anyone
dared to hinder his action. He was laughing, and I
thought I could read in his eyes a will to murder which
might be exercised on me. The longer he stared at me,
the more I had the feeling that he read in me the same
determined will to be exercised against him. So he grew
taut. His eyes were harder, his temples metallic, his facial
muscles more knotted. In response, I hardened accord-
ingly. I prepared an arsenal. I watched him. If someone
had entered at that moment, we would, I felt, uncertain
as we were of one another, have killed each other out of
fear lest one of us oppose the terrible decision of the
other.)*

I continued doing other jobs with Stilitano. We knew
a night watchman who tipped us off. Thanks to him, we
lived off our burglaries alone for a long time. The boldness of a thief's life—and its light—would have meant
nothing if Stilitano at my side had not been proof of it.
My life became magnificent by men's standards since I
had a friend whose beauty derived from the idea of
luxury. I was the valet whose job was to look after, to
dust, polish and wax, an object of great value which, however, through the miracle of friendship, belonged to me.

"When I walk along the street," I wondered, "am I
being envied by the loveliest and wealthiest of señoritas?
What roguish prince, what infanta in rags, can walk about
and have so handsome a lover?"

I speak of this period with emotion, and I magnify it,
but if glamorous words, I mean words charged in my
mind with more glamor than meaning, occur to me, they
do so perhaps because the poverty they express, which

was mine too, is likewise a source of wonder. I want to
rehabilitate this period by writing of it with the names
of things most noble. My victory is verbal and I owe it to
the richness of the terms, but may the poverty that
counsels such choices be blessed. In Stilitano's company,
during the period when I was to experience moral abjection, I stopped desiring it, and I hated that which must
be its sign: my lice, rags and filth. Perhaps his power
alone was enough for Stilitano to inspire respect without
having to perform a bold deed; nevertheless, I would
have liked our life together to be more brilliant, though it
was sweet for me to encounter in his shadow (his shadow,
dark as a negro's must be, was my seraglio) the looks of
admiration of the whores and their men when I knew that
we were both poor thieves. I kept inciting him to ever
more perilous adventures.

"We need a revolver," I said to him.

"Would you know what to do with it?"

"With you around, I wouldn't be afraid to bump a guy
off."

Since I was his right arm, I would have been the one
to execute. But the more I obeyed serious orders, the
greater was my intimacy with him who issued them. He,
however, smiled. In a gang (an association of evil-doers)
the young boys and inverts are the ones who display
boldness. They are the instigators of dangerous jobs. They
play the role of the fecundating sting. The potency of the
males, the age, authority, friendship and presence of the
elders, fortify and reassure them. The males are depend-
ent only upon themselves. They are their own heaven,
and, knowing their weakness, they hesitate. Applied to
my particular case, it seemed to me that the men, the
toughs, were composed of a kind of feminine fog in which
I would still like to lose myself so that I might feel more
intensely that I was a solid block.

A certain distinction of manner, a more assured gait,

proved to me my success, my ascension into the secular domain. In Stilitano's presence, I walked in the wake of a duke. I was his faithful but jealous dog. My bearing grew proud. Along the Ramblas, toward evening, we passed a woman and her son. The boy was good looking. He was about fifteen. My eyes lingered on his blond hair. We walked by them and I turned around. The youngster showed no reaction. Stilitano likewise turned around to see whom I was looking at. It was at that moment, when both Stilitano's eyes and mine were staring after her son, that the mother drew him to her, or drew herself to him, as if to protect him from the danger of our two gazes, of which, however, she was unaware. I was jealous of Stilitano whose mere movement of the head had, so it seemed to me, just been sensed as a danger by the mother's back.

One day, while I was waiting for him in a bar on the Parallelo (the bar was, at the time, the meeting place of all the hardened French criminals: pimps, crooks, racketeers, escaped convicts. Argot, sung with somewhat of a Marseille accent, and a few years behind Montmartre argot, was its official tongue. Twenty-one and poker were played there rather than ronda), Stilitano blew in. He was welcomed by the Parisian pimps with their customary, slightly ceremonious politeness. Severely, but with smiling eyes, he solemnly placed his solemn behind on the straw-bottomed chair whose wood groaned with the shamelessness of a beast of burden. This wailing of the seat expressed perfectly my respect for the sober posterior of Stilitano, whose charm was neither all nor always contained there, though it would assemble in that spot—or rather on it—and would there accumulate and delegate its most caressing waves—and masses of lead!—to give the rump a reverberating undulation and weight.

I refuse to be prisoner of a verbal automatism, but here again I must have recourse to a religious image: this posterior was a Station. Stilitano sat down. With his usual elegant lassitude—"I palmed them," he would say on all and every occasion—he dealt the cards for the poker game, from which I was excluded. None of the gentlemen would have required that I leave the game, but of my own accord, out of courtesy, I went to sit down behind Stilitano. As I was about to take my seat, I saw a louse on the collar of his jacket. Stilitano was handsome and strong, and welcome at a gathering of similar males whose authority likewise lay in their muscles and their awareness of their revolvers. The louse on Stilitano's collar, still invisible to the other men, was not a small stray spot; it was moving; it shifted about with disturbing velocity, as if crossing and measuring its domain—its space rather. But it was not only at home; on Stilitano's collar it was the sign that he belonged to an unmistakably verminous world, despite his eau de Cologne and silk shirt. I examined him more closely: his hair near the neck was too long, dirty, and irregularly cut.

"If the louse continues, it'll fall on his sleeve or into his glass. The pimps'll see it. . . ."

As if out of tenderness, I leaned on Stilitano's shoulder and gradually worked my hand up to his collar, but I was unable to complete my movement. With a shrug, Stilitano disengaged himself, and the insect continued its meanderings. A Pigalle pimp (who was said to be tied up with an international band of white slavers) made the following remark:

"There's a nice one climbing on you."

All eyes turned—without, however, losing sight of the game—to the collar of Stilitano, who, twisting his neck, managed to see the insect.

"You're the one who's been picking them up," he said to me as he crushed it.

"Why me?"

"I'm telling you it's you."

The tone of his voice was unanswerably arrogant, but his eyes were smiling. The men continued their card game.

It was the same day that Stilitano informed me that Pépé had just been arrested. He was in the Montjuich jail.

"Who told you?"

"I read it in the paper."

"How long can they give him?"

"Life."

We made no other comment.

This journal is not a mere literary diversion. The further I progress, reducing to order what my past life suggests, and the more I persist in the rigor of composition— of the chapters, of the sentences, of the book itself—the more do I feel myself hardening in my will to utilize, for virtuous ends, my former hardships. I feel their power.

In the urinals, which Stilitano never entered, the behavior of the faggots would make matters clear: they would perform their dance, the remarkable movement of a snake standing on its tail and undulating, swaying from side to side, tilted slightly backward, so as to cast a furtive glance at my prick which was out of my fly. I would go off with the one who looked most prosperous.

In my time, the Ramblas were frequented by two young mariconas who carried a tame little monkey on their shoulders. It was an easy pretext for approaching clients: the monkey would jump up on the man they pointed out to it. One of the mariconas was called Pedro. He was pale and thin. His waist was very supple, his step quick. His eyes in particular were splendid, his lashes immense.

In fun, I asked him which was the monkey, he or the

animal he carried on his shoulder. We started quarreling. I punched him. His eyelashes remained stuck to my knuckles; they were false. I had just discovered the existence of fakes.

Stilitano got money occasionally from the whores. Most often he stole it from them, either by taking the change when they paid for something, or at night from their handbags, when they were on the bidet. He would go through the Barrio Chino and the Parallelo heckling all the women, sometimes irritating them, sometimes fondling them, but always ironic. When he returned to the room, toward morning, he would bring back a bundle of children's magazines full of gaudy pictures. He would sometimes go a long roundabout way in order to buy them at a newsstand that was open late at night. He would read the stories which, in those days, corresponded to the Tarzan adventures in today's comic books. The hero of these stories is lovingly drawn. The artist took the utmost pains with the imposing physique of this knight, who was almost always nude or obscenely dressed. Then Stilitano would fall asleep. He would manage so that his body did not touch mine. The bed was very narrow. As he put out the light, he would say,

"Night, kid!"

And upon awakening:

"Morning, kid!"[1]

Our room was very tiny. It was dirty. The wash basin was filthy. No one in the Barrio Chino would have dreamed of cleaning his room, his belongings or his linen —except his shirt and, most often, only the collar. Once a

---

[1] I used to toss my things any old place when we went to bed, but Stilitano laid his out on a chair, carefully arranging the trousers, jacket and shirt so that nothing would be creased. He seemed thereby to be endowing his clothes with life, as if wanting them to get a night's rest after a hard day.

week, to pay the room rent, Stilitano screwed the land-
lady who, on other days, called him Señor.

One evening he had to fight. We were going through
the Calle Carmen. It was just about dark. Spaniards'
bodies sometimes have a kind of undulating flexibility and
their stances are occasionally equivocal. In broad daylight
Stilitano would not have made a mistake. In this incipient
darkness he grazed three men who were talking quietly
but whose gesticulations were both brisk and languorous.
As he neared them, Stilitano, in his most insolent tone
of voice, hurled a few coarse words at them. Three quick
and vigorous pimps replied to the insults. Stilitano stood
there, taken aback. The three men approached.

"Do you take us for mariconas, talking to us like that?"

Although he recognized his blunder, Stilitano wanted
to strut in my presence.

"Suppose I do?"

"Maricona yourself."

A few women drew up, and some men. A circle
gathered around us. A fight seemed inevitable. One of
the young men provoked Stilitano outright.

"If you're not fruit, come on and fight."

Before getting to the point of fists or weapons, hoodlums gab it out for a while. It's not that they try to soft-
pedal the conflict; rather, they work themselves up to
combat. Some other Spaniards, their friends, were egging
the three pimps on. Stilitano felt he was in danger. My
presence no longer bothered him. He said:

"After all, boys, you're not going to fight with a cripple."

He held out his stump. But he did it with such simplicity, such sobriety, that this vile hamming, instead of
disgusting me with him, ennobled him. He withdrew, not
to the sound of jeers, but to a murmur expressing the
discomfort of decent men discovering the misery about
them. Stilitano stepped back slowly, protected by his out-

stretched stump, which was placed simply in front of him. The absence of the hand was as real and effective as a royal attribute, as the hand of justice.

Those whom one of their number called the Carolinas paraded to the site of a demolished street urinal. During the 1933 riots, the insurgents tore out one of the dirtiest, but most beloved pissoirs. It was near the harbor and the barracks, and its sheet iron had been corroded by the hot urine of thousands of soldiers. When its ultimate death was certified, the Carolinas—not all, but a formally chosen delegation—in shawls, mantillas, silk dresses and fitted jackets, went to the site to place a bunch of red roses tied together with a crape veil. The procession started from the Parallelo, crossed the Calle São Paolo and went down the Ramblas de Las Flores until it reached the statue of Columbus. The faggots were perhaps thirty in number, at eight A.M., at sunrise. I saw them going by. I accompanied them from a distance. I knew that my place was in their midst, not because I was one of them, but because their shrill voices, their cries, their extravagant gestures seemed to me to have no other aim than to try to pierce the shell of the world's contempt. The Carolinas were great. They were the Daughters of Shame.

When they reached the harbor, they turned right, toward the barracks, and upon the rusty, stinking sheet iron of the pissoir that lay battered on the heap of dead scrap iron they placed the flowers.

I was not in the procession. I belonged to the ironic and indulgent crowd that was entertained by it. Pedro airily admitted to his false lashes, the Carolinas to their wild larks.

Meanwhile, Stilitano, by denying himself to my pleasure, became the symbol of chastity, of frigidity itself. If he did screw the whores often, I was unaware of it. When

he lay down to sleep in our bed, he had the modesty to
arrange his shirt tail so artfully that I saw nothing of his
penis. The purity of his features corrected even the
eroticism of his walk. He became the representation of a
glacier. I would have liked to offer myself to the most
bestial of negroes, to the most flat-nosed and most powerful face, so that within me, having no room for anything
but sexuality, my love for Stilitano might be further
stylized. I was therefore able to venture in his presence
the most absurd and humiliating postures.

We often went to the Criolla together. Hitherto, it had
never occurred to him to exploit me. When I brought
back to him the pesetas I had earned around the pissoirs,
Stilitano decided that I would work in the Criolla.

"Would you like me to dress up as a woman?" I murmured.

Would I have dared, supported by his powerful shoulder, to walk the streets in a spangled skirt between the
Calle Carmen and the Calle Mediodia? Except for foreign
sailors, no one would have been surprised, but neither
Stilitano nor I would have known how to choose the dress
or the hair-do, for taste is required. Perhaps that was
what held us back. I still remembered the sighs of Pedro,
with whom I had once teamed up, when he went to get
dressed.

"When I see those rags hanging there, I get the blues!
I feel as if I were going into a vestry to get ready to con-
duct a funeral. They've got a priestish smell. Like incense.
Like urine. Look at them hanging! I wonder how I manage to get into those damned sausage skins."

"Will I have to have things like that? Maybe I'll even
have to sew and cut with my man's help. And wear a
bow, or maybe several, in my hair."

With horror I saw myself decked out in enormous bows,
not of ribbons, but of sausage meat in the form of pricks.

"It'll be a drooping, dangling bow," added a mocking

inner voice. An old man's droopy ding-dong. A bow limp, or impish! And in what hair? In an artificial wig or in my own dirty, curly hair?

As for my dress, I knew it would be sober and that I would wear it with modesty, whereas what was needed to carry the thing off was a kind of wild extravagance. Nevertheless, I cherished the dream of sewing on a cloth rose. It would emboss the dress and would be the feminine counterpart of Stilitano's bunch of grapes.

(Long afterward, when I ran into him in Antwerp, I spoke to Stilitano about the fake bunch hidden in his fly. He then told me that a Spanish whore used to wear a muslin rose pinned on at cunt level.

"To replace her lost flower," he said.)

In Pedro's room, I looked at the skirts with melancholy. He gave me a few addresses of women's outfitters, where I would find dresses to fit me.

"You'll have a *toilette*, Juan."[1]

I was sickened by this butcher's word (I was thinking that the *toilette* was also the greasy tissue enveloping the guts in animals' bellies). It was then that Stilitano, perhaps hurt by the idea of his friend in fancy dress, refused.

"There's no need for it," he said. "You'll manage well enough to make pick-ups."

Alas, the boss of the Criolla demanded that I appear as a young lady.

As a young lady!

> *Myself a young lady*
> *I alight on my hip. . . .*

I then realized how hard it is to reach the light by puncturing the abscess of shame. I once managed to ap-

---

[1] The term *la toilette* also refers to certain kinds of wrappings or casings, for example, a tailor's or dressmaker's wrapper for garments, as well as to the caul over mutton.—Translator's note.

pear in woman's dress with Pedro, to exhibit myself with
him. I went one evening, and we were invited by a group
of French officers. At their table was a lady of about fifty.
She smiled at me sweetly, with indulgence, and unable to
contain herself any longer, she asked me:

"Do you like men?"

"Yes, madame, I do."

"And . . . when did it start?"

I did not slap anyone, but my voice was so shaken that
I realized how angry and ashamed I was. In order to pull
myself together, I robbed one of the officers that very
same night.

"At least," I said to myself, "if my shame is real, it hides
a sharper, more dangerous element, a kind of sting that
will always threaten anyone who provokes it. It might not
have been laid over me like a trap, might not have been
intentional, but since it is what it is, I want it to conceal
me so that I can lie in wait beneath it."

At Carnival time, it was easy to go about in woman's
dress, and I stole an Andalusian petticoat with a bodice
from a hotel room. Disguised by the mantilla and fan,
one evening I walked across town quickly in order to get
to the Criolla. So that my break with your world would
be less brutal, I kept my trousers on under the skirt.
Hardly had I reached the bar when someone ripped the
train of my dress. I turned around in a fury.

"I beg your pardon. Excuse me."

The foot of a blond young man had got caught in the
lace. I hardly had strength enough to mumble, "Watch
what you're doing." The face of the clumsy young man,
who was both smiling and excusing himself, was so pale
that I blushed. Someone next to me said to me in a low
voice, "Excuse him, señora, he limps."

"I won't have people limping on my dress!" screamed
the beautiful actress who smoldered within me. But the

people around us were laughing. "I won't have people limping on my toilette!" I screamed to myself. Formulated within me, in my stomach, as it seemed to me, or in the intestines, which are enveloped by the "toilette," this phrase must have been expressed by a terrible glare. Furious and humiliated, I left under the laughter of the men and the Carolinas. I went straight to the sea and drowned the skirt, bodice, mantilla and fan. The whole city was joyous, drunk with the Carnival that was cut off from the earth and alone in the middle of the Ocean. I was poor and sad.

("Taste is required. . . ." I was already refusing to have any. I forbade myself to. Of course I would have shown a great deal of it. I knew that cultivating it would have—not sharpened me but—softened me. Stilitano himself was amazed that I was so uncouth. I wanted my fingers to be stiff: *I kept myself from learning to sew.*)

Stilitano and I left for Cadiz. Changing from one freight train to another, we finally got to a place near San Fernando and decided to continue our journey on foot. Stilitano disappeared. He arranged to meet me at the station. He didn't show up. I waited for a long time; I returned the following day and the day after, two days in succession, though I was sure he had deserted me. I was alone and without money. When I realized this, I again became aware of the presence of lice, of their distressing and sweet company in the hems of my shirt and trousers. Stilitano and I had never ceased to be nuns of Upper Thebaid who never washed their feet and whose shifts rotted away.

San Fernando is on the sea. I decided to get to Cadiz, which is built right on the water, though connected to the mainland by a very long jetty. It was evening when I started out. Before me were the high salt pyramids of the San Fernando marshes, and farther off, in the sea, silhouetted by the setting sun, a city of domes and minarets. At the outermost point of Western soil, I suddenly had before me the synthesis of the Orient. For the first time in my life I neglected a human being for a thing. I forgot Stilitano.

In order to keep alive, I would go to the port early in the morning, to the piscatoria, where the fishermen always throw from their boats a few fish caught the night before. All beggars are familiar with this practice. Instead of going, as in Malaga, to cook them on the fire of the other tramps, I went back alone, to the middle of the rocks overlooking Porto Reale. The sun would be rising when my fish were cooked. I almost always ate them without bread or salt. Standing up, or lying among the rocks, or sitting on them, at the easternmost point of the island, facing the mainland, I was the first man lit up and warmed by the first ray, which was itself the first manifestation of life. I had gathered the fish on the wharves in the darkness. It was still dark when I reached my rocks. The coming of the sun overwhelmed me. I worshiped it. A kind of sly intimacy developed between us. I honored it, though without, to be sure, any complicated ritual; it would not have occurred to me to ape the primitives, but I know that this star became my god. It was within my body that it rose, continued its curve and completed it. If I saw it in the sky of the astronomers, I did so because it was the bold projection there of the one I preserved within myself. Perhaps I even confused it in some obscure way with the vanished Stilitano.

I am indicating to you, in this way, the form that my sensibility took. Nature made me uneasy. My love for Stilitano, the roar with which he burst upon my wretchedness, and any number of other things, delivered me to the elements. But they are malicious. In order to tame them I wanted to contain them. I refused to deny them cruelty; quite the contrary, I congratulated them for having as much as they had; I flattered them.

As an operation of this kind cannot succeed by means of dialectics, I had recourse to magic, that is, to a kind of deliberate *predisposition*, an intuitive complicity with nature. Language would have been of no help to me. It was then that things and circumstances became maternal to me, though alert within them, like the sting of a bee, was the point of my pride. (Maternal: that is, whose essential element is femininity. In writing this I do not want to make any Mazdaean allusion: I merely point out that my sensibility required that it be surrounded by a feminine order. It could do so inasmuch as it could avail itself of masculine qualities: hardness, cruelty, indifference.)

If I attempt to recompose with words what my attitude was at the time, the reader will be no more taken in than I. We know that our language is incapable of recalling even the pale reflection of those bygone, foreign states. The same would be true of this entire journal if it were to be the notation of what I was. I shall therefore make clear that it is meant to indicate what I am today, as I write it. It is not a quest of time gone by, but a work of art whose pretext-subject is my former life. It will be a present fixed with the help of the past, and not vice versa. Let the reader therefore understand that the facts were what I say they were, but the interpretation that I give them is what I am—now.

At night I would stroll about the city. I would sleep against a wall, sheltered from the wind. I thought about Tangiers, whose proximity fascinated me, as did the glamor of the city, that haunt, rather, of traitors. To escape my poverty, I invented the boldest acts of treason, which I would have calmly performed. Today I know that only my love of the French language attaches me to France, but then!

This taste for treason will have to be better formulated when I am questioned at the time of Stilitano's arrest.

"Should I squeal on Stilitano for money and under the threat of a beating?" I asked myself. "I still love him, and I answer no. But should I squeal on Pépé who murdered the ronda player on the Parallelo?"

I would have accepted, though with great shame, the knowledge that my soul was rotten within since it emitted the odor that makes people hold their noses. Now the reader may remember that my periods of begging and prostitution were to me a discipline which taught me to utilize ignoble elements, to apply them to my own ends, indeed, to take pleasure in my choosing them. I would have done the same (strong in my skill in turning my shame to account) with my soul that had been decomposed by treason. Fortune granted that the question be put to me at the time when a young ship's ensign was sentenced to death by the maritime court of Toulon. He had turned over to the enemy the plans of a weapon or of a war port or of a boat. I am not talking of an act of treason causing the loss of a naval battle, which is slight, unreal, hanging from the wings of a schooner's sails, but of the loss of a combat of steel monsters wherein dwelt the pride of a people no longer childlike, but severe, helped and supported by the learned mathematics of technicians. In short, it was an act of treason in modern times. The newspaper reporting these facts (I learned of the matter in Cadiz) said, stupidly no doubt, for what could the reporter know about it: ". . . out of a taste for treason." Accompanying the text was the photograph of a young, very handsome officer. I was taken with his picture, which I still carry with me. As love is exalted in perilous situations, secretly within me I offered to share the exile's Siberia. The maritime court, by arousing my hostility, further facilitated my climb toward him whom I approached with heavy yet wingèd foot. His name was Marc Aubert. I shall go to Tangiers, I said to myself, and perhaps I may be summoned among the traitors and become one of them.

I left Cadiz for Huelva. Chased by the Municipal Guard, I returned to Jerez and then, following the coastline, went on to Alicante. I traveled alone. Occasionally, I would meet or overtake another tramp. Without even sitting down on a stone pile, we would tell each other which village was more friendly to beggars, which mayor less inhuman, and we would continue on our solitary way. Joking about our sacks, we would say, "He's out hunting with a canvas gun." I was alone. I walked humbly along the outer edge of the roads, near the ditches, where the dust from the white grass powdered my feet. By this shipwreck, sunk by all the woes of the world in an ocean of despair, I still knew the sweetness of being able to cling to the strong, terrible prick of a negro. It was stronger than all the currents of the world, more certain, more consoling, and by a single one of my sighs more worthy than all your continents. Toward evening my feet would be sweating; on summer evenings I would therefore walk in the mud. The sun filled my head with a lead ballast which served as thought and at the same time emptied it. Andalusia was lovely, hot and barren. I went all across it. At that age, fatigue was unknown to me. I carried with me such a burden of sorrow that I was sure my whole life would be spent in wandering. Vagrancy was no longer a detail which would embellish my life, but a reality. I no longer know what I thought, but I remember that I offered all my woes to God. In my solitude, remote from men, I came quite close to being all love, all devotion.

"I am so remote from them," I must have said to myself, "that I no longer have any hope of returning. Let me
therefore cut myself off completely. Between them and
me there will be even fewer bonds, and the last will be
broken if to their contempt for *me* I oppose my love of
them."

Thus, reversing steam, there I was granting you my
pity. My despair was probably not expressed in this form.
Indeed, everything in my thoughts frittered away, but
the pity I speak of must have crystallized into exact reflections which, in my sun-scorched head, assumed a final
and obsessive form. My weariness—I do not think it was
fatigue—prevented me from resting. I no longer went to
drink at fountains. My throat was parched. My eyes
burned. I was hungry. Copper glints played over my
tough beard in the sunlight. I was dry, young and sad.
I learned to smile at things and meditate upon them. As
a young Frenchman on that shore, from my solitude,
from my beggar's state, from the dust of the ditches that
rose up in tiny individual clouds about each foot, renew-
ing themselves at every step, my pride derived a consoling singularity which contrasted with the banal sordidness of my apparel. Never did my broken-down shoes or
dirty socks have the dignity that lifts the sandals of the
Carmelites and bears them through the dust, never did
my dirty jacket accord my movements the slightest nobility. It was during the summer of 1934 that I trudged
along the Andalusian highways. At night, after begging
a few coins in a village, I would continue into the countryside, and I would lie down to sleep at the bottom of a
ditch. The dogs would scent me—my odor further isolated
me—they would bark whenever I left a farm or arrived
at one.

"Shall I go or not?" I would ask myself as I neared a
white house surrounded by whitewashed walls.

I would not hesitate long. The dog tied to the door would still be yapping. I would approach. It would yap louder. In very bad Spanish I would ask the woman who appeared, though without leaving the threshold, for a penny—being a foreigner protected me a little. If alms were refused me, I would withdraw, my head bowed, my face expressionless.

I dared not even notice the beauty of that part of the world—unless it were to look for the secret of that beauty, the imposture behind it, of which one will be a victim if he trusts it. By rejecting it, I discovered poetry.

"All this beauty, however, is meant for me. I am registering it, and I know that it is so conspicuous in order to show how woebegone I am."

Along the shores of the Atlantic and the Mediterranean I went through fishing ports where the elegant poverty of the fishermen wounded my own. Without their seeing me, I would brush against men and women standing in a patch of shade, against boys playing on a square. The love that human beings seem to feel for one another tortured me at the time. If two men exchanged a greeting or a smile in passing, I would retreat to the farthest edges of the world. The glances exchanged by the two friends—and sometimes their words—were the subtlest emanation of a ray of love from the heart of each. A ray of very soft light, delicately coiled: a spun ray of love. I was amazed that such delicacy, so fine a thread and of so precious, and so chaste, a substance as love could be fashioned in so dark a smithy as the muscular bodies of those males, though they themselves always emitted that gentle ray in which there sometimes sparkled the droplets of a mysterious dew. I would fancy hearing the elder say to the other, who was no longer I, speaking of that part of the body which he must have loved dearly:

"I'm going to dent your halo for you again tonight!"

I could not take lightly the idea that people made love without me.

(Maurice G. and Robert B. met at the Belle-Isle Reformatory. They were seventeen years old. I had known them in Paris and had made love to each of them several times, though neither knew about the other. They saw each other one day at Belle-Isle when they were tending cows or sheep. I don't know how it happened, but in talking about Paris, the first person whose name came up was mine. They were amused and amazed to learn that the other had also been my lover. It was Maurice who told me about it.

"We became real pals by thinking about you. I used to feel depressed at night. . . ."

"Why?"

"I used to hear him groaning behind the partition that separates the men. He was better looking than me and all the toughs were ramming it into him. There was nothing I could do about it."

I am always moved whenever I learn that the miraculous unhappiness of my childhood at the Mettray Reformatory is forever perpetuated.)

Inland, I went through landscapes of sharp rocks that gnawed the sky and ripped the azure. This rigid, dry, malicious indigence flouted my own and my human tenderness. Yet it incited me to hardness. I was less alone upon discovering in nature one of my essential qualities: pride. I wanted to be a rock among rocks. I was happy to be one, and proud. Thus did I hold to the soil. I had my companions. I knew what the mineral kingdom was.

"We'll stand up to wind, rain and blows."

My adventure with Stilitano was retreating in my mind. He himself was dwindling. All that remained of him was a gleaming point, of marvelous purity.

"He was a man," I said to myself.

Had he not confessed to me to having killed a man in the Foreign Legion? And did he not justify himself as follows:

"He threatened to bump me off. I killed him. He had a higher caliber gun than mine. I'm not guilty."

The only thing about him which retained any meaning for me was the manly qualities and gestures that I knew were his. Frozen, fixed forever in the past, they composed a solid object, indestructible since it had been achieved by those few unforgettable details.

At times, in the interior of this negative life, I would allow myself to perform an act, occasional thefts to the detriment of poor wretches, the gravity of which gave me a certain awareness.

The palms! They were gilded by a morning sun. The light quivered, not the palms. I came upon the first of them. They lined the Mediterranean. Frost on window-panes in winter had more variety, but the palms swept me in like manner—better perhaps—into a Christmas scene born paradoxically of the verse about the holy day preceding the death of God, about the entrance into Jerusalem, about the palms strewn beneath the feet of Jesus. My childhood had dreamed of palm trees. Now I was actually seeing them. I had been told that snow does not fall in Bethlehem. The name Alicante gave me a glimpse of the Orient. I was in the heart of my childhood, at its most preciously preserved moment. At a turn in the road I was about to discover beneath three palm trees the Christmas manger where, as a child, I used to be present at *my nativity* between the ox and the ass. I was the humblest of the world's poor. Wretchedly I walked in the dust and fatigue, at last deserving the palm, ripe for the penal colony, for the straw hats and the palm trees.

In the hands of a poor man, coins are no longer the sign of wealth but of its opposite. No doubt I robbed

some rich hidalgo in passing—rarely, for they know how
to protect themselves—but such thefts had no effect on
my soul. I shall speak of those I committed against other
beggars. The Alicante crime will clarify matters.

You will recall that, in Barcelona, Pépé, as he fled, had
time to hand me the money he had picked up in the
dust. Out of heroic loyalty to a hero, out of fear, too,
lest Pépé or one of his cronies find me, I had buried the
money at the foot of a catalpa in a little square near
Montjuich. I had the strength of character never to mention it to Stilitano, but when we decided to go south
together, I dug up the money (two or three hundred
pesetas) and sent it addressed to my name, care of general
delivery, to Alicante. Much has been said of the effect of
landscape upon the feelings, but not, it seems to me, of
the way it acts upon moral attitudes. Before entering
Murcia I crossed the palm grove of Elche, and I was
already so spontaneously excited by nature that my relations with men were beginning to be those which usually
exist between men and things. I reached Alicante at
night. I had to sleep in a workyard. Toward morning
there was revealed to me the mystery of the city and its
name: on the shores of a quiet sea and plunging into it;
white mountains, a few palms, a few houses, the port and,
in the sunrise, a cool and luminous air. (I was to experience a similar moment in Venice.) The connection among
all things was lightness. In order to be worthy of entering such a system, it seemed to me necessary to break
gently with men, to purify myself. As the bond linking
me to them was an emotional one, I had to detach myself from them without fanfare. All along the road I had
promised myself the bitter joy of withdrawing the money
from the post office and sending it to Pépé in the Montjuich jail. I drank a cup of warm milk at a stand that was
just opening and went to the general delivery window in

the post office. No difficulties were made about giving me
the bulky envelope. The money was there, intact. I left
and tore up the bills, meaning to throw them into a sewer,
but, the better to provoke the break, I pasted them together on a bench and then treated myself to a sumptuous lunch. Pépé must have been dying of hunger in jail,
but I thought that by means of this crime I had freed
myself of moral preoccupations.

However, I did not wander along the roads at random.
My path was that of all beggars and, like them, I was to
know Gibraltar. At night, the erotic mass of the rock,
filled, thronged, with soldiers and sleeping cannons, drove
me wild. I lived in the village of Linea, which is simply
one big brothel, and there I began the period of tin cans.
All the beggars in the world—I've seen the like in Central
Europe and in France—have one or more white tin cans
(which contain peas or stew) to which they add a wire
handle. They go along the roads and railroad tracks with
these cans hanging from the shoulder. I got my first one
in Linea. It was new. I had picked it out of a garbage
can where someone had thrown it the night before. Its
metal was gleaming. I pressed down the sheared edges
with a stone so that they wouldn't cut, and I went to the
barbed wire of Gibraltar to pick up the leftovers of the
English soldiers. In that way I abased myself further. I
no longer begged for money but for scraps of food. To
which was added the shame of begging them from soldiers. I would feel unworthy if some soldier's good looks
or the potency of his uniform excited me. At night, I tried
to sell myself to them, and I succeeded, thanks to the
darkness of the narrow streets. At noon, the beggars could
hang around anywhere in the enclosure, but in the evening we lined up in one of the trenches, near the barracks.
One evening I recognized Salvador on the line.

When, two years later in Antwerp, I met Stilitano, who

had put on weight, he was walking arm in arm with a
smart-looking tart who was wearing long artificial eyelashes and a tight black satin dress. Still very good-
looking, despite the heaviness of his features, wearing an
expensive woolen suit and a gold ring, he was being led
by a ridiculous, mean-tempered, tiny little white dog. It
was then that this pimp was revealed to me: he held his
folly in leash, his curly, frizzy, coddled meanness. It preceded him too and led him to a sad city which was always
wet with rain. I lived on the Rue du Sac, near the docks.
At night I hung around the bars on the docks of the
Scheldt. With that river, with that town of cut and stolen
diamonds, I associated the radiant adventure of Manon
Lescaut.[1] I felt myself involved in the novel, entering into
the picture, idealizing myself, turning into an idea of
jail and love intermingled. I teamed up with a young
Fleming who worked on a merry-go-round at a fair, and
we stole bikes in that city of gold, gems and naval vic-
tories. There where Stilitano was rich and loved, I continued in my poverty. I shall never dare reproach him for
having squealed on Pépé. Do I even know whether I was
not more excited by Stilitano's treachery than by the
gypsy's crime? Though unable to give me the exact details
—the fact that this indecision imparted to the tale a his-
torical tone further embellished it—Salvador was glad to
tell me what had happened. His drunken, joyous voice—
broken at times so as not to yield too fully to the song
of a victim—proved his hatred of Stilitano, and his bitterness. A feeling of that kind made Stilitano seem stronger,
bigger. Neither Salvador nor I was surprised to see one
another.

As he was one of the big shots and had a certain seni-
ority in Linea, I escaped having to pay the tithe of service

---

[1] The name of the Scheldt in French is *L'Escaut.*—Translator's
note.

that two or three strong, bullying beggars demanded of
me. I went to his side.

"I learned all about what happened," he said.

"What?"

"What? Stilitano's arrest."

"Arrested? Why?"

"Don't act innocent. You know more about it than I."

All of Salvador's gentleness had changed into a kind of
peevishness. He spoke to me maliciously and told me
about my friend's arrest. It was not for the theft of the
cape or any other theft but for the murder of the
Spaniard.

"He wasn't the one," I said.

"Of course not. Everyone knows that. It was the gypsy.
But it was Stilitano who spilled the beans. He knew the
name. The gypsy was found in the Albaïcin. They arrested
Stilitano so as to protect him from the gypsy's brothers
and pals."

On the road to Alicante, thanks to the resistance I had
to combat, thanks to what I had to bring into play to
abolish what is called remorse, the theft I had committed
became in my eyes a very hard, very pure, almost luminous act, which only the diamond can symbolize. I had, in
achieving it, destroyed once again—and, I thought to myself, once and for all—the dear bonds of brotherhood.

"After that, after this crime, what kind of moral perfection can I hope for?"

As the theft was indestructible, I decided to make it the
origin of a state of moral perfection.

"It's cowardly, weak, dirty, low . . . (I shall define it
only with words expressing shame). None of the elements
composing it leaves me a chance to magnify it. Yet I do
not deny this most monstrous of my sons. I want to fill
the world with its loathsome progeny."

But I cannot go into great detail about this period of

my life. My memory would like to forget it, would like to dim its contours, powder it with talcum, offer it a formula comparable to the milk bath which the elegants of the sixteenth century called *a bath of modesty*.

I got my mess-tin filled with leftover stew and went off to eat in a corner. I preserved within me the memory of a sublime and debased Stilitano, with his head under his wing. I was proud of his strength and was strong in his complicity with the police. All day long I was sad, though sober. A kind of dissatisfaction inflated each of my acts, including the most simple. I would have liked a visible, dazzling glory to be manifest at my fingertips, would have liked my potency to lift me from the earth, to explode within me and dissolve me, to shower me to the four winds. I would have rained over the world. My powder, my pollen, would have touched the stars. I loved Stilitano. But loving him in the rocky dryness of this land, under an irrevocable sun, exhausted me, rimmed my eyelids with fire. Weeping a little would have deflated me. Or talking a lot, at great length, brilliantly, before an attentive and respectful audience. I was alone and friendless.

I stayed in Gibraltar a few days, but chiefly in Linea. At mealtime, in front of the English barbed wire, Salvador and I would meet with indifference. More than once I saw him some distance away pointing me out with his finger or chin to another bum. He was intrigued by the period in my life when I had stayed with Stilitano. He sought to interpret its mystery. Since this life had taken place in the company of a "man," had been mingled with his, its history, which, as a result of being related by a witness, was a veritable martyrdom, adorned me in the eyes of the other beggars with a curious glamor. By precise though subtle indications, I was aware of it, and I

bore its weight without arrogance, while within me I
pursued what I thought Stilitano had indicated to me.

I would have liked to embark for Tangiers. Movies and
novels have made of this city a fearful place, a kind of
dive where gamblers haggle over the secret plans of all
the armies in the world. From the Spanish coast, Tangiers
seemed to me a fabulous city. It was the very symbol of
treason.

At times I would go to Algeciras. I would wander along
the docks and gaze into the distance where the notorious
city could sometimes be seen.

"What orgy of treason, of haggling, could one indulge
in there?" I wondered.

Reason, to be sure, prevented me from thinking that
anyone would have used me for purposes of spying, but
so great was my desire that I felt it illuminated me, that
it singled me out. Inscribed on my brow, visible to all,
was the word "traitor." I therefore saved a little money
and paid for a trip in a fishing boat, but rough weather
forced us to return to Algeciras. Another time, with the
collusion of a sailor, I managed to get on board a steamer.
My ragged clothing, filthy face and long, dirty hair frightened the customs officers, who would not let me disem-
bark. Back in Spain, I decided to go by way of Ceuta;
when I got there, I was put into jail for four days and
had to go back to where I had come from.

Probably no more at Tangiers than elsewhere would I
have been able to carry through an adventure regulated
by an organization that had its headquarters in offices,
an adventure governed by the rules of international political strategy, but to me this city represented Treason
so accurately, so magnificently, that I felt I was bound
to land there.

"Nevertheless, I'd find such fine examples there!"

There I would find Marc Aubert, Stilitano and others whose indifference to the rules of loyalty and rectitude I had suspected, without quite daring to believe it. Saying of them "They're treacherous" softened my heart. Still softens me at times. They are the only ones I believe capable of all kinds of boldness. Their sinuousness and the multiplicity of their moral lines form an interlacing which I call adventure. They depart from your rules. They are not faithful. Above all, they have a blemish, a wound, comparable to the bunch of grapes in Stilitano's underpants. In short, the greater my guilt in your eyes, the more whole, the more totally assumed, the greater will be my freedom. The more perfect my solitude and uniqueness. By my guilt I further gained the right to intelligence. Too many people think, I said to myself, who don't have the right to. They have not paid for it by the kind of undertaking which makes thinking indispensable to *your salvation*.

This *pursuit* of traitors and treason was only one of the forms of eroticism. It is rare—it is almost unknown—for a boy to offer me the heady joy that can only be offered me by the interlacings of a life in which I would be involved with him. A body stretched out between my sheets, fondled in a street or at night in the woods, or on a beach, affords me half a pleasure: I dare not see myself loving it, for I have known too many situations in which my person, whose importance lay in its grace, was the factor of charm of the moment. I shall never find them again. Thus do I realize that I have sought only situations charged with erotic intentions. That was what, among other things, guided my life. I am aware that there exist adventures whose heroes and details are erotic. Those are the ones I have wanted to live.

A few days later I learned that Pépé had been sen-

tenced to jail. I sent all the money I had to the imprisoned
Stilitano.

Two Criminal Records photographs have turned up.
In one of them I am sixteen or seventeen years old. I
am wearing, under a jacket of the *Assistance Publique*, a
torn sweater. My face is an oval, very pure; my nose is
smashed, flattened by a punch in some forgotten fight.
The look on my face is blasé, sad and warm, very serious.
My hair was thick and unruly. Seeing myself at that age,
I expressed my feelings almost aloud:
"Poor little fellow, you've suffered."
I was speaking kindly of another Jean who was not
myself. I suffered at the time from an ugliness I no longer
find on my childhood face. Nevertheless, crass insolence—
I was brazen—launched me forth into life with ease. If I
was anxious, it was not apparent at first. But at twilight,
when I was weary, my head would sink, and I would feel
my gaze lingering on the world and merging with it or
else turning inward and disappearing; I think it was
aware of my utter solitude. When I was a farmhand, when
I was a soldier, when I was at the orphanage, despite the
friendship and, occasionally, the affection of my masters,
I was alone, rigorously so. Prison offered me the first con-
solation, the first peace, the first friendly fellowship: I experienced them in the realm of foulness. Much solitude
had forced me to become my own companion. Envisaging
the external world, its indefiniteness, its confusion, which
is even more perfect at night, I set it up as a divinity of
which I was not only the cherished pretext, an object
of great care and caution, chosen and led in masterly
fashion, though through painful and exhausting ordeals,
to the verge of despair, but also the sole object of all this
labor. And little by little, through a kind of operation

which I cannot quite describe, without modifying the dimensions of my body, and perhaps because it was easier to contain so precious a reason for such glory, it was within me that I established this divinity—origin and disposition of myself. I swallowed it. I dedicated to it songs of my own invention. At night I would whistle. The melody was a religious one. It was slow. Its rhythm was somewhat heavy. I thought I was thereby entering into communication with God: which is what happened, God being only the hope and fervor contained in my song. Along the streets, with my hands in my pockets, my head drooping or held high, looking at houses or trees, I would whistle my clumsy hymns, which were not joyous, but not sad either: they were sober. I discovered that hope is merely the expression one gives to it. Likewise, protection. Never would I have whistled to a light rhythm. I recognized the religious themes: they create Venus, Mercury, or the Virgin.

In the second photo I am thirty years old. My face has hardened. The jaws are accentuated. The mouth is bitter and mean. I look like a hoodlum in spite of my eyes, which have remained gentle. Their gentleness is almost indiscernible because of the fixity of gaze imposed upon me by the official photographer. By means of these two pictures I can see the violence that animated me at the time: from the age of sixteen to thirty. In children's hells, in prisons, in bars, it was not heroic adventure that I sought; I pursued there my identification with the handsomest and most unfortunate criminals. I wanted to be the young prostitute who accompanies her lover to Siberia or the one who survives him, not in order to avenge him, but to mourn him and magnify his memory.

Without thinking myself magnificently born, the uncertainty of my origin allowed me to interpret it. I added to it the peculiarity of my misfortunes. Abandoned by my

family, I already felt it was natural to aggravate this
condition by a preference for boys, and this preference
by theft, and theft by crime or a complacent attitude in
regard to crime. I thus resolutely rejected a world which
had rejected me. This almost gleeful rushing into the
most humiliating situations is perhaps still motivated by
my childhood imagination which invented for me (so that
I might there squire about the slight and haughty person
of an abandoned little boy) castles, parks peopled with
guards rather than with statues, wedding gowns, bereave-
ments and nuptials, and later on, though just a trifle later,
when these reveries were thwarted to the extreme, to the
point of exhaustion in a life of wretchedness, by reformatories, by prisons, by thefts, insults, prostitution, I quite
naturally adorned my real situation as a man (but first as
a humiliated child whom knowledge of prisons was to
gratify to the full) with these objects of my desire, these
ornaments (and the rare diction pertaining to them)
which graced my mental habits. Prison offers the same
sense of security to the convict as does a royal palace to
a king's guest. They are the two buildings constructed
with the most faith, those which give the greatest certainty of being what they are—which are what they are
meant to be, and which they remain. The masonry, the
materials, the proportions and the architecture are in
harmony with a moral unity which makes these dwellings
indestructible so long as the social form of which they
are the symbol endures. The prison surrounds me with a
perfect guarantee. I am sure that it was constructed for
me—along with the Law Court, its annex, its monumental
vestibule. Everything therein was designed for me, in a
spirit of the utmost seriousness. The rigor of the rules,
their strictness, their precision, are in essence the same
as the etiquette of a royal court, as the exquisite and
tyrannical politeness of which a guest at that court is the

object. The foundations of the palace, like those of the prison, inhere in the fine quality of the stone, in marble stairways, in real gold, in carvings, the rarest in the realm, in the absolute power of their hosts; but they are also similar in that these two structures are one the root and the other the crest of a living system circulating between these two poles which contain it, compress it and which are sheer force. What security in the carpets, in the mirrors, in the very privacy of the palace latrines! Nowhere else does the act of shitting in the early morning assume the solemn importance which can result only from its being performed in a toilet through whose frosted windows can be discerned the sculptured façade, the guards, the statues and the court of honor; in a little privy where the tissue paper is of the usual kind but where some uncombed, unpowdered, powdery maid of honor in a satin dressing gown and pink slippers will shortly come to leave a heavy load; in a little privy from which the husky guards do not brutally expel me, for shitting there becomes an important act which has its place in a life to which the king has invited me. Prison offers me the same security. Nothing will demolish it, not blasts of wind, nor storms, nor bankruptcies. The prison remains sure of itself, and you in the midst of it sure of yourself. And yet it is this spirit of seriousness in which these structures were erected which is the source of their self esteem, of their mutual reserve and understanding; it is of this spirit of worldliness that they will perish. Were they established on the ground and in the world with more casualness, they might perhaps hold out for a long time, but their gravity makes me consider them without pity. I recognize that they have their foundations within myself; they are the signs of the most violent of my extreme tendencies, and my corrosive spirit is already working at their destruction. I pitched myself headlong into a miserable life which was the real appearance of destroyed palaces, of pillaged gardens, of dead splendors. It was their ruins, but, the more mutilated the ruins, the remoter seemed that of which they must have been the visible sign, more deeply buried in a sacred past, so that I no longer know whether I dwelt in sumptuous destitution or whether my abjection was magnificent. Finally, little by little, this idea of humiliation detached itself from what conditioned it; the cables connecting it with these ideal gildings were broken—gildings that justified it in the eyes of the world, in my eyes of flesh—almost excusing it—and it remained alone, by itself alone a reason for being, itself its only necessity and itself its only end. But it is the abandoned urchin's amorous imagining of royal magnificence that enables me to gild my shame, to carve it, to work over it like a goldsmith, until, through usage perhaps and the wearing away of the words veiling it, humility emerges from it. My love of Stilitano made me once again aware of so exceptional a disposition. Though I had known through him a certain nobility, now I was discovering the real direction of my life—as one says the direction through the woods—and that my life should manifest itself outside your world. I knew at the time a hardness and lucidity which explain my attitude toward the poor: so great was my destitution that it seemed to me I was composed of a dough that had been kneaded of it. It was my very essence, traversing and feeding my body as well as my soul. I am writing this book in an elegant hotel in one of the most fashionable cities in the world, where I am rich, though I cannot pity the poor: I am the poor. Though it is a pleasure for me to strut before them, I definitely deplore being unable to do so with more ostentation and insolence.

"I'd have a black, noiseless, shiny car. Idly, from inside, I would look out at poverty. Behind me would trail processions of myself in lavish finery so that poverty might watch me going by, so that the poor whom I shall not have ceased to be may see me slowing up nobly amidst the silence of a high-powered engine and in all the earth-ly glory prefiguring, if I wish, the other."

With Stilitano I was hopeless poverty, experiencing in the most fleshless country in Europe the dryest poetic formula, which was sometimes softened at night by my anxious trembling in the presence of nature. A few pages above I wrote: "a countryside at twilight." I did not imagine at the time that it contained grave dangers, that it concealed warriors who were going to kill or torture me; on the contrary, it became so sweet, so maternal and kind, that I was afraid to continue to be myself so that I might more easily melt into that kindness. I would often get off a freight train and wander into the night, to whose slow working I would listen; I would squat in the grass, or else I would not dare to and would remain standing motionless in the middle of a field. At times, I would pre-tend that the countryside was the scene of a crime story where I would place those heroes who will most effec-tively symbolize, as long as I live, my real drama: between two lone willows a young murderer who, with one hand in his pocket, levels a revolver and fires into a farmer's back. Did imaginary participation in a human adventure impart such receptive sweetness to the flora? I understood them. I stopped shaving the down that Salvador found disagreeable and began to look more and more like a mossy stalk.

Salvador did not say another word to me about Stili-tano. He was getting even homelier, but nevertheless gave pleasure to other tramps in some random alley or on some ragged litter.

"You've got to be pretty depraved to do it with that guy," Stilitano once said to me about Salvador.

Splendid depravity, sweet and kindly, which makes it possible to love those who are ugly, dirty and disfigured!

"You always find guys?"

"I get along," he answered showing his few black teeth. "Some of them give you what's left in their knapsacks or mess kits."

With faithful regularity he was still fulfilling his simple function. His begging was stagnant. It had become a still, transparent lake, never disturbed by a breath, and this poor shameful creature was the perfect image of what I would have liked to be. It was then perhaps that, had I met my mother and had she been humbler than I, we would have pursued together the ascension—though language seems to call for the word "fall" or any other that indicates a downward movement—the difficult, painful ascension which leads to humiliation. I would have carried out that adventure with her, I would have written of it so as to magnify, thanks to love, the terms—whether gestures or vocables—which were most abject.

I returned to France. I crossed the border without any trouble, but when I had got a few miles into the French countryside, I was arrested by French policemen. My rags were too Spanish.

"Your papers!"

I showed some scraps of paper that were torn and dirty as a result of folding and unfolding.

"What about your card?"

"What card?"

I learned of the existence of the humiliating "anthropometric card." It is issued to all tramps and stamped in every police station. I was thrown into jail.

After many stays in jail, the thief left France. He first went through Italy. The reasons he went there are ob-

scure. Perhaps it was the proximity of the border. Rome.
Naples. Brindisi. Albania. I stole a valise on the "Rodi,"
which set me ashore in Santi Quaranta. The port authori-
ties in Corfu refused to let me stay. Before I could leave
again, they made me spend the night on the boat I had
hired to bring me. Afterward it was Serbia. Afterward
Austria. Czechoslovakia. Poland, where I tried to circulate counterfeit zlotys. Everywhere it was the same: robbery, prison, and, from every one of these countries,
expulsion. I crossed borders at night, went through hopeless autumns when the lads were all heavy and weary,
and through springtimes when suddenly, at nightfall,
they would emerge from God knows what retreat where
they had been priming themselves to swarm in the alleys,
on the docks, the ramparts, in the parks, the movies and
the barracks. Finally it was Nazi Germany. Then Belgium. In Antwerp I ran into Stilitano again.

Brno—or Brünn—is a city in Czechoslovakia. I arrived
there on foot, in the rain, after crossing the Austrian border at Retz. Some petty thefts in stores kept me going
for a few days but I was without friends, astray amidst
a nervous people. I would have liked, however, to rest a
while after my turbulent trip through Serbia and Austria,
after my flight from the police of those countries and
from certain accomplices who were out to get me. Brno
is a wet, dismal city, oppressed by the smoke of factories
and the color of the stones. My soul would have relaxed
there, grown languid, as in a room whose shutters have
been drawn, if only I could have gone a few days without worrying about money. German and Czech were
spoken in Brno. There was a kind of war going on among
rival groups of young street singers. A group which sang
in German invited me to join them. There were six of us.
I took up the collection and handled the money.

Three of my companions played the guitar, one the accordion and the other sang. One foggy day, as I was leaning against a wall, I watched the group as they gave a concert. One of the guitarists was about twenty years old. He was blond and was wearing a plaid shirt and a pair of corduroy trousers. Beauty is rare in Brno; I was charmed by his face. I stood and looked at him for a long time and I caught him exchanging a smile of understanding with a fat, pink-cheeked man who was very conservatively dressed and was holding a leather briefcase. As I walked away, I wondered whether the young men realized that their companion made himself available to the city's rich queers. I walked away, but I made it my business to see them a number of times at various street corners. None of them was from Brno except Michaelis Andritch, the one who became my friend. His gestures were graceful without being effeminate. As long as he was with me, he never bothered with women. I had the surprise of seeing for the first time a homosexual whose bearing was manly, even somewhat blunt. He was the aristocrat of the troupe. They all slept in a cellar, where they also cooked their meals. Of the few weeks I spent with them there is nothing much to tell, except of my love for Michaelis, with whom I spoke Italian. He introduced me to the manufacturer. The man was rosy and fat, yet he did not seem to put much weight on the earth. I was sure that Michaelis felt no affection for him; nevertheless, I pointed out to him that theft would be more beautiful than prostitution.

"Ma, sono il uomo," he said to me arrogantly.

I doubted it but pretended to believe it. I told him about a few thefts and said that I had been in prison; he admired me for this. In a few days, with the help of my clothes, I became a glamorous figure to him. We pulled off a few jobs and I became his master.

I shall allow myself a certain coquetry and say that I was a clever thief. Never have I been caught red-handed, in *flagrante delicto*. But the fact that I know how to steal admirably for my earthly profit is unimportant; what I have sought most of all has been to be the consciousness of the theft whose poem I am writing; in other words, refusing to enumerate my exploits, I show what I owe them in the moral realm, what I build with them as a basis, what the simplest thieves are perhaps dimly seeking, what they themselves might achieve.

"A certain coquetry . . .": my extreme discretion.

This book, *The Thief's Journal*, pursuit of the Impossible Nothingness.

We very quickly decided to leave after robbing the gentleman. We were to go to Poland where Michaelis knew some counterfeiters. We planned to circulate counterfeit zlotys.

Although I had not forgotten Stilitano, the other was taking his place in my heart and against my body. What remained of the first was rather a kind of influence that imparted to my smile (which collided with the memory of his) a slight cruelty and to my gestures a certain rigor. I had been the beloved of so beautiful a bird of prey, a miscreant of the finest breed, that I could adopt a certain insolence with a charming guitarist, though he was so bright and alert that I had to go easy. I dare not venture a sketch of him. You would read in it the qualities I find in all my friends. (Pretexts for my iridescence, then for my transparence, and finally for my absence, the lads I speak of evaporate. All that remains of them is what remains of me: I exist only through them, who are nothing, existing only through me. They shed light on me, but I am the zone of interference. These men: my Twilight

Guard.) This one had, perhaps, a certain sweet roguishness, and he was so vibrant with grace that I am tempted, the better to define him, to use the old-fashioned expression:

"He was a sweet fiddle."

We crossed the border with little money, for the old fellow had been suspicious, and we arrived in Katowice. We found Michaelis' friends, but we were arrested by the police the second day for trafficking in counterfeit money. We stayed in prison, he for three months and I for two. At this point there occurred an event which has to do with my moral life. I loved Michaelis. Taking up a collection while the boys sang was not humiliating. Central Europe is used to such troupes of young men, and all our gestures were innocent because of their youthfulness and gaiety. I could love Michaelis tenderly, without feeling ashamed, and could tell him so. We had our luxurious hours at night, in secret, at his lover's home. Before being jailed, we lived together for a month at the Katowice police station. Each of us had a cell, but in the morning, before the offices were open, two policemen would come to get us; we had to empty the latrines and wash the tiles. The only time we could see each other was colored by shame, for the policemen were taking revenge on the Frenchman's and the Czech's elegance. They would wake us up early in the morning to empty the shit can. We would go down five flights. The stairway was steep. At every step a little wave of urine wet my hand and that of Michaelis, whom the policemen made me call Andritch. We would have liked to smile so as to make light of these moments, but the odor forced us to hold our noses, and fatigue contracted our features. The difficulty we had in using Italian did not help matters. Gravely, carefully, with solemn slowness, we took down the huge metal chamber pot into which, a whole night long, beefy policemen had been relieving themselves of a matter and liquid which at the time had been warm but in the morning was cold. We emptied it into privies in the court and went back upstairs. Had I met Andritch in a setting of shame and not given him a radiant image of myself, I could have remained calm as we carried down the jailors' shit, but to reduce his humiliation I stiffened myself to the point of becoming a kind of hieratic sign, a song that was, to him, superb, capable of stirring the humble: a hero. When the pot had been emptied, the policemen threw us a piece of sackcloth and we washed the floor. We crawled in front of them on our knees in order to rub and mop the flagstones. They would kick us with the heels of their boots. Michaelis must have understood my suffering. Unable to read his looks or behavior, I was not sure whether he pardoned my fall. One morning I thought of rebelling and spilling the pot on the cops' feet, but I pictured in my imagination what the revenge of those bullies would be—they'll drag me in the piss and shit, I told myself; in the wrath of all their muscles, in their trembling, they'll make me lick it—and I decided that this situation was exceptional, that it had been granted me because no other would have so well fulfilled me.

"This is definitely a rare situation," I said to myself. "It's exceptional. In the presence of the person I adore and in whose eyes I seemed an angel, here I am being knocked down, biting the dust, turning inside out like a glove and showing exactly the opposite of what I was. Why could I not likewise be this 'opposite'? The love that Michaelis bore me—his admiration, rather—being possible only in the past, I will do without that love."

This thought hardened my features. I knew that I was returning to the world from which all tenderness is banned, for it is the world of those feelings which are opposed to nobility and beauty. It corresponds in the physical world to the world of abjection. Without seeming to be unaware of this situation, Michaelis bore it lightly. He joked with the guards, he smiled often, his whole face sparkled with innocence. His well-meaningness toward me irritated me. He wanted to spare me drudgery, but I was snappish with him.

In order to thrust him further from me, I needed an excuse. I didn't have to wait long. One morning he stooped to pick up a pencil which one of the policemen had dropped. I insulted him on the stairs. He replied that he didn't understand. He wanted to calm me by acting more affectionate; he irritated me.

"You're a coward," I said. "You're a son of a bitch. The cops are still too good to you. One of these days you'll really lick their boots. Maybe they'll go pay you a visit in your cell and stick their pricks up your ass!"

I hated him for being the witness of my downfall after having seen what a Liberator I could be. My suit had faded; I was dirty, unshaved; my hair was unkempt; I was getting homely and again taking on the hoodlum look that Michaelis didn't like because it was his by nature. Nevertheless, I plunged into shame. I no longer loved my friend. Quite the contrary, this love—the first which I experienced that was protective—was followed by a kind of unhealthy, impure hatred because it still contained a few shreds of tenderness. But I know that had I been alone I would have adored the policemen. No sooner was I locked up in my cell than I dreamed of their potency, of their friendship, of a possible complicity between them and me, in which, by a mutual exchange of virtues, they revealed themselves, they as hoodlums and I as a traitor.

"It's too late," I continued. "It was when I was well-dressed, when I had a watch and shiny shoes that I could have been their equal. Now it's too late, I'm a bum."

It seemed to me to be definitely settled that I was to dwell in shame, though a happy effort for a few months would have put me back into the world. I made up my mind to live with my head bowed and to pursue my destiny toward darkness, in an opposite direction to yours, and to exploit the underside of your beauty.

Many literary men have often dwelt on the idea of bands. The country was said to have been infested with them. You then imagine rough bandits united by a will to plunder, by cruelty and hatred. Was it possible? It seems hardly probable that such men can organize themselves. I am afraid that the binding element of these bands was greed, but a greed camouflaged by anger, by the demand for justice. By giving oneself this kind of pretext, of justification, one quickly reaches the point of elaborating a rough-and-ready morality on the basis of these pretexts. Except among children, Evil, a zeal that goes counter to your morality, is never the element that unites outlaws and forms bands. In prison, every criminal may dream of a well-knit organization, closed but strong, which would be a refuge against the world and its morality: this is only a reverie. Prison is that fortress, the ideal cave, the bandit's retreat against which the forces of the world beat in vain. No sooner is he in contact with them than the criminal obeys the banal laws. If the current press speaks of bands formed by American deserters and French hoodlums, it is not a matter of organization, but of accidental and brief collaboration among three or four men at most.

When Michaelis came out of jail in Katowice, we got together again. I had been free for a month. I lived on petty pilferings in the neighboring villages and slept in a park just outside the town. It was summer. Other tramps came there to sleep on the lawns in the shelter of the shadow and the low branches of the cedars. At dawn, a thief would rise up from a clump of flowers, a young beggar would yawn in the first rays of the sun, others would be delousing themselves on the steps of a pseudo-Greek temple. I spoke to no one. I would go alone to some church a few miles away and by means of a gummed stick would steal the money from the collection box. In the evening, I would return to the park, always on foot. This Court of Miracles was bright. All its guests were young. Although in Spain they would get together and pool their information about the places where the pickings were good, here each beggar, each thief, ignored the others. He seemed to enter the park by a secret door. He would glide silently along the clumps and groves. Only the light of a cigarette or a furtive footfall signaled his presence. In the morning, all trace of him was gone. All this extravagance quickened my wings. Squatting in my patch of shade, I was astounded to find myself under the same starry sky that Alexander and Caesar had seen, since I was a mere beggar and a lazy thief. I had gone across Europe by my own means, which were the opposite of glorious means. Yet I was writing for myself a secret history, in details as precious as the history of the great conquerors. It was therefore necessary that these details make me out to be the rarest and most singular of characters. Following my line, I continued to experience the most dismal misfortunes. Perhaps I missed my shameless faggotty drag which I deeply regret not having taken along with me in my valises or under my secular garments. But it was this torn and spangled tulle that I secretly donned at night as soon as I was on the other side of the park railing.

Beneath a muslin scarf I sense the translucent pallor

of a naked shoulder: it is the purity of the morning when
the Carolinas of Barcelona went in procession to lay
flowers on the pissoir.[1] The city was awakening. Laborers
were going off to work. In front of every door, buckets
of water were being emptied on the sidewalk. Covered
with ridicule, the Carolinas were sheltered. No laughter
could hurt them; the squalor of their rags testified to their
abasement. The sun spared this garland which was emit-
ting its own luminosity. They were all dead. What we
saw walking in the street were Shades cut off from the
world. Fairies are a pale and motley race that flowers in
the minds of decent folk. Never will they be entitled to
broad daylight, to real sun. But, remote in these limbos,
they cause curious disasters which are harbingers of new
beauties. One of them, Theresa the Great, used to wait
for clients in the pissoirs. At twilight, she would bring a
camp chair to one of the circular urinals near the harbor
and would sit down inside and do her knitting or cro-
cheting. She would stop to eat a sandwich. She was at
home.

Señorita Dora was another. Dora would exclaim in a
shrill voice, "What bitches they are, those awful she-men!"

From the memory of this cry is born a brief but profound meditation on their despair, which was mine. Having escaped—for how long!—from abjection, I want to

---

[1] The reader is informed that this report on my inner life or what
it suggests will be only a song of love. To be exact, my life was the
preparation for erotic adventures (not play) whose meaning I now
wish to discover. Alas, heroism is what seems to me most charged
with amorous properties, and since there are no heroes except in
our minds, they will therefore have to be created. So I have recourse to words. Those which I use, even if I attempt an explanation by means of them, will sing. Was what I wrote true? False?
Only this book of love will be real. What of the facts which served
as its pretext? I must be their repository. It is not they that I am
restoring.

return to it. May my interlude in your world at least enable me to write a book for the Carolinas.

I was chaste. My dresses protected me, and I waited for sleep in an artistic pose. I detached myself from the ground even more. I flew over it. I was sure of being able to traverse it with similar ease, and my thefts in churches made me lighter still. The return of Michaelis weighed me down a bit, for though he helped me steal, he was almost always smiling, with a familiar smile.

I marveled at these nocturnal mysteries, and likewise marveled that even in daytime the earth is in darkness. Knowing almost all there was to know about poverty and how purulent it is, I now saw it silhouetted beneath the moon, projected like a shadow play in the shadow of the leaves. It no longer had depth; it was merely a silhouette which I had the dangerous privilege of traversing with my thickness of suffering and blood. I learned that even flowers are black at night, when I wanted to gather some to carry to the altars whose collection boxes I broke into every morning. I was not trying to use these bouquets to propitiate a saint or the Holy Virgin. Rather, I wanted to give my body and arms an opportunity to assume conventionally beautiful poses which might integrate me into your world.

It may surprise the reader that I describe so few picturesque characters. My gaze is filled with love and does not perceive, nor did it then, the striking features which cause individuals to be regarded as objects. I was immediately aware, without thinking, of a justification for any behavior, however strange. The most unaccountable gesture or attitude seemed to me to correspond to an inner necessity. I was unable, and still am, to make fun of people. Every remark I hear, even the most absurd, seems to me to come just at the right moment. I have gone through reformatories and prisons, known low dives, bars

and highways without being astonished. If I think back, I
find in my memory none of those characters which a
different, a more amused eye than mine, would have
mounted on a pin. This book will perhaps be disappoint-
ing. In order to break the monotony of it I would like to
try to tell a few anecdotes and report a few witty remarks.

In court. The judge: "Why did you steal the copper?"
The prisoner: "Because of poverty, your Honor."
The judge: "That's no excuse."

"I've been all over Europe," Stilitano said to me. "I've
even been to Greece."
"Did you like it?"
"It's not bad. But it's partly destroyed."

Michaelis, a handsome male, confessed to me that he
was more proud of the looks of admiration he received
from men than from women.
"I strut more."
"But you don't care for men."
"That doesn't matter. I enjoy seeing them drool when
they look at my pretty puss. That's why I'm nice to them."

When I was being followed on the Rue des Couronnes,
the terror that the plainclothesmen caused me was communicated by the ghastly swish of their rubberized rain-
coats. Every time I hear that sound again, my heart
contracts.

At the time of that arrest, for the theft of documents
concerning the Fourth International, I made the acquaint-
ance of B. He was about twenty-two or twenty-three. He
was afraid of being deported. While we were waiting to
be taken to the anthropometry department, he edged up
to me.

"I may get deportation too," I said.

"Really? Stay next to me. Maybe they'll put us in the same clink. (The prisoner gives his cell a friendly nickname.) We'll manage to be happy if we're deported."

When we got back from the records office, he sidled up to me and said, confidentially, "I knew a fellow who was twenty years old who once asked me to find him a guy. He felt like being fucked up the ass."

Finally he confessed to me the same evening:

"I was talking like a dope. I was the guy who felt like it."

"You'll find that here," I told him.

"That's why I'm not so worried."

B. was not deported. I came across him again in Montmartre. He introduced me to a friend of his, a priest, with whom he cruised at night.

"Why don't you chuck your curé?"

"I don't know. He's a swell guy."

When we meet, he often talks to me about him. He says "my curé" with a certain tenderness. The priest, who adores him, has promised him a wardenship in his parish.

Without suspecting what they were destroying, the police tore up ten or twelve drawings that were found in my possession. They were unaware that these arabesques represented the tooling (sides and back) of old bindings. When A., G. and I were planning to rob the museum in C., my job was to know the lay of the land and the possible loot. This theft, which was carried out by others, is, however, too recent for me to go into detail. Not knowing what excuse to give for my repeated visits, I hit upon the idea, after hearing someone speak very highly of the old books in certain locked showcases, of asking to be allowed to make brief sketches of the bind-

ings. I went back to the museum several days in succession and stayed for hours in front of the books, drawing
as best I could. When I got back to Paris, I made inquiries
about the value of the books; I was astounded to learn
that they were very valuable. Never before would I have
thought that books might be something to go after. We
didn't get hold of those, but that's how I got the idea of
browsing in bookstores. I rigged up a trick briefcase, and
I became so skillful that I pushed delicacy to the point of
always carrying out these thefts under the bookseller's
very nose.

Stilitano had Java's muscle-bound, slightly swaying
walk, as if he were cleaving the wind, and if Java gets
up to go, if he moves from one place to another, I feel
the same emotion as when I see a high-powered car get
under way smoothly and silently. Stilitano had perhaps
more sensitivity in the muscles of his buttocks. His rump
was more sinuous. But Java, like him, took pleasure in
betraying. Like him, he loved to humiliate whores.

"She sure is a bitch," he said to me. "You know what
she just told me? You'd never guess. That she can't come
tonight because she's got an appointment with an old
guy and that old guys pay better. She's a bitch. But I'll
fix her!"

He was so nervous that he broke the cigarette he was
taking out of the package. He was fuming:

"I'm going to shove my prick up her ass."

When I buggered this handsome twenty-two-year-old
athlete for the first time, he pretended to be sleeping.
With his face crushed against the white pillow, he let me
slip it in, but when he was stuck, he could not keep from
groaning delicately, the way one sighs.

Deeply threaded by my prick, he becomes something
other than himself, something other than my lover. He is

a strange part of me which still preserves a little of its own life. We form one body, but it has two heads and each of them is involved in experiencing its own pleasure. At the moment of coming, this excrescence of my body which was my lover loses all tenderness, clouds over. In the darkness, I sense his hardness and can feel that a veil of shadow is spreading over his face, which is contracted with pain and pleasure. I know that he knows he derives this pleasure from me, that he awaits it from my hand which is jerking him off, but I feel that the only thing that concerns him now is his coming. Though we are bound together by my prick, all our friendly relations are cut off. Our mouths, which could perhaps re-establish them are unable to meet. He wants only to be more deeply impaled. I cannot see him, for he has murmured "Put out the light," but I feel that he has become someone else, someone strange and remote. It is when I have made him come that I feel him hating me.

At the beginning, when, naked in bed, I would turn him over—the hoodlums I talk about say of themselves, with amused cynicism, "I turn over like a flapjack"—and start threading him, he frightened me, for he would groan. I would gently stroke his rump, as I would a horse's, so that he would remain still and not rebel when I started operating. His shuddering still excites me even today; it is the sign of the pleasure which his nostrils have just sniffed. I cling to him, to his twig, which I squeeze less hard so as to feel beneath my fingers the delicate pulsing of the flowing jissom which is about to penetrate the mattress.

On his wrists, the mark of the diving suit. And the openings of the white undershirt for the two arms, each of which has the vigor and elegant individuality of a nonchalant and obscene sailor.

I saw the letter A tattooed under his armpit.

"What's that?"

"My blood type. When I was in the S.S. We were all tattooed."

He added, without looking at me, "I'll never be ashamed of my letter. No one can ever take it away. I'd kill someone in order to keep it."

"Are you proud of having been in the S.S.?"

"I am."

His face bore a strange resemblance to Marc Aubert's. The same cold beauty. He lowered his arm; then he got up and straightened his clothes. He shook the bits of moss and bark out of his hair. We climbed over the wall and walked among the pebbles in silence. In the crowd, he looked at me with a touch of roguish sadness.

"People may say about us that we were screwed by Hitler. I don't give a damn what they say."

Then he burst out laughing. With his blue eyes protected by a sunny fur, he cleaves the crowd, air and wind with such lordliness that it is I who shoulder the burden of his shame.

"You like being screwed?"

"Sometimes. I like it when you're about to come. It relaxes me when you've got me groveling."

After knowing Erik, after loving and then losing him, whom did I meet but . . .[1] Like the former, he too knew the terrible joy of belonging to the vilified army. Though the former bodyguard of a German officer, he is gentle. He was given a brief training course in a camp where he was taught how to use a dagger, to be always on the alert, and to be ready to die to protect the officer. He saw the snows of Russia, pillaged the countries he went through, Czechoslovakia, Poland, and even Germany. He kept none of his booty. The court of justice sentenced him to a two-year prison term which he has just com-

[1] I have to leave this name blank.

pleted. He sometimes speaks to me of this period, and the memory that overshadows all the others is the deep joy he felt when he saw the pupils of the eyes of the man he was about to kill grow big with fear. He swaggers in the street; he walks only in the gutter. In the evening he offers his cock to whoever wants to suck it, or his ass for a ramming.

Murder is not the most effective means of reaching the subterranean world of abjection. Quite the contrary. The blood he has shed, the constant danger to which his body is exposed of eventually losing its head (the murderer withdraws but his withdrawal is upward), and the attraction he exerts—for he is assumed to possess, in view of the way he defies the laws of life, the most easily imagined attributes of exceptional strength—prevent people from despising the criminal. Other crimes are more degrading: theft, begging, treason, breach of trust, etc.; these are the ones I chose to commit, though I was always haunted by the idea of a murder which would cut me off irremediably from your world.

Having had a run of good luck in Poland, I paraded my elegance. Though the Poles never suspected me, the French consul sized up the situation and requested me to leave the consulate forthwith, Katowice within forty-eight hours and Poland itself as soon as possible. Michaelis and I decided to go back to Czechoslovakia together, but were both refused entry visas. We hired a car with its chauffeur so that he could take us to the border by a mountain road. I had a revolver.

"If the chauffeur refuses to drive us, we'll kill him and keep going in the car."

Sitting in the rear, with one hand on my weapon and the other in the hand of Michaelis, who was stronger than I though just as young, I would gladly have fired into the driver's back. The car was going slowly uphill. Michaelis was supposed to leap to the steering wheel, but just then the chauffeur stopped right in front of a border post that we had not seen. This crime was denied me. Escorted by two policemen, we returned to Katowice. It was night.

"If they find the revolver in my pocket," I thought, "they'll arrest us. Maybe they'll convict us."

The stairway leading to the office of the chief of police was dark. As we were going up, I got the bright idea of putting my weapon on one of the steps. I pretended to stumble, bent down and laid the gun in a corner near the wall. During the questioning (Why did I want to go to Czechoslovakia? What was I doing there?) I was all atremble lest my ruse be discovered. At that moment I experienced the anxious joy, fragile as the pollen on hazel blossoms, the golden morning joy of the murderer who escapes. Though I had not managed to commit the crime, I had at least been gently bathed in the fringe of its dawning.

Michaelis loved me. Perhaps the painful position he knew I was in transformed this love into a kind of pity. Mythologies are full of heroes who are changed into servants. Perhaps he dimly feared that in my contracted, my larval position, I might elaborate some cunning scheme and that my metamorphosis would be climaxed by a sudden sprouting of wings, like the stag at bay that God miraculously allows to escape from the hounds, before the very eyes of my guards who would be thunder-struck by my glory. The beginning of the execution of a murder is in itself sufficient, and Michaelis beheld me as in the past, but I no longer loved him. If I report my adventure with him, I do so only that it may be seen that a relentless fatality corrupted my attitudes; either my hero collapsed or I myself proved to be made of paltry clay. It will be no different with Java. I am already aware that his toughness is only an appearance; not that it is a mere *front,* but that it is made of the softest gelatine.

To speak of my work as a writer would be a pleonasm. The boredom of my prison days made me take refuge in my past life, even though it was vagrant, austere or destitute. Later on, when I was free, I wrote again, in order to earn money. The idea of being a professional writer leaves me cold. However, if I examine my work, I now perceive in it, patiently pursued, a will to rehabilitate persons, objects and feelings reputedly vile. Naming them with words that usually designate what is noble was perhaps childish and somewhat facile; I was in too much of a hurry. I used the handiest means, but I would not have done so were it not that, within me, those objects, those feelings (treason, theft, cowardice, fear), called for the qualifier generally reserved—by you—for their opposites. Perhaps at the moment, in the heat of writing, I wanted to magnify feelings, attitudes and objects that were honored by some splendid boy before whose beauty I bowed low; but today, as I reread what I have written, I have forgotten those boys: all that remains of them is the attribute which I have sung, and that is what will glow in my books with a brilliance equal to pride, heroism and boldness. I was not trying to make excuses for them. Nor to justify them. I wanted them to have the right to the honors of the Name. This operation will prove not to have been fruitless for me. I already feel its efficacity. In embellishing what you hold in contempt, my mind, weary of the game that consists of naming with a glamorous name that which stirred my heart, refuses any qualification. Without confusing them, it accepts them all, beings and things, in their equal nakedness. It then refuses to clothe them. Thus, I no longer want to write; I am dead to Letters. However, I gather from the news-papers of the past few days that the world is appre-hensive. People are talking about war again. As anxiety mounts, as preparations begin to take shape (no longer the high-sounding declarations of statesmen but the men-acing exactness of technicians), a strange peace comes over me. I turn inward. There I arrange for myself a fierce, delightful place from which I shall regard men's fury without fearing it. I long for the noise of cannon, for the trumpets of death, so that I may arrange an end-lessly recreated bubble of silence. I shall remove them from me even further by the multiple and ever thicker layers of my past adventures, chewed over and over, slobbered all over me, spun out and wrapped about like the silk of a cocoon. I shall work at conceiving my soli-tude and immortality, at living them, unless an idiotic desire for sacrifice makes me emerge from them.

My solitude in prison was total. Now that I speak of it, it is less so. Then I was alone. At night I would let myself be borne along by a current of abandon. The world was a torrent, a rapid of forces come together to carry me to the sea, to death. I had the bitter joy of knowing I was alone. I am nostalgic for the following sound: as I lie dreaming in my cell, my mind idly drifting, suddenly a convict in the cell above gets up and starts walking up and down, with an even pace. My reverie is also adrift, but this sound (in the foreground, as it were, because of its precision) reminds me that the body which is day-dreaming, the one from which the reverie has escaped, is in prison, prisoner of a clear, sudden, regular pacing. I would like to have my old comrades-in-misery, the chil-dren of sorrow. I envy the glory which they secrete and which I utilize for ends less pure. Talent is courtesy with respect to matter; it consists of giving song to what was dumb. My talent will be the love I feel for that which constitutes the world of prisons and penal colonies. Not that I want to transform them or bring them around to your kind of life, or that I look upon them with indulgence or pity: I recognize in thieves, traitors and murderers, in the ruthless and the cunning, a deep beauty—a sunken beauty—which I deny you. Soclay, Pilorge, Weidmann, Serge de Lenz, Gentlemen of the Police, crafty informers, at times you seem to me adorned, as if dressed in widows' weeds, with such lovely crimes that I envy some of them the mythologic fear they inspire, others their tortures, and all of them the infamy in which they finally merge. If I cast a backward look, I see only a succession of pitiful actions. My books narrate them. They have adorned them with qualifiers thanks to which I recall them with gladness. I have thus been that little wretch who knew only hunger, physical humiliation, poverty, fear and degradation. From such galling attitudes as these I have drawn reasons for glory.

"That's probably what I am," I would say to myself, "but at least I'm aware of it, and such awareness destroys shame and affords me a feeling that few know: pride. You who regard me with contempt are made up of nothing else but a succession of similar woes, but you will never be aware of this and thus will never possess pride, in other words, the knowledge of a force that enables you to stand up to misery—not your own misery, but that of which mankind is composed."

Are a few books and poems capable of proving to you that I put these misfortunes to use, that they were necessary to my beauty? I have written too much, I am weary. It has been so hard for me to achieve so inadequately what my heroes do so quickly.

When Java cringed with fright, he was stunning. Thanks to him, fear was noble. It was restored to the dignity of natural movement, with no other meaning than that of organic fright, panic of the viscera confronted with the image of death or pain. Java trembled. I saw a yellow diarrhea flow down his monumental thighs. Terror stalked and ravaged the features of his splendid face that had been so tenderly and greedily kissed. It was mad of that cataclysm to dare disturb such noble proportions, such inspiring, such harmonious relationships, and those proportions and relationships were the source of the crisis, they were responsible for it. So lovely were they that they were even its expression, since what I call Java was both master of his body and responsible for his fear. His fear was beautiful to see. Everything became a sign of it: his hair, muscles, eyes, teeth, penis, and the child's manly grace.

Thereafter, he ennobled shame. He bore it in my presence like a burden, like a tiger clinging to his shoulders, the threat of which imparted to his shoulders a most insolent submissiveness. His behavior has since been tempered by a delicate and delightful humility. His male vigor, his bluntness, are veiled, as the glare of the sun might be, by crape. As I watched him fight, I felt he was declining battle. Perhaps he was afraid of being the less strong or that the other fellow might punch his face in, but I saw him seized with terror. He shriveled up and wanted to fall asleep and dream of the Indies or of Java, or to be arrested by the police and condemned to death. He is thus a coward. But his example has shown me that fear and cowardice can be expressed by the most charming grimaces.

"I'm letting you off," the fellow sneered at him contemptuously.

Java didn't bat an eyelash. He accepted the insult. He got up from the dust, picked up his beret and left without brushing the dust off his knees. He was still very handsome.

Marc Aubert taught me that treason develops in a fine body. It is therefore plainly legible if it is ciphered with all the signs that formed both the traitor and treason. It was signified in blond hair, limpid eyes, a golden skin, a winning smile, by a neck, a torso, arms, legs, a member for which I would have given my life and have accumulated acts of treason.

"These heroes," I said to myself, "must have reached such a state of perfection that I no longer wish to see them live, so that their lives may be climaxed by a brazen destiny. If they have achieved perfection, behold them at the brink of death, no longer afraid of the judgment of men. Nothing can spoil their amazing success. May they therefore grant me what is denied the wretched."

Almost always alone, though aided by an ideal companion, I crossed other borders. My emotion was always equally great. I crossed Alps of all kinds. From Slovenia to Italy, helped by the customs men, then abandoned by them, I went upstream, along a muddy torrent. Fought by the wind, by the cold, by the thorns, by November, I gained a summit behind which was Italy. In order to reach it I affronted monsters hidden by the night or revealed by it. I got caught in the barbed wire of a fort where I heard the sentinels walking and whispering. Crouching in the shadow, my heart beating, I hoped that before shooting me they would fondle and love me. Thus I hoped that the night would be peopled by voluptuous guards. I ventured at random upon a road. It was the right one. I sensed it by the feel of my soles on its honest ground. Later on, I left Italy for Austria. I crossed fields of snow at night. The moon cast my shadow. In every country that I left behind I had stolen and had known prisons. Yet I was not going through Europe but through the world of objects and circumstances, and with an ever fresher ingenuousness. All the wonders I beheld made me uneasy, but I hardened myself further so as to penetrate, without danger to myself, their customary mystery.

I quickly realized that it was difficult to steal in Central Europe without danger because the police system was perfect. The paucity of the means of communication and the difficulty of crossing the borders, which were excellently guarded, prevented me from fleeing quickly, and my being a Frenchman made me all the more conspicuous. Furthermore, I noticed that very few Frenchmen in foreign countries are thieves or beggars. I decided to go back to France and there pursue—perhaps even limiting my activity to Paris alone—a thief's destiny. The idea of continuing my way around the world committing more or less important larcenies also tempted me. I chose France out of a concern for depth. I knew the country well enough to be sure of giving stealing all my attention and care, of handling it as if it were a unique substance whose devoted craftsman I would become. I was twenty-four or twenty-five at the time. In pursuit of a moral adventure, I sacrificed dispersion and ornament. The reasons for my choice, whose meaning is revealed to me only today perhaps because I have to write about it, were not clearly apparent. I think that I had to hollow out, to drill through, a mass of language in which my mind would be at ease. *Perhaps I wanted to accuse myself in my own language.* Neither Albania, Hungary or Poland, nor India or Brazil would have offered me so rich a matter as France. Indeed, theft—and what is involved in it: prison sentences, along with the shame of the profession of thief —had become a disinterested undertaking, a kind of active and deliberate work of art which could be achieved only with the help of language, my language, and which would be confronted with the laws springing from this same language. In a foreign country I would have been merely a more or less clever thief, but, as I would have thought of myself in French, I would have known I was a Frenchman—a status that allows none other to survive—among foreigners. To be a thief in my own country and to justify my being a thief who used the language of the robbed—who are myself, because of the importance of language—was to give to being a thief the chance to be unique. I was becoming a foreigner.

Perhaps the oppressively perfect police system of the Central European states is due to the uneasiness created there by political confusion. I am speaking, of course, of its swiftness. It seems that, owing to a network of informers, an offense is known before it is committed, but their police do not have the finesse of ours. Accompanied by Anton, an Austrian, I entered Yugoslavia from Albania, showing to the customs officers a passport which was simply a French military service certificate to which I had added four pages from an Austrian passport (issued to Anton) containing visas from the Serbian consulate. Several times, in the train, in the street, in hotels, I handed this strange document to Yugoslav policemen; it seemed to them normal. The stamps and the visas satisfied them. When I was arrested—for having shot at Anton with a revolver—the police returned it to me.

Did I love France? I was nimbused at the time with its brilliance. The French military attaché in Belgrade having demanded several times that I be extradited—which is contrary to international law—the Yugoslav police resorted to a compromise: I was escorted to the border of the country nearest France, Italy. I went through Yugoslavia from prison to prison. There I met handsome criminals, violent and somber, swearing in a savage language in which the oaths are the finest in the world.

"I fuck the Mother of God in the ass!"

"I bugger the wall!"

A few minutes later they would burst out laughing, and I could see their splendid teeth. The King of Yugoslavia was then a graceful boy of twelve or fifteen whose hair was parted on the side: Peter the Second, whose portrait, which also adorned the postage stamps, hung in the offices of all the prisons and police stations. The anger of the roughnecks and thieves rose up toward this child. They railed against him. The raucous insults of the spiteful men were like a street quarrel with a cruel lover. They called him a whore. When I got to the prison in Susak (Italian border)—after having been in ten others where I spent only a few nights—I was locked in a cell where there were about twenty of us. I immediately saw Rade Peritch. He was a Croat who was serving a two-year sentence for theft. In order to take advantage of my overcoat, he made me lie down next to him on the cot. He was dark and well built. He was wearing a pair of somewhat faded blue denim mechanic's overalls with a big wide pocket in the middle into which he stuck his hands. I spent only two nights in the Susak jail, but that was time enough for me to get a terrific crush on Rade.

The prison was separated from the highway not by a wall but by a ditch beneath our cell window. When the police and then the customs officers made me cross the Italian border, by the mountain route and on a freezing night, I headed for Trieste. In the lobby of the French consulate I stole an overcoat which I immediately resold. With the money, I bought thirty feet of rope and a saw and returned to Yugoslavia by way of Piedicolle. An automobile took me to Susak, where I arrived at night. I whistled from the road. Rade came to the window, and I very easily got the equipment to him. I returned the following night, but he refused to attempt an escape, though it would have been easy. I waited until dawn, hoping to persuade him. Finally, shivering with cold, I took the mountain path again, sad that this brawny fellow preferred the certainty of prison to adventuring with me. I managed to cross the Italian border and get to Trieste, then to Venice and finally to Palermo where I was put into jail. An amusing detail recurs to my memory. When I entered the cell in the Palermo jail, the prisoners asked me,

"Come va, la principessa?"

"No lo so," I replied.

During the morning walk in the yard, I was asked the same question, but I knew nothing about the health of the Princess of Piedmont, the king's daughter-in-law (the question concerned her). I learned later that she was pregnant and that the amnesty which is always granted upon the birth of a royal child depended on the child's sex. The guests of the Italian jails had the same preoccupations as the courtiers at the Quirinal.

When I was let out, I was taken to the Austrian border, which I crossed near Villach.

Rade did the right thing in refusing to leave. During my trip through Central Europe I was accompanied by his ideal presence. Not only did he walk and sleep at my side, but in making decisions I wanted to be worthy of the bold image of him that I had created. Once again a man with a handsome face and beautiful body gave me the opportunity to prove my courage.

Neither by the recital nor the interlacing or overlapping of the facts—and I don't know what they are, which limits them in time and space—nor by their interpretation, which, without destroying them, creates new ones, can I discover the key, nor, by means of them, my own key. I undertook, with a baroque intention, to cite a few, pretending to omit those—the first which make up the apparent texture of my life—which are the knots of the glistening threads. If France is an emotion communicated from artist to artist—a relay of neurons, so to speak—then to the very end I am only a string of tinglings, the first of which are beyond my range. The prongs of a boat hook that had been dug into a drowned man to pull him out of a stream made me suffer in my child's body. Could it really be that people searched for corpses with harpoons? I roamed about the countryside, delighted to discover in the wheat or beneath the firs the bodies of drowned men to whom I accorded the most incredible obsequies. Can I say that it was the past—or that it was the future? Everything has already been caught, until my death, in an ice floe of *being:* my trembling when a piece of rough trade asks me to brown him (I discover that his desire is his trembling) during a Carnival night; at twilight, the view from a sand dune of Arab warriors surrendering to French generals; the back of my hand placed on a soldier's basket, but especially the sly way in which the soldier looked at it; suddenly I see the ocean between two houses in Biarritz; I am escaping from the reformatory, taking tiny steps, frightened not at the idea of being caught but of being the prey of freedom; straddling the enormous prick of a blond legionnaire, I am carried twenty yards along the ramparts; not the handsome football player, nor his foot, nor his shoe, but the ball, then ceasing to be the ball and becoming the "kick-off," and I cease being that to become the idea that goes from the foot to the ball; in a cell, unknown thieves call me Jean; when at night I walk barefoot in my sandals across fields of snow at the Austrian border, I shall not flinch, but then, I say to myself, this painful moment must concur with the beauty of my life, I refuse to let this moment and all the others be waste matter; using their suffering, I project myself to the mind's heaven. Some negroes are giving me food on the Bordeaux docks; a distinguished poet raises my hands to his forehead; a German soldier is killed in the Russian snows and his brother writes to inform me; a boy from Toulouse helps me ransack the rooms of the commissioned and non-commissioned officers of my regiment in Brest: he dies in prison; I am talking of someone—and while doing so, the time to smell roses, to hear one evening in prison the gang bound for the penal colony singing, to fall in love with a white-gloved acrobat—dead since the beginning of time, that is, fixed, for I refuse to live for any other end than the very one which I found to contain the first misfortune: that my life must be a legend, in other words, legible, and the reading of it must give birth to a certain new emotion which I call poetry. I am no longer anything, only a pretext.

By moving slowly, Stilitano exposed himself to love as one exposes oneself to the sun. Offering to the rays all his facets. When I met him in Antwerp, he had put on weight. Not that he was fat, but a certain thickness had rounded his angles. In his gait I found the same savage suppleness, more powerful, less rapid and more muscular, but just as nervous. In the dirtiest street in Antwerp, near the Scheldt, beneath a gray sky, Stilitano's back seemed to me streaked by the alternate light and shade of a Spanish shutter. The woman in a black satin sheath walking with him was really his female. He was surprised to see me and, it seemed to me, glad.

"Jean! You in Antwerp?"

"How're things going?"

I shook hands with him. He introduced me to Sylvia. I barely recognized him in the exclamation, but hardly had he opened his mouth for a more softly uttered phrase when there again, veiling it, was the white blob of spit, and through the strange mucosity which formed it, though remaining intact, I recognized, between his teeth, the Stilitano of old. Without naming anything, I said,

"You've kept it."

"You noticed?"

"Of course. You're too proud of it."

"What are you talking about?" asked Sylvia.

"We're talking, baby. Mind your business."

This innocent complicity at once set up a relationship between us. All his former charms bore down on me: the power of his shoulders, the mobility of his buttocks, the hand that had perhaps been torn off in the jungle by another savage beast, and finally his member, so long denied me, buried in a dangerous darkness which was shielded from mortal odors. I was at his mercy. Without knowing anything about his activities, I was sure that he ruled over the people of the dives, docks and bars, hence over the entire city. To achieve harmony in bad taste is the height of elegance. Stilitano had unfalteringly chosen a pair of green and tan crocodile shoes, a brown suit, a white silk shirt, a pink tie, a multicolored scarf, and a green hat. It was all held in place by pins, links, and gold chains, and Stilitano was elegant. Standing before him, I became the same unhappy creature as in the past, and this did not seem to trouble him.

"I've been here three days," I said.

"Are you getting along?"

"The way I used to."

He smiled.

"Do you remember?"

"You see this guy?" he said to his girl. "He's a pal. He's a buddy. He can come to our room whenever he likes."

They took me to dinner in a restaurant near the harbor. Stilitano informed me that he was in the opium racket. His girl was a whore. With the words junk and opium

my imagination took wing; I saw Stilitano as a bold, rich
adventurer. He was a bird of prey flying in great circles.
Yet, though his gaze was sometimes cruel, he had none
of the rapacity of the birds of prey. Quite the contrary,
for, despite his affluence, Stilitano still seemed to be playing. It did not take me long to learn that only his appearance was prosperous. He was living in a small hotel. The
first thing I saw was a big pile of colored comic books
stacked on the mantelpiece. The text accompanying the
pictures was now in French instead of Spanish: the child-
ishness was the same, as were the handsomeness, vigor
and courage of the hero, who was almost always naked.
Every morning Sylvia brought him new ones, which he
read in bed. I thought that two years had rolled by, during which time he had been reading gaudy infantile
stories, and that meanwhile, on the side, his body had
been maturing—and perhaps his mind too. He sold opium,
which he bought from sailors, and supervised his girl. He
carried his wealth with him: his clothes, his jewels and
his wallet. He suggested that I work for him. For a few
days I carried tiny packets to the homes of shifty-looking
and anxious clients.

Just as in Spain, and with the same promptness, Stilitano had got in with the Antwerp riffraff. In the bars
he was treated to drinks and he kidded the whores and
queers. Fascinated by his new beauty, by his opulence,
and perhaps bruised by the memory of our friendship, I
let myself love him. I followed him everywhere. I was
jealous of his friends, jealous of Sylvia, and I would
suffer when I met him around noontime, fresh and per-
fumed, but with dark rings under his eyes. We would
stroll along the docks together and talk of old times. He
talked particularly about his exploits, for he was boastful.
Never did it occur to me to reproach him for his under-
handedness, or his treachery, or his cowardice. On the

contrary, I admired him for bearing the brand, in my memory, as simply and haughtily as he did.

"You still like men?"

"Of course I do. Why? Does it bother you?"

"Me?" he replied with a pleasant and quizzical smile. "You're crazy. On the contrary."

"Why on the contrary?"

He hesitated and wanted to delay answering.

"Huh?"

"You say on the contrary. You like them too."

"Me?"

"Yes."

"No, but sometimes I wonder what it's like."

"It gets you hot."

"Not a bit. I said it . . ."

He laughed in embarrassment.

"What about Sylvia?"

"Sylvia, she's my bread and butter."

"Is that all?"

"Yes. And that's enough."

If Stilitano were to add to his power over me by giving me any wild hope, he would reduce me to slavery. I already felt myself floundering in a deep, sad element. And what were Stilitano's flurries holding in store for me? I said to him, "You know I still have a soft spot for you, and I'd like to make love to you."

Without looking at me, he answered smilingly, "We'll see about it."

After a brief silence, he said, "What do you feel like doing?"

"With you, everything!"

"We'll see."

He didn't budge. No movement bore him toward me, though my whole being wanted to be swallowed up within him, though I wanted to give my body the supple-

ness of osier so as to twine round him, though I wanted
to warp, to bend over him. The city was exasperating.
The smell of the port and its excitement inflamed me.
Flemish dockers brushed against us, and the maimed
Stilitano was stronger than they. Perhaps he had in his
pocket, for his imprudence was exquisite, a few grains of
opium which made him precious and punishable.

In order to get to Antwerp I had just gone through
Nazi Germany, where I had stayed a few months. I
walked from Breslau to Berlin. I would have liked to
steal. A strange force held me back. Germany terrified
all of Europe; it had become, particularly to me, the
symbol of cruelty. It was already outside the law. Even
on Unter den Linden I had the feeling that I was strolling about in a camp organized by bandits. I thought that
the brain of the most scrupulous bourgeois concealed
treasures of duplicity, hatred, meanness, cruelty and lust.
I was excited at being free amidst an entire people that
had been placed on the index. Probably I stole there as
elsewhere, but I felt a certain constraint, for what governed this activity and what resulted from it—this particular moral attitude set up as a civic virtue—was being
experienced by a whole nation which directed it against
others.

"It's a race of thieves," I thought to myself. "If I steal
here, I perform no singular deed that might fulfill me. I
obey the customary order; I do not destroy it. I am not
committing evil. I am not upsetting anything. The outrageous is impossible. I'm stealing in the void."

I would feel a kind of uneasiness after stealing. It
seemed to me that the gods who govern the laws were
not revolted. They were merely surprised. I was ashamed.
But what I desired above all was to return to a country
where the laws of ordinary morality were revered, were

laws on which life was based. In Berlin I chose prostitution as my means of livelihood. It satisfied me for a few
days and then wearied me. Antwerp offered me legendary treasures, Flemish museums, Jewish diamond mer-
chants, ship owners loitering about at night, passengers
on transatlantic steamers. Exhilarated by my love, I
wanted to experience perilous adventures with Stilitano.
He seemed to want to join in the game and to dazzle me
by his boldness. Driving with only one hand, he arrived
at the hotel one evening on a police motorcycle.

"I just stole it from a cop," he said with a smile and
without even deigning to get off the machine. Yet he was
aware that the gesture of bestriding it would be to me a
maddening sight; he got off the seat, pretended to examine the motor and was off again with me behind.

"We'll get rid of it right away," he said.

"You're crazy. We can do things. . . ."

Exhilarated by the wind and the ride, I thought I was
being carried off on a highly dangerous chase. An hour
later, the motorcycle was sold to a Greek seaman who
immediately put it on board. But I had been granted the
sight of Stilitano at the center of a genuine, accomplished
feat, for the sale of the machine, the debating of the
price and the settling of the payment were a masterpiece
of finesse after the act of force.[1]

Stilitano was no more a mature man than I was. Although he really was a gangster, he played at being one,
that is, he invented gangster attitudes. I know no hoodlums who are not children. What "serious" mind going
by a jewelry shop or a bank would seriously work out, in

---

[1] When, a few days ago, Pierre Fièvre, the son of a state trooper
and himself a probationary policemen (he's twenty-one years old),
told me that he wanted to be a cop so as to have a motorcycle, I
got an erection. I again saw Stilitano's buttocks flattened against the
leather seat of the stolen machine.

minute detail, an assault or a burglary? Where else would you find the idea of a guild rooted—not in the interest of the members—in a pact of complicity bordering on friendship, for mutual aid, where else than in a kind of reverie, of gratuitous game, like something out of a story book? Stilitano was playing. He liked knowing that he was outside the law; he liked feeling that he was in danger. An aesthetic need placed him there. He was attempting to copy an ideal hero, the Stilitano whose image was already inscribed in a heaven of glory. In this way he obeyed the laws that govern gangsters, and give them form. Without them he would have been nothing. Blinded at first by his august solitude, by his calmness and serenity, I believed him to be anarchically self-creating, guided by the sheer impudence, the nerviness of his gestures. The fact is, *he was seeking a type.* Perhaps it was the one represented by the conquering hero of the comic books. At any rate, Stilitano's mild reverie was in perfect harmony with his muscles and his taste for action. Probably the hero of the pictures had finally come to be engraved in Stilitano's heart. I still respect him, for though he observed the externals of a protocol leading to them, within himself and without any witness he submitted to the constraints of his body and heart; he was never gentle with his girl.

Without quite becoming bosom friends, we got into the habit of seeing each other daily. I had lunch in his room, and in the evening, when Sylvia worked, we went out to dinner together. We would then make the round of the bars in order to get drunk. He also danced, almost all night long, with very pretty girls. Hardly would he arrive than the atmosphere changed, first at his table and then gradually at the others. It became both heavy and frenzied. He got into a fight almost every evening; he was savage and splendid, his one hand swiftly armed

with a switchblade which he flipped open in his pocket.
The stevedores, merchant-seamen and pimps would circle
around us or join forces with us. That kind of life exhausted me, for I would have liked to prowl around the
docks in the fog or rain. My memory of those nights is
shot through with sparks. A journalist, discussing a film,
writes: "Love blossoms amidst brawls." This absurd
phrase reminds me of the flowers known as "snapdragons"
which blossom among dry thistles, and thereby of my
velvety tenderness which Stilitano wounded.

Though he did not assign me any work, I sometimes
stole bicycles which I resold at Maestricht, in Holland.
When Stilitano learned that I knew how to get across
the border, he accompanied me one day and we went as
far as Amsterdam. The city didn't interest him. He
ordered me to wait for him in a café for a few hours and
then disappeared. I had learned that there was no use
questioning him. My work concerned him, but his was
none of my business. We returned in the evening, but at
the station he handed me a little package, tied and sealed,
about the size of a brick.

"I'm going ahead by train," he said.

"But what about customs?"

"Don't worry. I'm in order. You cross as usual, on foot.
And don't open the package. It belongs to a friend of
mine."

"What if they nab me?"

"Don't fool around. You'll get it in the neck."

Clever at manipulating conflicting charms between
which I would oscillate without ever coming to rest *at*
myself, he gave me a nice kiss and went off to the train.
I beheld this tranquil Reason, this guardian of the Tables
of the Law, walking before me, his authority contained
in the sureness of his gait, in his nonchalance, in the
almost luminous play of his buttocks. I did not know

what the package contained; it was the sign of confidence
and chance. Thanks to it, I was no longer going to cross
a border for my own paltry needs but rather out of
obedience, out of submission, to a sovereign Power.
When I took my eyes off Stilitano, the sole aim of my
preoccupations was to seek him, and it was the package
that directed me. During my expeditions (my thefts, my
reconnoiterings, my flights) objects were animated. When
I thought of night, it was with a big N. The stones and
pebbles on the roads had a sense through which I was to
make myself known. The trees were surprised to see me.
My fear bore the name of panic. It liberated the spirit of
every object, which awaited only my trembling to be
stirred. About me the inanimate world gently shuddered;
I could have chatted with the rain itself. I very quickly
began making an effort to consider this emotion as something quite special and to prefer it to the one that was its
pretext: fear, and the pretext of this fear: a burglary or
my flight from the police. Favored by night, the same
anxiety came at length to trouble my days. Thus, I moved
about in an enigmatic universe, for it had lost the sense
of the practical. I was in danger. Indeed, I no longer
considered objects from the point of view of their usual
purpose but rather from that of the friendly anxiety they
offered me. Stilitano's package between my chest and my
shirt betokened, made more precise, the mystery of each
thing, at the same time resolving it, thanks to the smile
(almost cropping out at my lips and revealing my teeth)
which it enabled me to venture so as to pass freely. Might
it be that I was carrying stolen jewels? What police problems, what goals of bloodhounds, of police dogs and
secret telegrams, derived their origin from this tiny
package? I therefore had to rout all the enemy forces,
Stilitano was waiting for me.

"He's a fine son of a bitch," I said to myself. "He's

careful not to run any risks. Just because he's got only
one hand, that's no reason."

When I got to Antwerp, I went straight to his hotel,
without shaving or washing, for I wanted to appear with
the attributes of my victory, with my beard and filth and
my arms laden with fatigue. Isn't that what is symbolized
when the victor is covered with laurel, flowers and gold
chains? But I carried my victory naked. In his room, in
front of him, I put on a show of exaggerated naturalness
as I handed him the package.

"Here it is."

He smiled, with a triumphant smile. I believe he was
not unaware that his power over me had managed everything.

"Were there any hitches?"

"None at all. It was easy."

"Ah!"

He smiled again and added, "That's fine." But I myself
dared not tell him that he would have managed the trip
without any more danger, for I already knew that Stilitano was my own creation and that its destruction depended upon me. I understood, nevertheless, why God
needs an angel, which He calls a messenger, to carry out
certain missions which He Himself is unable to.

"What's in it?"

"Junk, of course."

I had smuggled opium.[1] I did not despise Stilitano for
having exposed me to the danger of being caught in his
stead.

"It's perfectly natural," I said to myself. "He's a prick
and I'm a cunt."

For his revealing himself to me in this way, my grati-

---

[1] 1947. I have just read in an evening paper that he was arrested
for an armed assault in the dark. The article says: ". . . the handsome cripple was pale . . ." Reading this causes me no emotion.

tude rose up to him. Had he revealed himself to me by a number of bold deeds in which I had been forbidden to take part, thus becoming both cause and end, Stilitano would have lost all power over me. I dimly suspected him of being incapable of an act involving his whole person. The care he took of his body was proof. His baths, his perfumes, his sleeping all morning, the very form that his body had taken, its softness. Realizing that it was through me that he had to act, I attached myself to him, sure of drawing strength from the elementary and disorganized power that shaped him.

What with the time of year (autumn), the rain, the dark color of the buildings, the stolidity of the Flemings, the peculiar character of the city, and saddened too by my poverty, I was led by a deep melancholy to discover within me the objects in whose presence I felt uneasy. During the German occupation I saw in the newsreels the funeral services for the hundred or hundred and fifty victims of the bombardment of Antwerp. The coffins, covered with tulips or dahlias and exposed amidst the Antwerp ruins, were all flower stalls, and a host of priests and choir boys in lace surplices were filing by to bless them. This scene, which was the last, still helps me believe that Antwerp revealed to me areas of shadow. "They're celebrating," I thought to myself, "the cult of this city, the spirit of which—I gathered as much at the time—is Death." However, the mere appearance of things must have caused me that anxiety which at first was born of fear. Then the anxiety disappeared. I felt I was perceiving things with blinding lucidity. Even the most trivial of them had lost their usual meaning, and I reached the point of wondering whether it was true that one drank from a glass or put on a shoe. As I discovered the particular meaning of each thing, the idea of number deserted me. Little by little Stilitano lost his fabulous

power over me. He thought I was dreamy: I was attentive. Without being silent, I was elsewhere. As a result of
the relationships suggested by objects that seemed to
have conflicting purposes, my conversation took on a
humorous turn.

"You sure are going nuts!"

"Nuts!" I repeated, opening my eyes wide. Hence, I
think I remember having the revelation of an absolute
perception as I considered, in the state of luxurious
detachment of which I have been speaking, a clothespin
left behind on a line. The elegance and oddness of this
familiar little object *appeared before me without astonishing me.* I perceived events themselves in their auton-
omy. The reader can imagine how dangerous such an
attitude must have been in the life I was leading, when
I had to be wide-awake every minute and ran the risk of
being caught if I lost sight of the usual meaning of
objects.

With Stilitano's help and advice I had managed to
dress elegantly, though with a quite personal elegance.
Disdaining the rigid styles of the riffraff, I displayed a
certain fancy in my attire. Thus, the moment I stopped
being a beggar whom shame cut off from the practical
world, this world eluded me. I distinguished the essence
of objects, not their qualities. In short, my humor disen-
tangled me from the beings to whom I had passionately
bound myself. I felt lost and absurdly light.

A young pimp in a bar, squatting on his haunches and
playing with a puppy: this playfulness seemed to me so
odd in such a place that I smiled with pleasure at pimp
and puppy; I had understood them. And also that the
bus, which was full of serious and hurried people, could
courteously stop at the diminutive sign of a child's fingers.
Seeing a stiff hair threateningly emerge from Stilitano's
nostril, without trembling I took a pair of scissors to cut
it off.

Later on, when, without refusing to get excited about a handsome boy, I applied the same detachment, when I allowed myself to be aroused, and when, refusing the emotion the right to rule me, I examined it with the same lucidity, I realized what my love was; on the basis of this awareness I established relationships with the world; this was the birth of intelligence.

But Stilitano was disenchanted. I no longer served him. If he struck me or bawled me out, he taught me the meaning of insults and blows. Antwerp no longer had for me its sad character and its sordid maritime poetry. I saw clearly, and anything could have happened to me. I could have committed a crime. This period lasted about six months. I was chaste.

Armand was away on a trip. Although I heard that he was sometimes called by other names, we shall keep this one. Am I myself not up to my fifteenth or sixteenth name, including Jean Gallien, my current one? He was returning from France where, as I learned later, he was smuggling opium. A face need appear before me only a few seconds for me to be able to express its quality in a single word. If, however, it lingers, instead of the straight-forwardness, limpidity or frankness which it suggested, a curl of the lip or a gaze or a smile which I then perceive complicates the interpretation. The face becomes more and more complex. The signs overlap: it is illegible. In Stilitano's I made an effort to see the hardness which was marred only by a sign of irony at the corner of the eyes or mouth, I'm not sure which. Armand's face was false, cunning, mean, sneaky, brutal. No doubt it is easy for me to discover these things after knowing the man, but I know that the impression I had at the time could have been the result only of the miraculous union of these qualities on a single face. Hypocrisy, meanness, stupidity, cruelty and savagery are all reducible to a single term. Rather than their being detailed on his face, what could be read there (I mean not in space but in time) depended on either my own mood or what provoked, within Armand, the appearance of such qualities on his features. He was a brute. He exhibited no regular beauty, but the presence on his face of what I have mentioned—and which was pure because so unmarred by its opposite—gave him a somber though sparkling appearance. His physical strength was prodigious. He was about forty-five at the time. Having lived so long in the company of his own vigor, he carried it lightly. He had been clever enough to make the most of it, so that this vigor, this muscular power, visible in the shape of the skull and the base of the neck, further proclaimed, and imposed, those detestable qualities. It made them sparkle. His face was flat, I believe naturally so, as his nose did not look as if it had been damaged by a blow. His jaw was strong and solid. His skull was very round and almost always shaved. The skin on the back of his neck had three folds which were delineated by thin streaks of dirt. He was tall and splendidly built. He generally moved slowly and with deliberation. He laughed little and without frankness. His voice. It was deep, hollow, almost bass. Not that it could be called a gruff voice, though its timbre did seem muffled. When Armand spoke very fast or when he spoke while walking quickly, he achieved, by the contrast of the acceleration of his delivery and the deep tone of his voice, an ingenious musical effect. With so hurried a movement one expected a high-pitched timbre or, from so deep a voice, that it would move heavily, with difficulty: it was agile. This contrast also produced some elegant inflections. Armand barely articulated. The syllables did not collide. As his speech, though simple, flowed freely, the words linked up with a horizontal tranquillity. It was his voice in particular that made you realize that throughout his youth he had been admired,

especially by men. Males who are admired by men for
their strength or beauty can be recognized by a kind of
impertinent assurance. They are both more sure of themselves and more accessible to gentleness. Armand's voice
touched a spot in my throat and took my breath away.
It was a rare thing for him to hurry, but if, once in a
great while, he had to rush to an appointment, as he
walked between Stilitano and me, his head high, leaning
slightly forward, despite his massive stature and his free
and easy bearing, his voice, growing increasingly rapid
with the depth of the timbre, achieved almost too bold a
masterpiece. Whenever there was a bit of fog, there issued from this leaden athlete a voice of azure.

One assumes that it had belonged to a hurried, nimble,
joyous, glorified adolescent, sure of his grace, strength,
beauty and strangeness, and of the beauty and strangeness of his voice.

Within him, in his organs, which I imagined to be
elementary though of solid tissue and of very lovely
speckled shades, couched in warm and generous guts, I
think he spun out his will to impose, apply and render
visible hypocrisy, stupidity, meanness, cruelty and servility and thereby achieve for his entire person the most
obscene success possible. I saw him in Sylvia's room.
When I entered, Stilitano told him at once that I was
French and that we had met in Spain. Armand was
standing up. He did not offer me his hand, but he looked
at me. I remained near the window without seeming to
pay any attention to them. When they decided to go to
the bar, Stilitano said to me, "Are you coming, Jean?"

Before I had a chance to answer, Armand asked, "Do
you usually take him along?"

Stilitano laughed and said, "If it bothers you, we can
leave him."

"Oh, bring him along."

I followed them. After having a drink, they separated, and Armand did not shake my hand. Stilitano said not a word about him to me. A few days later, when I met him near the docks, Armand ordered me to follow him. Almost without speaking, he took me to his room. With the same apparent scorn, he subjected me to his pleasure.

Dominated by his strength and age, I gave the work my utmost care. Crushed by that mass of flesh, which was devoid of the slightest spirituality, I experienced the giddiness of finally meeting the perfect brute, indifferent to my happiness. I discovered the sweetness that could be contained in a thick fleece on torso, belly and thighs and what force it could transmit. I finally let myself be buried in that stormy night. Out of gratitude or fear I placed a kiss on Armand's hairy arm.

"What's eating you? Are you nuts or something?"

"I didn't do any harm."

I remained at his side in order to serve his nocturnal pleasure. When he went to bed, Armand whipped his leather belt from the loops of his trousers and made it snap. It was flogging an invisible victim, a shape of transparent flesh. The air bled. If he frightened me then, it was because of his powerlessness to be the Armand I see, who is heavy and mean. The snapping accompanied and supported him. His rage and despair at not being *him* made him tremble like a horse subdued by darkness, made him tremble more and more. He would not, however, have tolerated my living idly. He advised me to prowl around the station or the zoo and pick up customers. Knowing the terror inspired in me by his person, he didn't deign to keep an eye on me. The money I earned I brought back intact. He himself operated in the bars. He carried on various kinds of traffic with the dockers and seamen, who respected him. Like all the local pimps and hoodlums of the time, he wore sneakers. Being silent, his footstep was heavier and more elastic. Often he wore a pair of blue woolen sailor pants, the flap of which was never completely buttoned, so that a triangle would hang down in front of him, or sometimes it was a slightly rolled pocket that he wore on his belly. No one had such a sinuous walk as he. I think that he slid along that way in order to recapture the memory of the body he had had as a twenty-year-old hoodlum, pimp and sailor. He was faithful to it, as one is to the fashions of one's youth. But, himself a figure of the most provocative eroticism, he wished also to express it by language and gesture. Accustomed to Stilitano's modesty and to the crudeness of the dockers in their bars, I was the witness of, often the pretext for, proceedings which were the height of audacity. In front of anybody Armand would grow lyrical over his member. No one interrupted him. Unless some tough, annoyed by his tone and remarks, retorted.

"My cock," he once said, "is worth its weight in gold."

"It's not heavy," said a seaman.

"Heavier than that beer mug you've got in your hand!"

"I doubt it."

"You want to weigh them?"

"O.K."

Bets were quickly laid, and Armand, who was already unbuttoned and had a stiff hard-on, put his prick on the seaman's flat palm.

"The beer mug," he said.

At times, with his hand in his pocket he would stroke himself as he stood drinking at the bar. He would boast at other times that he could lift a heavy man on the end of his cock. Not knowing what this obsession with his member and strength corresponded to, I admired him. In the street, though he would draw me to him with his arm as if to embrace me, a brutal push of the same arm would thrust me aside. Since I knew nothing about his life, except that he had been around the world and that he was Flemish; I tried to distinguish the signs of the penal colony from which he must have escaped, bringing back with him that cropped skull, those heavy muscles, his hypocrisy, his violence, his fierceness.

Meeting Armand was such a cataclysm that though I continued to see Stilitano often, he seemed to move off from me in time and space. It was long ago and far away that I had wedded this youngster whose toughness, with its veil of irony, had suddenly been transformed to a delicious gentleness. Never, during all the time I lived with Armand, did Stilitano joke about us. His discretion became delicately painful to me. He soon came to represent Bygone Days.

Unlike Stilitano, Armand was not a coward. Not only did he not refuse single combat, but he accepted dangerous jobs involving force. He even dared conceive them and work out the details. A week after our meeting, he told me that he would be gone for a while and that I was to wait for him to return. He asked me to take care of his belongings, a suitcase containing some linen, and he left. For a few days I felt lighter, I no longer carried the weight of fear. Stilitano and I went out together several times.

Had he not spat into his hands to turn a crank, I would not have noticed a boy of my own age. This typical workman's gesture made me so dizzy that I thought I was falling straight down to a period—or region of myself— long since forgotten. My heart awoke, and at once my body thawed. With wild speed and precision the boy registered on me: his gestures, his hair, the jerk of his hips, the curve of his back, the merry-go-round on which he was working, the movement of the horses, the music, the fair ground, the city of Antwerp containing them, the Earth cautiously turning, the Universe protecting so precious a burden, and I standing there, frightened at possessing the world and knowing I possessed it.

I did not see the spit on his hands: I recognized the puckering of the cheek and the tip of the tongue between his teeth. I again saw the boy rubbing his tough, black palms. As he bent down to grab the handle, I noticed his crackled, but thick, leather belt. A belt of that kind could not be an ornament like the one that holds up the trousers of a man of fashion. By its material and thickness it was penetrated with the following function: holding up the most obvious sign of masculinity which, without the strap, would be nothing, would no longer contain, would no longer guard its manly treasure but would tumble down on the heels of a shackled male. The boy was wearing a windbreaker, between which and the trousers could be seen his skin. As the belt was not inserted into loops, at every movement it rose a bit as the trousers slid down. I stared at the belt, spellbound. I saw it operating surely. At the sixth jerk of the hips, it girdled—except at the fly where the two ends were buckled—the chap's bare back and waist.

"It's nice to see, huh?" said Stilitano.

Watching me watch, he spoke not of the merry-go-round but of its guardian spirit.

"Go tell him you like him. Go on."

"Don't kid around."

"I'm talking seriously."

He was smiling. As neither my age nor bearing would have permitted me to approach or observe him with the light or amused arrogance assumed by distinguished-looking gentlemen, I wanted to go away. Stilitano grabbed me by the sleeve.

"Come on."

I shook him off.

"Let me alone," I said.

"I can see that you like him."

"What of it?"

"What of it? Invite him for a drink."

He smiled again and said:

"Are you scared of Armand?"

"You're crazy."

"Well? You want me to go up to him?"

Just at that moment, the boy stood up straight, his face
flushed and gleaming: he was a congested prick. As he
adjusted his belt, he approached us. We were on the
pavement and he was standing on the baseboards of the
merry-go-round. Since we were looking at him, he smiled
and said:

"That's a real workout."

"It must make you thirsty," said Stilitano. And turning
to me he added, "You going to treat us to a drink?"

Robert went with us to a café. The joyousness of the
event and its simplicity set my head spinning. I was no
longer at Robert's side, nor even at Stilitano's. I was
scattering myself to all corners of the world and was
registering a hundred details which burst into light stars,
I no longer know which. But when I accompanied Lucien
for the first time, I had the same feeling of absence. I
was listening to a housewife bargaining over a geranium.

"I'd like to have a plant in the house . . ." she was
saying, "a nice plant. . . ."

This need for possession, which made her want to have
a plant of her own, chosen, with its roots and earth, from
among the infinity of plants, did not surprise me. The
woman's remark made clear to me the sense of ownership.

"She'll water her plant," I said to myself. "She'll buy
it a majolica flowerpot. She'll put it out in the sun. She'll
cherish it. . . ."

Lucien was walking at my side. The only live things I had ever owned were lovely pricks, whose roots were buried in black moss. I cherished several such, and I wanted them in all the flower of their strength. Those plants were my pride. Such was my fervor that their bearers themselves were amazed at their unwonted beauty. Nevertheless, each remained fastened, by a mysterious and solid base, to the male whose chief branch it was; he owned it more than I did. It was his. Some flies were buzzing around Lucien. My hand mentally made the gesture of chasing them away. This plant was going to belong to me.

"From where could such a marvelous result (the flower crowning it is a lump of thistle) have been transplanted? It must have been chosen from a childpatch. . . . I will cherish it. . . ."

Not only his prick, but all of Lucien was mine. Before him, Robert. At night, rolled up in a blanket, he slept under the canvas covers of the merry-go-round. I invited him to share my room. He came to sleep there the second night. As he was late, I went looking for him. Without his being aware, I saw him in a bar near the docks talking to a man who had the manners of a queer. I said nothing to him, but I let Stilitano know about it. The next morning, before Robert went off to work, Stilitano came to see us. Still encumbered with his unbelievable modesty, he found it embarrassing to say what he wanted to say. He finally spoke up.

"We'll work together. You'll lure them into a pissoir or a room and then Jean and I'll come around. We'll say we're your brothers and we'll make the guy pay up."

I almost said, "What about Armand? What'll he do?" I kept my mouth shut.

Robert was sitting up in bed with the covers over his legs. I was careful not to brush against him so as not to embarrass him. He pointed out to Stilitano the risk involved, but I realized that he himself regarded these risks as something vague and remote, as if wrapped in a heavy fog. Finally he said he would. Stilitano's charm had just acted upon him. It made me feel ashamed. I loved Robert and I would not have succeeded in getting him to agree, but what was particularly cruel for me was the repetition and use of the same details of our intimacy in Spain which only Stilitano and I knew of. When Stilitano had gone, Robert slid under the covers and snuggled up to me.

"He's your guy, huh?"

"Why do you ask that?"

"Anyone can see that he's your guy."

I hugged him and wanted to kiss him, but he moved away.

"You're crazy. We're not going to do that together!"

"Why not?"

"Huh? I don't know. We're the same age. It wouldn't be any fun."

That morning he got up late. We had lunch with Stilitano and Sylvia, and then Robert went to get his pay and tell his boss that he was giving up his job at the merry-go-round. We spent the whole night drinking. During the week of Armand's absence we didn't hear from him. I first thought of clearing out of Antwerp, and even Belgium, and taking his things with me. But his power acted from a distance and I was held back, not by fear but by the attraction of the violence of this mature man, matured in evil, a genuine bandit, capable, and he alone, of drawing me, almost carrying me, into the frightening world from which I felt he had emerged. I did not move out of his room, but my anxiety increased daily. Stilitano had promised me not to tell him about my passion for Robert, but I was not sure whether the boy himself would not be so malicious as to tell on me. Robert acted very much at ease with the cripple. Not the least bit shy, he was playful, bantering, even a bit impudent. When they spoke of possible jobs to be pulled off, I noticed that his expression suddenly became attentive, and when the explanation was finished, Robert would crown it with an explicit gesture: his thumb and middle finger came together and seemed to be insinuating themselves into the inner pocket of an invisible jacket and delicately withdrawing an invisible jewel. The gesture was light-fingered. Robert outlined it in the air slowly, with broken movements: one, when the hand seemed to be leaving the victim's pocket; the other, as it entered his own.

Robert and I served Stilitano the way one serves a priest or a piece of artillery. Kneeling before him, each of us would lace one of his shoes. The thing got complicated when it came to the single glove. Almost always it was Robert who had the privilege of pressing the snap button.

An account of the few operations we carried out would not teach you anything about such practices. Generally Robert or I would go upstairs with the queer. While he was asleep, we would throw the money down to Stilitano, who was posted beneath the window. In the morning the client would accuse us. We would let him search us, but he dared not lodge a complaint. In the beginning, Robert tried to justify his thefts. A novice crook always wants to punish a louse by robbing him.

"Those people," he would say, "are degenerates."

His attempts to find fault with the queers he robbed made him boring. With brutal frankness Stilitano told him off.

"If you go on preaching like that you'll wind up as a priest. There's only one reason for what we're doing and that's dough."

That kind of language loosened Robert up. Sure of

being upheld by Stilitano, he really let himself go. His talk became very funny. He amused Stilitano, who went out only with him. My mood became grayer and grayer. I was jealous of my two friends. In addition, Robert, who was fond of girls, smiled at all of them. They liked him. As a result, I felt that, with Stilitano, he was not against me but rather out of reach. Since he was better looking than I, Stilitano gave him my clothes to make it easier for him to attract men. Robert wore them, smiling and unembarrassed. All I had was a pair of trousers, a jacket and some torn shirts. I concocted trivial schemes of revenge on Stilitano. Compared to Armand, he became flatter and flatter, lacking in thickness. His good looks seemed insipid, his speech dreary. I hoped for new revelations from Armand.

As for Armand's immodest attitudes, I cannot quite say that they were the cause of my decision to write pornographic books, but I certainly was flabbergasted by the insolence of the answer he gave Stilitano who had asked him very calmly, though with a kind of casual indifference, the reason why he got so passionately lyrical.

"It's my balls," he said, "my balls! Women walk with their tits bulging, don't they? They parade them, don't they? Well, I've got a right to let my balls stick out so people can see them, and even to offer them on a platter. I've got a great pair of balls and I've even got a right to send them as a present to Pola Negri or the Prince of Wales."

Stilitano was capable of cynicism, not of song. Long buried—where, in accumulating, they thickened my rancor —his cowardice, flabbiness and laziness rose up to poison my breath. The qualities which had once embellished him—as an ulcer sculpts and paints meat—now became reasons for contempt. The two of them seemed unaware

that I was jealous and furious and that this was damaging our relationship. One day when I was alone with
her, Sylvia took my arm in the street. She pressed herself against me. Two men whom I loved were, by their
mutual and unambiguous friendship, cutting themselves
off from me, refusing me access to free—and joyous—
cordiality, but the woman of one of them was degrading
me even further by her desire, which was akin to comforting the poor. Her hip and breast against my body
made me feel like vomiting. She dared say in Stilitano's
presence, no doubt to hurt him, that she rather liked me.
Robert and he burst out laughing.

"The two of you can go gallivanting. We're going out
together."

Driven out by their laughter, I saw myself tumbling
down the steps of light, of which Stilitano was lord. I was
back in Spain, with my rags, my nights among the poor,
enriched by some happy memories, but hopeless: there
I was, sure that all I would ever do was bite the dust and
lick boots—my own, dusty with weary tramping. The idea
of lice was already breeding its insects on me. As it was
almost time to hatch them, I stopped cutting my hair. I
resolved to kill Stilitano and Robert. Failing to be a hoodlum in glory, I wanted to be one in affliction. I chose the
penal colony or an ignominious death. To sustain me I
had, nevertheless, the memory of Armand and the hope
of his returning, but he did not appear.

We were in Belgium. Only the French police have a
fabulous glamor for me. Likewise the whole penitentiary
apparatus. What I committed outside of France was not
a sin but an error. What would I find in the Belgian penal
settlements and prisons? Only the boredom, probably, of
being deprived of freedom. I suggested to Stilitano and
Robert that we do a job in Maubeuge.

"If I kill them in the Ardennes, I'll be arrested by the French police and condemned to Devil's Island."

Neither of them was willing to follow me. One day, when I was alone in Stilitano's room, I stole his revolver from the pocket of a jacket that was hanging in a closet.

The life I have been telling about was lived between 1932 and 1940. Here are the loves with which I have been preoccupied while writing about it. Having noted them, I now make use of them. May they serve the purposes of this book.

I bit Lucien until blood flowed. I was hoping to make him scream; his insensitivity conquered me. But I know that I would go so far as to rip my friend's flesh and lose myself in an irreparable carnage wherein I would preserve my reason and know the exaltation of the fall.

"May the signs of it grow on me," I said to myself, "long nails and hair, sharp teeth, drool; and despite my bites may Lucien preserve his indifferent expression, for the signs of extremely great pain would immediately make me loosen my jaws and beg his pardon." When my teeth bit into his flesh, my jaws clenched until they trembled and made my whole body shudder. I'm in a fury, and yet how tenderly I love my littler fisherman from Le Suquet. When he lies pressed against me, he gently twines his legs about mine and our legs are merged by the soft cloth of our pajamas; then he very carefully chooses the right spot to cuddle his cheek. So long as he is not sleeping, I feel the quivering of his eyelids and

upturned lashes against the very sensitive skin of my
neck. If he feels a tickling in his nostrils, his laziness and
drowsiness keep him from lifting his hand, so that in
order to scratch himself he rubs his nose against my
beard, thus giving me delicate little taps with his head,
like a young calf sucking its mother. He is then completely vulnerable. A cross look or harsh word from me
would wound him or, without leaving a trace, would cut
through a substance that has become very tender, almost
soft, elastic. It sometimes happens that a wave of tenderness, rising up from my heart without my even anticipating it, passes into my arms, which hug him tighter,
and he, without moving his head, presses his lips against
the part of my face or body with which they are in contact. This is the automatic response to the sudden pressure of my arm. The wave of tenderness is always met by
this simple peck, in which I feel, blossoming on the surface of my skin, the sweetness of a simple, candid boy.
By this sign I recognize his docility to the injunctions of
the heart, the submission of his body to my mind. I
whispered, with my voice choked by the weight of his
head, "When you're like that, crushed against me, I feel
as if I were protecting you."

"Me too," he said. And quickly he gave me one of his
peck-answers.

"What do you mean 'me too'?"

"I feel I'm protecting you too."

"You do? Why? Do I seem weak to you?"

Gently he sighed to me, "Yes . . . I'm protecting you."

After kissing my closed eyes, he leaves my bed. I hear
him shutting the door. Images take shape beneath my
eyelids: in the clear water I see a world, agile gray insects
moving about on the slimy bottom of certain fountains.
They scurry about in the shade and clear water of my
eyes, whose bottom is covered with slime.

It amazes me that so muscular a body dissolves so readily in my heat. In the street he sways his shoulders as he walks: his hardness has melted. That which was sharp edges and splinters has grown smooth—except the eyes, which gleam in the crumbling snow. That punching, butting, kicking machine lies down, stretches out, uncoils, proves to my astonishment that it was merely a contracted, taut gentleness, coiled about several times, knotted and swollen, and I learn how that gentleness, that supple docility in responding to my tenderness, will be transformed into violence, into meanness, if gentleness no longer had the opportunity to be itself, if, for example, my tenderness ceased, if I abandoned the child, if I deprived weakness of the possibility of its occupying that splendid body. I see what would govern the sudden starts. The rage at being so awakened. His gentleness would become knotted, would contract, would coil about itself several times to form a dreadful spring.

"If you left me, I'd go wild," he said. "I'd become the worst kind of tramp."

Sometimes I fear that his docility may suddenly stop obeying my love. I have to be very careful and take quick advantage of what he offers my happiness. Toward evening, when Lucien holds me tight in his arms and covers my face with kisses, a sadness clouds my body. It is as if my body were growing dark. A shadow covers it with crape. My eyes turn inward. Shall I let this child detach himself from me? Fall from my tree? Crash to the ground?

"My love is always sad."

"That's true. As soon as I kiss you, you get sad. I've noticed it."

"Does it bother you?"

"No, it doesn't matter. I'm happy instead of you."

I murmur to myself:

"I love you. . . . I love you. . . . I love you. . . ."

My love may end, I say to myself, by going out of me, swept off by these words, as a poison is swept out of the body by milk or a purge. I hold his hand in mine. My fingertips linger over his. Finally I cut the contact: I still love him. The same sadness clouds my body. I see him for the first time: Lucien was coming down from Le Suquet barefoot. He walked through the town barefoot and went into the movie theater. He was wearing a fault-lessly elegant outfit: a pair of blue dungarees and a white and blue striped sailor's jersey with short sleeves rolled up to the shoulders. I dare write that he was also *wearing* bare feet, so keenly did I feel that they were accessories which had been wrought to complete his beauty. I often admired his mastery and the authority conferred upon him, amidst the city's conceited throng, by the sweet, simple assertion of his beauty, by his elegance, youth, strength and grace. In the center of this profusion of hap-piness, he seemed to me solemn, and he smiled.

The leaves of the araucaria plant are red, thick and fuzzy, slightly oily and brown. They adorn the graves and cemeteries of fishermen long dead who for centuries walked along this coast, which was still wild and gentle. The men bronzed their muscles, which were already dark, as they hauled their boats and nets. They wore at the time an outfit whose forgotten details changed very little: a very low-cut shirt, a multicolored scarf around their dark, curly heads. They walked barefoot. They are dead. The plant, which also grows in public parks, makes me think of them. The people of shades which they have become continues its pranks and eager chatter: I reject their death. Having no other finer means of resurrecting a young fisherman of 1730 so that he might live more vividly, I would sit out in the sun on the rocks or in the

evening in the shadow of the pines and make his image
serve my pleasure. The company of a youngster was not
always enough to distract me from them. One evening I
shook off the dead leaves clinging to my hair and jacket;
I buttoned my trousers and asked Bob:

"Do you know a guy named Lucien?"

"Yes, why?"

"Nothing. He interests me."

The boy didn't bat an eyelash. He was gingerly brushing off pine needles. He ran his fingers subtly through his
hair to feel for bits of moss. He emerged slightly from the
shadow to see whether any jissom had spattered his
soldier pants.

"What kind of guy is he?" I asked.

"Him? A little tramp. He used to hang around with the
guys from the Gestapo."

Once again I was the center of a soul-stirring whirl-
wind. The French Gestapo contained two fascinating elements: treason and theft. With homosexuality added, it
would be sparkling, unassailable. It would possess the
three virtues, which I set up as theological, capable of
composing so hard a body as Lucien's. What could be
said against it? It was outside the world. It betrayed
(betraying means breaking the laws of love). It engaged
in pillage. And lastly, it banned itself from the world by
homosexuality. It thus established itself in an indestructible solitude. I was to learn more about it from Java and
shall speak of it later on.

"Are you sure of what you're saying?"

Bob looked at me. With a toss of his head, he threw
back his dark curls. He was walking at my side, in the
shadow.

"Of course I'm sure."

I remained silent. I was observing myself intently.
Within me were unfurling the waves formed by the word

Gestapo. Lucien was walking on them. They bore up his graceful feet, his muscular body, his litheness, his neck, his head crowned with gleaming hair. I was filled with wonder at the knowledge that this palace of flesh was the seat of perfect evil, which composed that perfect balance of limbs and torso, of light and shade. The palace slowly sank into the waves; it swam to the middle of the sea which beats against the coast where we were walking and, gradually becoming liquid, it turned into sea. How filled I was with peace and tenderness in the presence of so precious a solitude in so rich a case! I would have liked to fall asleep without sleeping, to close my arms over the waves. The shadow of the world, of the sky, of the road and trees, entered through my eyes and settled within me.

"What about you? Didn't you ever think of joining up so that you could get your hands on things?"

Bob turned his head slightly in my direction. His face, alternately luminous and dark, remained impassive.

"You're crazy. Where would I be now? In the jug like the rest of them."

In the jug or dead, like the chiefs of the organization: Laffon, Bony, Clavié, Pagnon, Labussière. The reason I tore out and saved the scrap of newspaper with their photographs was the desire to draw from it food for argument in favor of treason, which I have always endowed with a radiant visage. Maurice Pilorge, he of the fair morning face, was as tricky as they come. He used to lie. He lied to me and smilingly betrayed all his friends. I loved him. When I learned that he had murdered Escudero, I was momentarily stunned because once again drama came so close as to touch me; it entered my life, exalted me, gave me a new importance (the guttersnipes say: "He don't feel himself shitting no more!"). And I worshiped him as I still do eight years or so after his beheading. During the time from murder to death, Pilorge became greater than I. Thinking also of his severed life, of his rotting body, it was when I could say "Poor kid" that I loved him. I then accepted his being, for me, not an example, but a help in making my way to a heaven where I hope to join him (I do not write rejoin him). I had in front of me faces (except Labussière's) that were bored and baggy with fear and cowardice. Against them were the bad quality of the paper and printing and their having been snapped at a trying moment. They had the look of people caught in a trap, but one which they had set for themselves, an inner trap. In the very beautiful photo which shows him bandaged, wounded by the cop who arrested him, Weidmann is also an animal caught in a trap, but a mantrap. His own truth does not turn against him to disfigure him. What I saw and what I sometimes see when I look at the picture of Laffon and his friends is the way they themselves turn against themselves.

"A genuine traitor, a traitor for the love of it," I say to myself, "doesn't have a false look."

Each of the men I am speaking of had periods of glory. They were luminous then. I knew Labussière. I have seen him going out with girl friends, in luxurious cars. He was sure of himself, ensconced in his truth, tranquilly established at the center of his activity as a well paid stool pigeon. Nothing tormented him.

"Scruples and feelings which in others create such uneasiness that you can see it on their faces leave Lucien's candor intact," I said to myself.

Bob hoped, by describing him to me as a rat, to detach him from me. On the contrary, he attached me to him even more. I amorously imagined him "bumping off" and torturing people. I was wrong. He never betrays. When I asked Lucien whether he would be willing to lead my life with me, including the dangers involved, he looked

me in the eyes and never have I seen so fresh a gaze. It
was a spring flooding a damp meadow, where you find
forget-me-nots and that graminaceous plant which in
Le Morvan is called trembling grass. Then he said to me:

"I would."

"I can count on you, on your friendship?"

"You can. I'll lead the same life as you, except that I
don't want to steal."

"Why?"

"No. I'd rather work."

I remained silent.

"You say that if I left you, you'd become a bandit.
Why?"

"Because I'd be ashamed of myself."

A few days later I said to him:

"You know, we'll have to manage with what's left.
We're almost broke."

Lucien was walking with his eyes lowered.

"If only we could find something to swipe," he said.

I was careful to handle gently, so as not to break it,
the fragile mechanism which made him utter such a remark, careful to say nothing too brutally victorious. I
spoke of something else. The day after a visit to G. H.
he became more precise.

G. H. lives in an apartment which he furnished in four
days when the Germans entered Paris. He and three
friends put on Wehrmacht uniforms (uniforms stolen by
whores from soldiers groggy with fatigue, liquor and sex)
and rifled a few private mansions of Parisians who had
taken flight. His loaded truck traveled back and forth
from Passy to the garage. Now he owns furniture and
rugs. Carpets of that kind, I say to myself, in homes
where discretion enters me by the feet, create silence—
even the solitude and quietude offered by a mother's

heart. There one may utter the vilest words, prepare the most abominable of crimes. The chandeliers are stacked in his apartment. His friends had an equal share of the booty. Two are dead, killed in Italy while fighting in the Darnand militia.[1] The other one has just been condemned to hard labor for life. These two deaths and the conviction have sanctified G. H.'s proprietary rights. They have authenticated it. Sure—or not—of never being discovered, he walks on his rugs and lolls in his armchairs with an authority he did not hitherto have.

"Let them come and put me out," he said to me.

He draws his strength from the certainty of his right to occupy this conquered furniture, these rich spoils which Lucien admires. The apartment, *qua* fact, as an action continuing to unfold, is an element of the drama. It is the infinitely precious tabernacle where the witness keeps vigil. Now that I know about these deaths, I myself enter G. H.'s home with more assurance, with less awe. Each object no longer looks as if it belonged to another master, as if it were submissive to another mind. Everything here quite definitely belongs to its present possessor. When we left the apartment, Lucien said to me on the stairs:

"It must be fun working with that guy."

"What work?"

"His."

"Which?"

"You know well enough—robbery."

Perhaps Armand lives in similar luxury or perhaps he has been shot. When the Germans occupied France, to which he had returned, it was natural for him to enlist in the Gestapo. I learned the fact from a police inspector

[1] A French Fascist organization of storm troopers.—Translator's note.

who found his photo on me when I was arrested. That was where he was bound to go and where I should have followed him. His influence had been leading me there.

(Having lost a large part of this journal, I can no longer remember the words in which I recalled the adventure of Albert and D., which I witnessed, though without taking part in it. I don't feel I have the heart to go into the whole story again, but a kind of respect for the tragic tone they gave their love makes it my duty to mention it. Albert was twenty years old. He came from Le Havre. D. had met him at the Santé Prison. When they got out, they lived together. As the Germans were in France, D. joined the Gestapo. One day, in a bar, he shot and killed a German officer who was making fun of his friend In the confusion, he had time to slip Albert his weapon.
"*Ditch the gun.*"
"*Beat it. Beat it, Dédé!*"
Before he had gone fifty yards, he was prevented from fleeing by a barrier. He doubtless foresaw with lightning speed the torture he was in for.
"*Hand me the gun,*" *he said to Albert. Albert refused.*
"*I'm telling you to hand it to me! I want to shoot myself.*"
It was too late. The Germans were near them.
"*Bébert, I don't want them to get me alive. Kill me.*"
Albert fired a bullet into Dédé's head and then committed suicide.
When I wrote the lost fragment of this journal, I was haunted for a long time by Albert's beauty. He always wore a bargeman's cap (the black ribbon of which is brocaded with flowers). D. used to strut insolently around Montmartre with his boots. They were always quarreling (D. was forty at the time), right up to that death, which I did not witness. In the form in which I first cast this

account, I must have made it serve some moral con-
clusion, which I no longer remember. I don't feel impelled
to rewrite it.)

I know the extraordinary calmness one feels at the
moment of performing the theft, and the fear that accompanies it. My body is afraid. In front of a jeweler's
window: as long as I'm not inside, I don't think I'm going to steal. No sooner do I get inside than I'm sure I'll
come out with a jewel: a ring or handcuffs. This certainty
is expressed by a long shudder which leaves me motionless but which goes from the back of my neck down to
my heels. It peters out at my eyes and dries their lids.
My cells seem to be transmitting to one another a wave,
an undulating movement which is the very substance of
calm. I am alive with thought from my heels to the back
of my neck. I accompany the wave. It is born of fear.
Without it there would not be this calm in which my
body bathes—which my body attains. I have to be very
careful not to flee. When I leave the store, it is very difficult for me to run, or even to walk fast. A kind of elastic
holds me back. My muscles are heavy and tight. But a
sharp vigilance directs them in the street. I cannot see
Lucien in that kind of situation. Would he falter? And
what happens during a burglary? When I have broken
the lock, as soon as I push the door it thrusts back *within*
me a heap of darkness, or, to be more exact, a very thick
vapor which my body is summoned to enter. I enter. For
a half hour I shall be operating, if I am alone, in a world
which is the reverse of the customary world. My heart
beats loudly. My hand never trembles. Fear does not
leave me for a single second. I do not think specifically
of the proprietor of the place, but all my gestures evoke
him in so far as they see him. I am steeped in an idea of
property while I loot property. I recreate the absent pro-

prietor. He lives, not facing me, but about me. He is a fluid element which I breathe, which enters me, which inflates my lungs. The beginning of the operation goes off without too much fear, which starts mounting the moment I have finally decided to leave. The decision is born when the apartment contains no more secret spots, when I have taken the proprietor's place. And this is not necessarily when I have discovered the treasure. Guy almost always sits down and eats in the kitchen or the looted drawing room. Some burglars go to the can after ransacking a place. I won't have Lucien undergoing such rites. His is not a religious nature. When the treasure has been discovered, I have to leave. Fear then invades my body. I would like to hasten everything. Not hasten myself, not go more quickly, but act in such a way that everything is magically sped up. To be out of here and far away. But what gestures shall I make in order to go more quickly? The heaviest, the slowest. Slowness brings fear. Not only my heart but my whole body is now beating. I am one enormous temple, the throbbing temple of the looted room. I have sometimes preferred to sleep there for an hour behind a door so as to calm down rather than go out into the street and be off, for though I know that I am not being followed, I shall zigzag in and out, I shall take certain streets, I shall retrace my steps, as if trying to cover up my tracks. After a rapid theft, the experience is even more exciting: I go more quickly, I accelerate; the sections making up the broken lines are shorter. It is as if I were being carried away by the speed itself with which I perform the theft. I wouldn't put up with Lucien's exposing himself in that way. His bearing isn't furtive. In his movements and behavior there is, as it were, a slight hesitation, a holding back, comparable to the holding back of the last syllables at the corners of the moist mouths of young Americans. Lucien is modest.

One day I threatened to leave him.

"Once is enough, but one of these days I'm going to blow up. I'm fed up with your whims."

I went out without kissing him. For three days I refused to see him. He never complained.

"How am I going to get rid of him?" I wondered. I was visited by scruples which, along with my thoughts, weighed on my mind and embittered the course of a life that was already full of anxiety. I hoped that he would throw himself on my neck. I awaited a miracle, but a storm was needed to clear the sky. The evening of the third day I entered his room.

"Haven't you eaten?"

"I didn't have any money left."

"Couldn't you have asked me for some?"

"I thought you wouldn't give me any."

He spoke simply; then he remained silent. He made no effort to hold on to life. His insensitivity to his own misery exasperated me.

"He may be dying to do it," I thought, "but his lack of imagination prevents him from finding the necessary gestures."

All at once he seemed to be walled up in an underground cavern from which he was unable to make his voice heard—a voice that was no doubt very discreet and very soft. He was a paralytic whose soul was pining away in a motionless body. But what finally melted my rigor was my remembering something he had said about his dislocated shoulder: "It's not my fault." He had uttered this excuse in such a humble tone that I thought I could feel him blushing in the dark.

"I can't leave the poor kid all alone," I said to myself. "He may remember saying this to me and he'll know I'm hardhearted."

Two minutes later, when he was in my arms, I took

hold of his hair to lift up his face which he had buried
in my neck; I saw that he was crying. During those three
days he had known utter grief. I was then at peace with
my soul for having brought peace to the child. I was
proud of being the cause of a child's tears, of his joy and
suffering. By virtue of my grace, he was a kind of jewel
which his tears and pain hardened until it sparkled. His
despair embellished both himself and his return to life.
They made him precious. His tears and sobs on my neck
proved my virility. I was his man. Hardly had he sponged
his face and stretched out beside me on the bed than
he began straightening the rim of my ear. He rolled it,
unrolled it, bent it.

"It's getting creased," he said.

He abandoned my ear for my cheek, then for my forehead, which he creased with his cruel fingers. (His fingers
are kneading my skin with stern precision. His gesture is
not mechanical. Lucien is paying very close attention to
what he is doing.) He seemed to be trying various faces
on me, none of which satisfied him. I let myself be
worked on by the child; the game enabled him to work
off his grief. It amused him to invent wrinkles, hollows
and bumps, but it seemed to amuse him solemnly. He was
not laughing. Under the inventive fingers I felt his kindness. They made it seem a blessing to be kneaded and
molded, and I knew the love that matter must feel for the
one who fashions it with such joy.

"What are you doing to my cheek?"

My question is far away. Where am I? What's going
on here, in this hotel room, on a brass bed. Where am I?
I am indifferent to what he is doing. My mind is resting.
In a little while that roaring plane will crash to the
ground. I shall remain here, my face finally on his neck.
He won't move. I shall be stuck in love, the way one is
stuck in ice, or mud, or fear.

Lucien was pawing away and kneading my skin, my eyebrows, my chin, my cheek. I opened my eyes wider, looked at him and, without smiling, for I did not have the strength to, said to him sadly (nor did I have the strength to change my tone):

"What are you doing to my cheek?"

"I'm making knots in it."

He replied simply, the way one speaks about a natural thing to someone who ought to understand, or who will never understand anything so simple, so mysterious. His voice was somewhat hollow. When he raised my eyebrow in order to massage it, I drew my head slightly back. He put out his hands to take it again, to pull it closer. I drew it farther back. He held out his arms and appealed plaintively, almost like a baby:

"Jean, please, let me."

"You're hurting me."

"Only a tiny little bit, my nice little Jean. Your little eyebrow, a tiny little bit."

I understand what binds the sculptor to his clay, the painter to his paints, each workman to the matter he works with, and the docility and acquiescence of the matter to the movements of the one who animates it; I know the love that passes from the fingers into the folds, the holes, the swellings.

Shall I abandon him? Lucien would prevent me from living. Unless his quiet tenderness, his blushing modesty, became beneath my sun of love a tiger or a lion. If he loves me, will he follow me?

"What would become of him without me?"

Being proud, he will refuse to return to his family. In my company he will acquire habits of laziness and luxury. Will he hang around bars? He will become mean and cruel out of revenge, out of defiance, out of hatred of all men. One misfortune in the world, among so many others, is a matter of indifference to me, but I suffer at the thought of this child's taking the path of shame. My love is exalted at the edge of his abyss. At the point of ending, every evening it lights up the apotheosis of the setting sun.

"What will become of him?"

Grief unfurls over me, covers me over. I see Lucien: his numb, purple, sluggish, sensitive fingers, frozen to the bone, painfully open to enter the stiff, filthy pockets of his trousers; I see him standing and tapping his toes on the sidewalk, in the dry cold, in front of cafés he dares not enter; perhaps a new dance may be born from his aching feet, a parody. He turns up the collar of his jacket. Despite the wind that chaps his lips, he will smile at the old queens. Grief unfurls over me, but what happiness in my body and heart spreads its fragrance when, by the same thought which makes me abandon him, I save him from all the evil to which I doom him. He will not hate me. Nauseating whiffs of my Spain rise to my nostrils.

Can I do better than place him for a few pages in one of the most humiliating situations which I myself had been in? An awkward, childish and perhaps proud sense of redemption makes me believe that I underwent all those humiliations so that he might be spared them. But to make the experiment more effective I shall make Lucien live for a moment in my wretched skin. In a book entitled *Miracle of the Rose* I take upon myself the ignominy of the situation of a young inmate whose cheeks and eyes are spat on by fellow inmates, and in speaking of him I say "I . . ." Here it's the reverse. It was raining. Lucien and some other ignominious bums were squatting against a block of stone in a lot near the harbor where beggars were tolerated. Each of them was tending a little brushwood fire in which he was heating the rice and beans that had been handed out at the barracks and brought back in a tin can. Coming from the splendid soldiers, among whom he would have been the handsomest, this food, this unnamable stew, which had been left by them, which had been stirred by their pity and disdain that had now become part of it, turned to stone as it went down his throat. His heart was contracted. The tears he held back hardened his eyelids. The rain had put out all the fires, though they were still smoking. The beg-

gars protected their stew as best they could, covering the
can with the flaps of their jackets or with a sack thrown
over their shoulders. As the lot was situated at the lower
level of a wall supporting a boulevard that joins the
Ramblas, the strollers leaning on the parapet looked down
on a veritable Court of Miracles where, at all times, one
witnessed paltry disputes, paltry fights, petty transac-
tions. Every act was a parody. The poor are grotesque.
What they were doing there was only a distorted reflection
of sublime adventures which take place perhaps in rich
dwellings, to persons worthy of being seen and heard. The
beggars who fought and insulted one another attenuated
the violence of their gestures and cries so as not to adorn
themselves thereby with any noble attribute reserved for
your world. The other beggars watching these battles
looked on casually, for this gesture too should be only a
reflection. To a witticism, to a high-sounding and humorous insult, to a sudden rush of eloquence as well as to a
blow cleverly, too skillfully delivered, they refused the
smile or admiring word. Quite the contrary, though in
silence, and in the secrecy of their hearts, they blamed
it as though it were an incongruity. Which it was, and
their sense of decency rejected it. For example, no beggar
would have said to another, in a pitying tone of voice,
"Poor fellow, don't worry. You'll get over it." Those
gentlemen had tact. For their own security, so as to avoid
any flaw through which grief might enter, they observed
an indifference bordering on the most extreme courtesy.
Their language preserved the restraint of the classics.
Knowing that they were distorted and unhappy shadows
or reflections, they strove piously to possess the unhappy
discretion of gestures and feelings. They spoke not in a
low voice, but in an intermediate tone between low and
high. The scene that I wish to describe took place in the
rain, but even at noon, in the July sun, rain seemed to

fall on them gently and to make them shiver. Sometimes a soldier would appear. He would say a few words in Spanish, and five or six of the humblest, oldest and homeliest would rush forward miserably: the soldier would take two of them to the wash house where they would wring and hang out the laundry. Lucien never responded to these calls. He would look out, from within a shelter of sadness, at the sea getting wet in the distance. His eyes were staring. He was sure he would never emerge from this dream. Dirt sharpened his features. Sweat made his face smooth and oily, perfect for a camera shot. He shaved rarely and badly, soaping his beard with his hand. Not having—nor had I at that time—cut the cables that hold captive a man whose only chance is detachment, he remained in contact with your world through his youth, his beauty, his concern for elegance, his hunger, his need for earthly glory. It is painful for me to degrade him. I would be overjoyed if I could call him scoundrel, blackguard, riffraff, guttersnipe, hoodlum, crook, charming names whose function is to evoke what you, derisively, call a pretty world. But these words sing. They hum. They also evoke for you the sweetest and spiciest pleasures, since, placing before them, under your breath, the words tender, dear, adorable or beloved, which they subtly attract, you murmur them to your lovers. May Lucien despair and may I suffer thereby! The veil of modesty torn, the shameful parts shown, I know—with my cheeks aflame—the need to hide myself or die, but I believe that by facing and enduring this painful anxiety I shall, as a result of my shamelessness, come to know a strange beauty. (I use this word at random, for I assume that I shall discover a fairer world where, without disturbing the emotion, without disturbing the love, a discreet—and futile—laugh will be permitted.) Lucien suffered, though secretly, for he was steeping. If he

looked at his dirty hands, a burst of rage would sometimes drive him to a fountain. He would zealously wash
his torso, then his feet, and his hands; he would scrub
his face and comb his hair with a toothless comb. This
attempt to return to your world was futile. A few days
later the dirt would eat away his courage. More and more
he was chilled by the wind, weakened by hunger—not
with the noble weakness of sickly languishment; his body
remained just as beautiful and he was unable to disdain
it, for that would have been insolence—and alienated
from you by a frightful odor.

I have said enough about what happened when French
tourists passed by and leaned over the parapet. When
their ship put in at Barcelona, they would go ashore for a
few hours. Foreigners in this country, wearing fine gabar-
dines, rich, they recognized their inherent right to find
these archipelagoes of poverty picturesque, and this visit
was perhaps the secret, though unavowed, purpose of
their cruise. Without considering that they might be
wounding the beggars, they carried on, above their heads,
an audible dialogue, the terms of which were exact and
rigorous, almost technical.

"There's a perfect harmony between the tonalities of
the sky and the slightly greenish shades of the rags."

"... something out of Goya ..."

"It's very interesting to watch the group on the left.
There are things of Gustave Doré in which the composition ..."

"They're happier than we are."

"There's something more sordid about them than those
in the shantytown, you remember, in Casablanca? There's
no denying that the Moroccan costume gives a *simple*
beggar a dignity that no European can ever have."

"We're seeing them when they're all frozen. They have
to be seen when the weather is right."

"On the contrary, the originality of the poses . . ."

From within their warm fleeces the strollers observed this population that sat hunched up with their chins on their knees, unsheltered from the wind and water. Never did I feel in my heart envy or hatred of the rich who turned aside from us in disgust. Prudence recommended repressed feelings: submissiveness, servility. The rich obey the laws of wealth. When Lucien saw them approaching, he felt a kind of anxiety. It was the first time he had seen men come to examine his behavior, his aberrations, his oddities. All at once he was dizzily swept to the depths of the nameless; the fall took his breath away and made his heart leap. Between their gloved hands he saw the malicious gleam of the cruel lenses of their cameras. A few beggars understood French, but he alone could distinguish the shades of the blend of insolence and authoritarian benevolence. Each one wearily undid his covers or rags and raised his head a little.

"Do you want to earn . . . ?"

Like the others, Lucien stood up, leaned on his elbow, squatted, depending on the shots the tourists wanted to take. He even smiled, as ordered, at an old beggar, and he even allowed them to muss his dirty hair and make it fall down over his wet forehead. The poses took a long time since the weather was gray. The tourists complained about the light, but they praised the quality of their films. Though the beggars might have felt a naïve vanity in serving a picturesqueness without which Spain would be less beautiful, Lucien felt shame overflowing and drowning him. They belonged to an illustrious site. Did I myself realize, in Marseille, when I was sixteen years old, amidst other kids waiting for the gentlemen who were to choose us, that I was being used to compose a group of fifteen or twenty hoodlums whom people come to see from all over the world and who are the extensible but essential element of that city dear to queers. I know a few who are my age, and if they meet me they say, "Oh! yes, I remember, you were from the Rue Bouterie," or "You were from Belzunce Square."

With an excess of servility, the beggars arranged themselves in the filthiest spots, disdainful of the slightest precaution for their own person. Lucien had sat down on a step that was soaking wet, with his feet in another puddle. He made no further effort to go back to your world; he was in a state of despair. His pitiful image was destined to illustrate the trip of a millionaire connoisseur.

"I've taken you five times," said a man. He handed ten pesetas to Lucien who thanked him in Spanish.

The beggars showed a discreet joy and gratitude. Though a few went off to drink, the others resumed their hunched position, seemingly asleep, but in reality secreting a kind of truth which would be their own and which would save them: penury in the pure state.

This scene is only one among many by which I should like the idea of Lucien to be purified so as to emerge perfect, and worthy of the good fortune I earned for him at the time.

What I know about him: tenderness, sweetness, vulnerability, rather than strong points and weaknesses (but as in the saying: "the weak spot in his armor"), bringing him before me in situations in which he would be so unhappy as to kill himself. However, in order to love him more than myself I have to feel that he is weak and fragile so as never to be tempted (against my will) to desert him. He is served by my adventures. I have lived them. Upon my chosen image of Lucien I cruelly impose the same ordeals. Save that it is my body which has suffered them, and my mind. Then, with them as a basis, I shall shape an image of him which he will imitate.

I have just given a poor description of the operation which consists of taking upon oneself the sufferings of others, but, aside from the fact that I indicate its mechanism rather confusedly, it's too late; I'm too weary to make the effort to cast more light on it.

In order not to establish Lucien in happiness, but rather that he may emit happiness, I want to fashion him in accordance with an image of him which I shall have first prepared, worked out and sketched by my own adventures. Thus, I gradually accustomed him to hearing me talk about them, to knowing that I was steeped in them, to talking about them himself without blushing, without pitying me or feeling sorry for me, for he has to know that I have decided he will benefit from them. I therefore require that he know about my prostitution and that he acknowledge it. That he know the details of my pettiest larcenies, that he suffer thereby and that he accept them. That he also know about my background and my homosexuality, my cowardice, my peculiar imagination which wishes on me a mother who is an old thief with a pale, shifty-looking face; my gesture for begging alms; my voice, which I used to crack and muffle, in keeping with a convention recognized by both beggars and bourgeoise; my ingenious way, which I myself invented, of accosting queers; my faggoty carryings-on; my shame in the presence of good-looking boys; the scene in which one of them rejected my tenderness for the grace and impudence of a guttersnipe; another in which the French consul held his nose when he saw me coming in and had me thrown out; and those interminable jaunts through Europe in rags, hunger, contempt, fatigue and vice.

When I was deserted by Stilitano near San Fernando, my grief was even greater, my sense of poverty even deeper. (When Arabs talk about the poor, they say "meskine." I was *mesquin* [shabby].) It was no longer even the memory of him that I carried away with me but rather the idea of a fabulous creature, the origin and pretext of all desires, terrifying and gentle, remote and close

to the point of containing me, for, now being something
dreamed, he had, though hard and brutal, the gaseous
insubstantiality of certain nebulae, their gigantic dimensions, their brilliance in the heavens and their name as
well. I trampled Stilitano beneath my feet as he lay battered by sun and fatigue; the dust I raised was his im-
palpable substance, while my burning eyes tried to make
out the most precious details of an image of him that was
more human and equally inaccessible.

*In order to achieve poetry here, that is, to communi-
cate to the reader an emotion of which I was ignorant at
the time—of which I am still ignorant—my words make
appeal to the carnal sumptuousness, the pomp, of the
ceremonies of the here-below, not, alas, to the supposedly
rational disposition of our epoch, but to the beauty of
those that are dead or dying. I had hoped, by expressing
it, to rid it of the power exercised by objects, organs, sub-
tances, metals and humors which were for long the object
of a cult (diamonds, purple, blood, sperm, flowers, ori-
flammes, eyes, fingernails, gold, crowns, necklaces, weapons, tears, autumn, wind, chimeras, seamen, rain, crape)
and to free myself of the world which they signify (not
the one which they name, but the one which they evoke
and in which I am mired); my attempt remains futile. I
always have recourse to them. They proliferate and snap
me up. It is their fault that I make my way through
genealogical strata, the Renaissance, the Middle Ages,
Carolingian, Merovingian, Byzantine and Roman times,
the epics and invasions, in order to arrive at the Fable
where all creation is possible.*

I used to wonder what could possibly be hidden behind
that veil of saliva, what the secret meaning was of the
unctuousness and whiteness of his spittle, which was not

sickly but, on the contrary, thrillingly vigorous, able to stir up orgies of energy. I would also conjure up the vision of his prick. At times I would imagine it black, alive, detached from him and standing upright and rigid, like a leech, and similarly swollen with blood. (Excited in my random readings by coming upon terms evoking religiosity, I quite naturally made use of them in musing on my loves, which by being so named took on monstrous proportions. I would be swallowed up with them in an original adventure governed by elemental forces. Perhaps love, the better to create me, acquainted me with those elements which summon forth the heady words that are used to name them: cults, ceremonials, visitations, litanies, royalty, magic. . . . By such a vocabulary, by the amorphous universe which it offers and which I contained, I was dispersed, annihilated). In this disorder, in this incoherence, I wandered from village to village, begging my way.

Every two or three miles along the coast of Spain the coast guard has put up little sheds overlooking the sea. One night someone entered the shed where I had lain down to sleep. When I walked miserably along in the rain and wind, the tiniest crag, the most meager shelter became habitable. I would sometimes adorn it with an artful comfort drawn from what was peculiar to it: a box in the theater, the chapel of a cemetery, a cave, an abandoned quarry, a freight car and so on. Obsessed by the idea of a home, I would embellish, in thought, and in keeping with its own architecture, the one I had just chosen. While everything was being denied me, I would wish I were meant for the fluting of the fake columns that ornament façades, for the caryatids, the balconies, the stone, for the heavy bourgeois assurance which these things express.

"I shall have to love and cherish them," I would tell

myself. "I shall have to belong to them so that they may belong to me and that the order which they support may be mine."

Alas, I was not yet meant for them. Everything set me apart from them and prevented this love. I lacked a taste for earthly happiness. Now, when I am rich but weary, I ask Lucien to take my place.

All doubled up, wrapped in my coat so as to keep out the ocean dampness, I forgot my body and its fatigue by imagining details which would make the cane and reed hut a perfect dwelling, built expressly for the man I became in a few seconds, so that my soul might be in perfect harmony with the site—sea, sky, rocks and heaths—and the fragility of the structure. A man stumbled against me. He swore. I was no longer afraid at night. Quite the contrary. It was a coast guard of about thirty. Armed with his rifle, he was on the lookout for the fishermen and sailors who engaged in smuggling between Morocco and Spain. He wanted to put me out; then, turning his flashlight on my face and seeing that I was young, he told me to stay. I shared his supper (bread, olives and a few herring) and I drank some wine. We talked for a while and then he began to caress me. He told me that he was Andalusian. I don't remember whether he was good looking. The water could be seen through the opening. We heard oars striking the water and voices speaking, but were unable to see any boat. He knew he ought to leave, but my caresses grew more artful. He couldn't tear himself away; the smugglers must have landed peacefully.

In submitting to the whims of the coast guard I was obeying a dominating order which it was impossible not to serve, namely, the Police. For a moment I was no longer a hungry, ragged vagabond whom dogs and childred chased away, nor was I the bold thief flouting the cops, but rather the favorite mistress who, beneath a starry sky, soothes the conqueror. When I realized that it was up to me whether or not the smugglers landed safely, I felt responsible not only for them but for all outlaws. I was being watched elsewhere and I could not back out. Pride bore me up. After all, since I held back the guard by feigning love, I shall hold him back more surely, I said to myself, if my love is more potent, and, unable to do better, I loved him with all my might. I granted him the loveliest of my nights. Not so that he might be happy but that I might take upon myself—and deliver him from—his own ignominy.

Betrayal, theft and homosexuality are the basic subjects of this book. There is a relationship among them which, though not always apparent, at least, it seems to me, recognizes a kind of vascular exchange between my taste for betrayal and theft and my loves.

When I had sated him with pleasure, the coast guard asked me whether I had heard anything. The mystery of the night, of the sea where invisible thieves were prowling, made me uneasy.

The very particular emotion which, quite at random, I have called poetic, left behind in my soul a kind of wake of anxiety which gradually petered out. In my peculiar situation, the murmur of a voice at night and the sound of invisible oars on the sea had excited me. I remained on the alert to seize those vagrant moments which seemed to me in quest, as a lost soul is in quest of a body, of a consciousness to register and feel them. Having found it, they cease: the poet drains the world dry. But if he offers up another, it can be only his own reflection. When, in the Santé Prison, I began to write, it was never because I wanted to relive my emotions or to communicate them, but rather because I hoped, by expressing them in a form that they themselves imposed, to construct an order (a moral order) that was unknown (above all to me too).

"Yes," I said.

He asked me where I thought they had landed. His gaze seemed to be trying to peer through the darkness. He was holding his gun in his hand, ready to fire. Now, I am so concerned about exactitude that I almost indicated the right direction: it was as a result of reflection that I owed my fidelity to the smugglers. Together, as if I were his dog, we walked a few steps among the rocks and returned to the hut to go on with our love-making.

I continued traveling along the shore route. Sometimes by night, sometimes by day. I registered stupefying visions. Fatigue, shame and poverty forced me to have recourse only to a world where every incident had a meaning which I cannot define but which is not the one it suggests to you. In the evening I would hear singing: peasants were gathering oranges. I would enter churches during the day in order to rest. As the origin of the moral order is in Christian precepts, I wished to familiarize myself with the idea of God: in a state of mortal sin, I would take communion at morning mass. The priest (a Spanish curé!) would take a host from the ciborium.

"What sauce do they steep in?" I wondered. The sauce was the unction of the priest's pale fingers. In order to separate the hosts and take only one, he manipulated them with an unctuous gesture, as if he were stirring a thick liquid in a golden vase. Now, as I knew that they were flakes of dry white dough, I was astonished. Refusing to accept a God of light in accordance with the explanations of the theologians, I felt God—or, rather than Him, a sickening impression of mystery—by means of a few evil and sordid details (arising from a childish imagination) of the Roman liturgy.

"From this nausea," I said to myself, "has arisen the magnificent structure of the laws in which I am caught."

In the shadow of the church, facing the priest in his chasuble, I was frightened. But as the kneeling hidalgos beside me did not shrink from my rags, as they received the same host on the tips of their tongues, knowing full well that its power manifests itself within our souls and not elsewhere, in order to catch its imposture in *flagrante delicto* and make it my accomplice, I mentally cursed it as I chewed it. At other times I recommended myself not to God but to the nausea induced in me by the religious services, by the shadow in the chapels where Virgins and tapers dressed for a ball keep vigil, by the hymn for the dead or the simple candle-snuffer. I note this curious impression for it was not without analogy to the one I was to know throughout my life in circumstances far different from those I am describing. The army, police stations and their hosts, prisons, a looted apartment, the soul of the forest, the soul of a river (the threat—reproach or complicity of their presence at night) and, increasingly, every event I have witnessed, create in me the same sensation of disgust and fear which leads me to think that the idea of God is something I harbor in my bowels.

Still afoot, leaving the south, I headed for France. What I knew of Seville, Triana, Alicante, Murcia and Cordova was mainly the flop house and the bowl of rice that was served there. Nevertheless, under all the tinsel and idiotic gilding, I could see the angular and muscular force which, suddenly taut and erect, was to bring the whole thing down a few years later. Deep within my wretchedness I was not unaware of the presence of sensuality, of a touch of fury.

(I have clipped a poem from a Communist periodical. It was written with the purpose of flaying the warriors of the Blue Legion, the Fascists, the Nazis. Though written against them, it actually hymns them. I quote:

ROMANCE OF THE BLUE LEGION

We're all Good Catholics,
We're all good killers too,
To hell with the republic,
Let's hear of some good floggings,
Let's talk of castor oil.

. . . .

It's snowing in Castile
To the whistling of the winds,
We'll all have iron crosses
We'll all be dressed in green
We'll all have iron crosses
And the lips of all the girls.
It's snowing in Castile.

Written by a Spaniard, a mediocre rhymester, this poem epitomizes Spain. The Blue Legion was a team of killers sent to Russia to help Hitler. The color of the sky helping the devil!)

Neither the state guards nor the municipal police stopped me. What they saw going by was no longer a man but the curious product of misfortune, something to which laws could not be applied. I had exceeded the bounds of indecency. I might, for example, without anyone's being surprised, have welcomed a prince of the blood, a Spanish grandee, might have called him cousin and addressed him in elegant terms. It would have caused no surprise.

"Welcomed a Spanish grandee. But in what palace?"

If I use this rhetorical device in order to give you a clearer notion of the degree to which I had achieved a solitude that conferred sovereignty upon me, I do so be-cause it is forced upon me by a situation, by a success which is expressed in words intended to express the tri-umph of the century. A verbal kinship denotes the kin-ship of my glory with nobiliary glory. I was a kinsman of princes and kings through a kind of secret connection unknown to the world, the kind which permits a shep-herdess to chat familiarly with a king of France. The palace of which I speak (for it has no other name) is the architectural ensemble of the increasingly tenuous delicacies which the labor of pride won from my solitude. Jupiter carries off Ganymede and screws him: I could have indulged in every kind of debauchery. I had the simple elegance, the easy bearing of the hopeless. My courage consisted of destroying all the usual reasons for living and discovering others. The discovery was made slowly.

It was later on that I discovered the virtues of the discipline—not the formal rules—observed at the Mettray Reformatory. In order to become a colonist, as the chil-dren were called, I had to force myself. Like most of the little hoodlums, I might spontaneously, without giving thought to them, have performed the many actions which *realize the colonist.* I would have known naïve joys and sorrows; life would have offered me only trivial thoughts, those which anyone could utter. Mettray, which gratified my amorous taste to the full, always wounded my sensi-bility. I suffered there. I felt the cruel shame of having my head shaved, of being dressed in unspeakable clothes, of being confined in that vile place; I knew the contempt of the other colonists who were stronger or more ma-licious than I. In order to weather my desolation when I withdrew more deeply into myself, I worked out, with-out meaning to, a rigorous discipline. The mechanism was somewhat as follows (I have used it since): to every charge brought against me, unjust though it be, from the bottom of my heart I shall answer yes. Hardly had I uttered the word—or the phrase signifying it—than I felt within me the need to become what I had been accused of being. I was sixteen years old. The reader has understood: I kept no place in my heart where the feeling of my innocence might take shelter. I owned to being the coward, traitor, thief and fairy they saw in me. An accusation can be made without proof, but it will seem that in order to be found guilty I must have committed the acts which make traitors, thieves or cowards; but this was not at all the case: within myself, with a little patience, I discovered, through reflection, adequate reasons for being named by these names. And it staggered me to know that I was composed of impurities. I became abject. Little by little I grew used to this state. I openly admit it. The contempt in which I was held changed to hate: I had succeeded. But what torments I suffered![1]

Two years later I was strong. Training of this kind—similar to spiritual exercises—was to help me set poverty up as a virtue. As for the triumph, I won it over myself

---

[1] I envy, as a privilege, the shame suffered by a young bridal couple whose experience was reported in the newspaper *France-Dimanche*. To Nadine, the girl, the inhabitants of Charleville mockingly presented her with a floral swastika on her wedding day. During the German occupation Nadine had been the mistress of a Berlin captain who died at the Russian Front. "She had a mass said for him and wore mourning." The newspaper photo shows Nadine and her husband leaving the church where the priest has just married them. She is stepping across the swastika. The people of Charleville are looking at her with hostility. "Give me your arm and close your eyes," her husband is said to have murmured to her. She walks smilingly past the French flags which are bedecked with crape.

I envy this young woman's bitter and haughty happiness. I'd "give" the world to re-experience it.

alone. Even when I faced the scorn of children or men, it was I alone whom I had to conquer, since it was a matter of modifying not others but myself. My power over myself became great, but by thus exercising it over my inner being I became very clumsy in doing so over the world. Neither Stilitano nor my other friends were of any use to me, since in relation to them I was too preoccupied with my attitude as perfect lover. My wanderings over Europe might perhaps have resulted in my gaining a certain poise were it not that I rejected everyday concerns in favor of a kind of contemplation. Before the occurrence of what I am about to relate, I had performed certain acts but had not examined any of them with the keenness I applied to my mental life. I knew the intoxication of action when, one evening in Antwerp, near the docks, I succeeded in tying up a man who had gone off with me. Stilitano had gone dancing with Robert. I was alone, sad and jealous. I went into a bar and had a drink. For a moment I thought of looking for my two friends, but the mere idea of looking for them proved that they were lost. The smoky, noisy bars where they drank and danced were the earthly image of a moral region where, that very morning, they had isolated themselves from me and the rest of the world when, upon entering the room, I saw Stilitano, who was about to leave, extend his gloved hand and raise it slightly, and Robert, smiling, almost without touching it, press the snap button. I was no longer Stilitano's right arm.

A heavy-set man asked me for a light and offered me a drink. When we left, he wanted me to go home with him, but I refused. He hesitated, then decided for the docks. I had noticed his gold watch, wedding ring and wallet. I knew he wouldn't call for help, but he looked strong. I couldn't carry the thing off except by some trick.

I prepared nothing. Suddenly I thought of using the
cord that Stilitano had given me. When we got to a corner
of the docks, the man asked me to screw him.

"All right. Let your pants down."

I had him lower his trousers as far as his heels so that
he would get tangled up in them if he tried to run.

"Spread your ass."

With both hands he did what I ordered, and I quickly
tied them up, behind his back.

"What are you doing?"

"Can't you tell, you big lug?"

I had just used the same language and tone of voice I
had heard Stilitano use when we were once caught stealing a bike.

When at rest on humble things, Stilitano's gaze was
softened by a kind of gentleness. His lone hand would,
with a certain kindness, take the greasy menu from the
restaurant table. Objects could attach themselves to him
who had no contempt for them. Merely to touch a thing
was, for Stilitano, to recognize at once its essential quality
and to turn it to splendid use. As he smiled at it, it would
become his bride.

I am more charmed by the smile on a youngster's face
than by his pout. I sometimes contemplate it for a long
time. It fascinates me. It becomes a thing detached from
the face, animated by a peculiar soul. It is rather a
precious animal, with a tough, yet fragile life; it is a lovely
and fabulous beast. If I could manage to peel it off, to
remove it from the face over which it plays, to carry it
away in my pocket, its malicious irony would help me
achieve prodigies. I sometimes try to adorn myself with
it—this amounts to protecting myself against it—but in
vain. It is this smile which is the real thief.

"Hey, untie me! Look, I'll give you . . ."

"Shut up! I'll help myself."

The fear of being caught or of the man's breaking the rope gave me knowledge of the surest twists and knots. I searched his pockets. With keen joy my fingers recognized banknotes and personal papers. Trembling with fear, he dared not move.

"Come on, let me . . ."

"Shut up!"

There is no reason for such moments to end. I had one of my victims at my mercy and I wanted to make him pay dearly for being so. The place was dark but unsafe. A customs officer might make his rounds and discover us.

"You old son of a bitch, you thought I was going to stick it in!"

I tore his watch from the buttonhole of his vest where it was held by the chain.

"It's a souvenir," he murmured.

"That's just it. I like souvenirs."

I smashed him in the face. He whimpered, though in silence. With the same dispatch as Stilitano, I opened my knife in front of him and showed him the blade. I should like to tell with greater precision what this moment meant to me. The cruelty into which I was forcing myself gave amazing power not only to my body but to my mind. I felt myself capable of being magnanimous toward my victim and untying him. Capable also of killing him. He himself must have recognized my force. In spite of the darkness I knew he was humble, well-disposed, inclined to serve my intoxication.

"And don't yell or I'll kill you."[1]

---

[1] René, whom I shall mention again later, told me that a queer in Nice used to do the same sort of thing. The anecdote he related drew me even closer to him.

I took a step in the darkness.

"Listen . . ."

"What?"

He murmured in a gentle voice, trembling perhaps with a foreboding of my refusal:

"At least, let me blow you a little."

The next time I saw Stilitano I had a few thousand Belgian francs and a gold watch. I first thought of telling him about my exploit in order to rile him, and Robert too. Then gradually, as my walk slowed up, I became less vainglorious. I decided to remain the sole repository of this adventure. I—and I alone—knew what I was capable of. I concealed my booty. It was the first time I saw the look on the face of the people I robbed: it was ugly. I was the cause of such ugliness, and the only thing it made me feel was a cruel pleasure which, I thought, was bound to transfigure my own face, to make me resplendent. I was then twenty-three. From that moment on, I felt capable of advancing in cruelty. The possession of the money and the watch eliminated whatever remained of my taste for dire poverty. (Without destroying the taste for unhappiness, but for pompous unhappiness.) Nevertheless, I profited—so as to persevere in cruelty or indifference to the suffering of others—from my rigorous discipline in begging. I committed other aggressions. They succeeded. I was thus spared the shifty condition of the shame-faced thief. For the first time I went after man. I fought him openly, unmasked. I felt myself growing vibrant, mean, icy, stiff, gleaming, cutting, like a sword blade. No one, neither Stilitano nor Robert, noticed this transformation. They lived in a comradely partnership, looking for women or neglecting them in each other's company. My attitude to Stilitano did not change. I displayed the same deference toward him, and Robert the same impertinence. The personality of Stilitano, in whose depths what was most precious in me kept watch and maintained order, protected me like a hero's armor, or was it that I was using my friend's voice, words and gestures the way one touches relics whose magic is urgently needed? It was Stilitano who fought in my place. He was ready to drink with the queers, he preened himself in their presence, he skinned them. He haunted me. It pained me to know this, but I also knew that had I been proudly rid of this support I would have collapsed. As for him, he was unaware of the secret purpose I was making him serve and that he was what is called the homeland: the entity which fights in the soldier's place and sacrifices him. I trembled as I went down the stairs from the room where I had just made the client hand over his money, for Stilitano was withdrawing from me, at headlong speed. When I counted my loot, it was no longer with the idea of offering it to him. So I was alone.

I grew restless again. I was dominated by the world of males. When they were merged in shadow, each group of lads offered me a puzzle, the solution of which could not be given me in a straightforward way. The still, silent males had the violence of electronic corpuscles gravitating about a sun of energy: love. Suppose, I asked myself, suppose I managed to bombard one of them? What disintegration would result, what sudden annihilation? They must, I added, be aware of this in some obscure way and that's why they stay so fast in place.

Exhausted by the effort which had just enabled me to confront men, I was delivered up to the powers of darkness. I became lucid. A retrospective fear invaded me. I decided to give up such dangerous activity. In the evening, hardly would some man turn about as I passed, than Stilitano would subtly insinuate himself into me; he would fill out my muscles, loosen my gait, thicken my gestures, he would almost color me. He was in action. I felt, in my footsteps on the sidewalk, his crocodile leather shoes creaking with the weight of the ponderous body of that monarch of the slums. Thus possessed, I knew I was capable of every kind of cruelty. I was more clear-sighted. Instead of causing fright, my transformation adorned me with manly graces. I felt myself becoming lively, impetuous. One evening, in anger, confronted with a snooty queen, my fist made the gesture of beating an invisible drum.

"You dirty louse," I muttered between my teeth, while within me my conscience grieved at having wounded and insulted those who were the wretched expression of my dearest treasure: homosexuality.

Excluded by my birth and tastes from the social order, I was not aware of its diversity. I wondered at its perfect coherence, which rejected me. I was astounded by so rigorous an edifice whose details united against me. Nothing in the world was irrelevant: the stars on a general's sleeve, the stock-market quotations, the olive harvest, the style of the judiciary, the wheat exchange, flower-beds . . . Nothing. This order, fearful and feared, whose details were all interrelated, had a meaning: my exile. Hitherto I had acted against it slyly, in the shadow. Now I dared touch it, dared show I was touching it, by insulting those who composed it. Whereupon, recognizing my right to do so, I recognized my place in it. It seemed to me natural that waiters in cafés should call me "Monsieur."

I might, with a bit of patience and luck, have widened the breach. However, I was held back by my ingrained habit of living, with my head bowed and in accordance with an ethic contrary to the one which governs the world. In short, I was afraid of losing the benefit of my laborious and painful effort in the direction opposite to yours.

Stilitano behaved toward his woman in the same brutal way, which I envied, though he tolerated Robert's gentle mockery. He would then smile delightfully, revealing his white teeth. If he smiled at me, the smile was the same, but, perhaps because I did not take it by surprise, I was unable to read in it the same freshness, the same complicity. At Stilitano's feet all was as the bounding of fauns. Robert twined his garlands about him. The cripple was the column, the other the wisteria. I was disturbed by the fact that, though they loved each other so, they never made love. Stilitano seemed to me more and more inaccessible. I discovered, I have forgotten how, that he had not stolen the black motorcycle from the policeman. He hadn't even stolen it at all. They had come to an agreement beforehand: it had been abandoned for a few seconds, and Stilitano had merely to mount it and sell it. They divided the money. A discovery of this kind ought to have estranged me from him; it made him dearer to me. I was in love with a fake hoodlum who was in cahoots with a cop. As a team, they were a traitor and an impostor. Made of mud and mist, Stilitano was indeed a divinity to whom I could still sacrifice myself. In both senses of the word, I was possessed.

I was familiar with Stilitano's past in the Foreign Legion, which I knew about from trivial details that he mentioned from time to time, and I also knew how his time had been spent between our separation and our meeting. In the intervening four or five years he had wandered around France selling cheap lace at a very high price. He smiled as he told me the following story. A friend had concocted for him an agent's card authorizing him—and him only—to sell lace made by the young consumptives of the Cambo Sanatorium.

"In Cambo, I'm telling you, because there's no sanatorium in Cambo. That way, they couldn't accuse me of

fraud. So in each town I'd go see the priest. I'd show him
my card, my one arm and my lace. I'd tell him that it
would be nice if his church had altar cloths made by
sick kids. It didn't work with the priests, but they'd send
me to all the women with dough. Since I came from the
priest, they didn't dare kick me out. They didn't dare
refuse to buy. So I'd get a hundred francs for the little
machine-made lace squares that cost me five francs on
the Rue Myrrha."

That was how Stilitano told it, without any frills, in
his toneless voice. He said he had made a lot of money,
but I didn't believe him because he wasn't very industri-
ous. What must have attracted him more than anything
else was the idea of such a racket.

One day, while he was away, I found a lot of military
medals in a drawer, *croix de guerre* and so on. He admitted that he had put on a French uniform, plastered
his chest with them and gone through the subways showing his stump and making a collection.

"I made my couple of hundred francs a day," he said.
"I sure put it over on those Parisians."

He informed me of other details which I haven't time
to go into. I still loved him. His qualities (like those of
Java) make me think of certain drugs, certain odors
which can't be called agreeable but from which one can't
escape.

However, Armand returned when I had stopped waiting for him. I found him lying in bed, smoking a cigarette.

"Hello, kid," he said.

He offered me his hand for the first time.

"Well, did it work out all right? No hitches?"

I have already spoken of his voice. It seemed to me to
have the same coldness as his blue eyes. Just as he looked
at things or people, without resting his eyes on them, so
he spoke, with an unreal voice, as if hardly taking part

in the conversation. Certain gazes have a kind of radiance (Lucien's, Stilitano's, Java's), but not Armand's. Nor did his voice radiate either. It was emitted by a group of tiny characters whom he kept secretly hidden in the depths of his heart. It betrayed nothing and would not have betrayed. However, I could discern a vaguely Alsatian accent: the characters of his heart were Boches.

"Yes, it worked out all right," I said. "I kept your things, as you see."

Even now I sometimes wish that the police would arrest me in order to say: "Indeed, sir, I see that it wasn't you who committed the thefts; the guilty ones have been arrested." I would like to be innocent of everything. When I answered Armand, I would have liked him to know that someone else—who, nevertheless, was myself—had robbed him. Almost shuddering, I triumphed in my fidelity.

"Oh that? I was sure you would."

"What about you, everything all right?"

"Oh, me? Things worked out."

I dared sit down on the edge of the bed and put my hand on the covers at the spot where I judged his prick to be. That evening, beneath the light falling from above, he had the strength and physique of his great days. I suddenly saw the possibility of escaping from the uneasiness and anxiety in which I was being smothered by the inexplicable relationship between Stilitano and Robert. If he were willing, not to love me but to let me love him, Armand, by his greater age and vigor, would have saved me. He arrived in the nick of time. Already admiring him, I was ready to lay my cheek tenderly on his dark hairy chest. I moved my hand forward. He smiled. He smiled at me for the first time and that was enough. I loved him.

"I swung some good deals," he said.

He turned on his side. A very slight stiffening at my fly made me aware that I was hoping for his terrible hand to

lower my head in obedience to the imperious gesture by
which he demanded that I bend forward for his pleasure.
Were I in love today, I would have resisted slightly so
that he might get excited, that he might desire me more.

"I feel like having a drink. I'm going to get up."

He got out of bed and dressed. When we were in the
street, he congratulated me on the way I'd been frisking
the queers. I was dumbfounded.

"Who told you about it?"

"Don't let that bother you."

He even knew that I had tied one of them up.

"Good work. I wouldn't have believed it."

He then informed me that the men on the waterfront
knew about my method. Each victim would pass the
word on about me, or would mention me to the docker
(they've all been with the queers) whom he took out for
a night. I was now known and feared by the queers.
Armand came to tell me about my reputation and to explain that it was a danger to me. He had heard about it
as soon as he got back. If Robert and Stilitano were still
unaware of it, they would know before long.

"What you've done is all right, my boy. I like it."

"Oh, it's not hard. They get scared."

"It's all right. I wouldn't have believed it. Let's go have
a drink."

When we returned, he demanded nothing of me, and
we went to sleep. The following days we saw Stilitano
again. Armand met Robert and wanted to have him as
soon as he laid eyes on him, but the boy roguishly eluded
him. One day he said laughingly, "You've got Jean. Isn't
that enough for you?"

"It's not the same thing."

As a matter of fact, since learning about my nocturnal
boldness, Armand had been treating me like a pal. He
would talk to me and give me advice. His contempt dis-

appeared and was replaced by a somewhat gentle, maternal solicitude. He advised me about how to dress. And in the evening, as soon as we finished our cigarettes, he would say good night and go to sleep. As I lay beside him whom I now loved, it grieved me to be unable to give him proof of my love by inventing artful caresses. The form of friendship he granted me bound me to the utmost severity. Though I was aware of the faking in my crimes and the fear in my boldness, I forced myself to be the man Armand saw in me. I told myself that the gestures which conventionally deny heroic acts should correspond to them. The simple Armand would not have allowed me to serve his pleasure. Respect alone kept him from using my body, as he had done earlier, whereas such use would have swelled me with force and courage.

Stilitano and Robert lived on Sylvia's earnings. Robert, having really forgotten about our tricky dealings with the queers, pretended to be contemptuous of my work.

"You call that work?" he said. "Fine work. You go after old men who couldn't stand up straight if it weren't for their stiff collars and their canes."

"He's doing the right thing in picking his victims."

I did not realize that Armand's reply would immediately bring about one of the boldest revolutions in ethics. Before Robert had even a chance to answer, he continued in a more subdued voice, "And what about me? What do you think, eh?" And turning to Stilitano: "When it's necessary, it's not old men I go after. It's old women. You get me? It's not men, it's women. And I pick the weakest. What I need is dough. A job is good when you pull it off. When you get it into your head that chivalry's not our line, you'll have learned a lot. Him (Armand, who never called me by my name or its diminutive, pointed at me), he's way ahead of you and he's right."

His voice was not trembling, but my emotion was so

great that in the midst of it all I was afraid that Armand
might let fall disastrous confidences. The solid matter of
the last word assured me. He stopped talking. Within me
I felt a host of thoughts welling up (opening out into a
sea of regrets), all reproaching me with having yielded to
the appearances of honor. Armand never took the matter
up again (Stilitano and Robert would not have dared
argue it), but it left its seed in my mind. The code of
honor peculiar to hoodlums seemed to me laughable.
Armand gradually became the Almighty in the realm of
ethics. No longer seeing him as a block, I could feel that
he was a sum of painful experiences. However, his body
remained just as bulky, and I loved him for protecting
me. Finding such authority in a man devoid of fear—so
I wish to believe—I began to feel myself thinking, with a
strange, new lightness. No doubt it was much later that
I decided to develop and exploit the many feelings of
ambiguity wherein, with mingled shame and delight, I
discovered that I was an abode and jumble of contradic-
tions, but I already sensed that it is for us to declare what
will serve us as principles. Later, as a result of reflection
and of Armand's attitude, my will was disengaged from
the mists of ethics and I was able to apply it in my way
of considering the police.

It was in Marseille that I met Bernardini. When I
came to know him better, I called him Bernard. For me,
only the French police has the monstrous potency of a
mythology. When I was twenty-two, Bernard was thirty.
I wish I could describe him exactly, but my memory
retains only the impression of physical and moral force
which he made upon me at the time. We were in a bar
on the Rue Thubaneau. A young Arab pointed him out
to me.

"He's a first-class pimp," he said. "He always has good-
looking girls."

The girl who was with him seemed to me very pretty. I might not have noticed him had I not been told he was a cop. The police of the various European countries inspired me with fear, just as they do any other thief. The French police moved me more through a kind of terror, the source of which was in my feeling of native and irrevocable guilt, than by the danger in which I was placed by my casual delinquencies. The world of the police, like the underworld, was a world which I would never enter. My lucidity (my awareness) kept me from drifting into that formless, moving, hazy universe, constantly self-creating, elementary and fabulous, of which the motorcycle police, with its attributes of force, is the delegation here below. That was what the French police, more than any other, meant to me. Perhaps because of its language, in which I discovered abysses. (It was no longer a social institution but a sacred power, acting directly upon my soul and troubling me. Only the German police, in Hitler's time, succeeded in being both Police and Crime. This masterly synthesis of opposites, this block of truth, was frightful, charged with a magnetism that will continue to perturb us for a long, long time.)

Bernardini was to me the visible, though perhaps brief manifestation on earth of a demoniacal organization as sickening as funeral rites, as funereal ornaments, yet as awe-inspiring as royal glory. Knowing that there, in that skin and flesh, was a particle of what I would never have hoped could be mine, I looked at him with a shudder. His dark hair was flat and glossy, as Rudolph Valentino's used to be, with a straight white part on the left side. He was strong. His face looked rugged, somewhat granite-like, and I wanted his soul to be cruel and brutal.

Little by little I came to understand his beauty. I even think I created it, deciding it would be precisely that face and body, on the basis of the idea of the police which

they were to signify. The popular expression for the
entire organization added to my disturbance:

"The Secret Police. He's in the Secret Police."

I cleverly managed to follow him and see him from
a distance during the next few days. I worked out a
subtle way of shadowing him. Without his suspecting it,
he belonged to my life. Finally I left Marseille. I preserved, in secret, a memory of him that was both painful
and tender. Two years later I was arrested at the Saint
Charles Station. The inspectors were brutal with me,
hoping to make me confess. The door of the police station
opened and to my amazement there was Bernardini. I
was afraid he might add his blows to those of his col-
leagues. He made them stop. He had never noticed me
when I used to follow him lovingly. Even had he seen my
face a few times, he would have forgotten it after two
years. It was not sympathy or kindness that bade him
spare me. He was a cop, like the others. I cannot explain
why, but he protected me. When I was released two days
later, I managed to see him. I thanked him.

"You, at least, were pretty swell."

"Forget it. There's no use knocking a guy silly."

"Have a drink with me."

He accepted. The following day I met him again. It
was he who invited me. We were the only customers in
the bar.

With my heart racing away, I said:

"I've known you for a long time."

"Have you? Since when?"

With tension in my throat, fearing he might get angry,
I confessed my love and told him about my ruses for
following him. He smiled.

"So you had a crush. What about now?"

"A little still."

His smile broadened. Perhaps he was flattered. (Java

has just admitted to me that he is prouder of a man's love or admiration than a woman's.) I was standing beside him and telling him about my love; I clowned about it, for I was still afraid that the gravity of this admission might remind him of the gravity of his functions. With a smile and a somewhat lecherous air, I said, "What do you expect? I like good-looking guys."

He looked at me indulgently. His manliness, protecting him, prevented cruelty.

"What if I'd grilled you the other day?"

"That would have really made me feel bad."

But I refrained from saying more. Had I gone on in this tone, I would have admitted not only to a passing fancy but to so deep a love that it would have wounded the detective's modesty.

"You'll get over it," he said with a laugh.

"I hope so."

However, he was not aware that, beside him, at the bar, crushed by his huskiness and assurance, I was excited chiefly by the invisible presence of his inspector's badge. That metal object had for me the power of a cigarette lighter in the fingers of a workman, of the buckle of an army belt, of a switchblade, of a caliper, objects in which the quality of males is violently concentrated. Had I been alone with him in a dark corner, I might have been bold enough to graze the cloth, to slip my hand under the lapel where cops usually wear the badge, and I would have then trembled just as if I had been opening his fly. His virility was centered in that badge as much as in his penis. Had the latter been roused at the touch of my fingers, it would have drawn from the badge such force that it might have swelled up and taken on monstrous proportions.

"Can I see you again?"

"Sure, drop in and say hello."

Lest my eagerness irritate him, I refrained from seeing him for a few days. We finally became fond of each other. He introduced me to his wife. I was happy. One evening, as we walked along the banks of the Joliette, the solitude which suddenly sprang up about us, the proximity of Fort Saint Jean, packed with men of the Foreign Legion, the maddening desolateness of the port (the most heart-breaking thing that could happen to me was to be with him in that place), suddenly made me extremely bold. I was lucid enough to notice that his pace slowed up as I drew near him. With trembling hand I clumsily touched his thigh; then, not knowing how to go on, I mechanically used the formula with which I approached timid queers.

"What time is it?" I asked.

"Eh? Look, mine says noon."

He laughed, for he had a stiff hard-on.

I saw him frequently. I would walk beside him in the street, keeping in step with him. If it was broad daylight, I would place myself so that he projected his shadow on my body. This simple game filled me with joy.

I continued as before, robbing the queer who picked me for the night. The whores of the Rue de la Bouterie (the quarter had not yet been destroyed) bought the objects I stole. I was no different. Perhaps I was a little too ready to take out my brand new identity card (which Bernard himself had stamped at police headquarters) and flash it under the eyes of the cops. Bernard knew about my life and never reproached me. Once, however, he tried to justify his being a cop; he talked to me about morality. Merely from the aesthetic viewpoint with regard to an act, I could not listen to him. The good will of moralists cracks up against what they call my dishonesty. Though they may prove to me that an act is detestable because of the harm it does, only I can decide, and that by the song it evokes within me, as to its beauty and elegance; only I can reject or accept it. No one will bring me back to the path of righteousness. At most, someone might undertake my artistic re-education—at the risk, however, of the educator's being convinced and won over to my cause if its beauty is proved by the more masterly of the two personalities.

"I'm not blaming you for being a cop, you know."

"It doesn't bother you?"

Knowing it would be impossible to explain to him the dizziness which hurled me toward him, I felt a malicious desire to hurt him.

"It does annoy me a little."

"You think you don't need courage to be in the police? It's more dangerous than people think."

But he was talking about physical courage and danger. Besides, he asked himself few questions. With rare exceptions (Pilorge, Java, Soclay, whose faces, though suggesting rugged virility, conceal muddy swamps, like the tropical regions known as muskegs) the heroes of my books and the men I chose to love had the same bulky appearance and the most immoral serenity. Bernard resembled them. Wearing a ready-made suit, he had the exaggerated elegance of the men of Marseille whom he poked fun at. He wore tan shoes with rather high heels that forced him to arch his whole body. He had the handsomest wop kisser I ever saw. Happily I found in him the very opposite of the rigorous, the steadfast qualities found in movie cops. He was a real bastard. With all his defects, what a wonderful knowledge of the heart he might have had, and what kindness, had he managed to be intelligent!

I would imagine him chasing a dangerous criminal, catching up with him the way a rugby player throws himself on the opponent who has the ball, holds him around the waist and is dragged along by him, his head

pressing against an enemy thigh or fly. The thief would
hold fast to his treasure; he would protect it; he would
struggle a while; then, the two men, unable to ignore the
fact that they had the same solid and utterly fearless
body, and the same mind, would exchange a friendly
smile. Imposing a conclusion upon this brief drama, I
would hand the bandit over to the detective.

What obscure desire was I obeying in requiring (and
so fervently!) that each of my friends have his double in
the police? I adorned neither hoodlum nor cop with the
knightly virtues ascribed to heroes. One was never the
shadow of the other, but as both seemed to me to be
outside society, rejected and cursed by it, perhaps I
wanted to merge them so as to make more precise their
merging by the average man when he says:

"Cops aren't picked from among choir boys."

If I wanted my policemen and hoodlums to be handsome, it was so that their dazzling bodies might avenge
the contempt in which you hold them. Hard muscles and
harmonious faces were meant to sing and glorify the
odious functions of my friends and to impose them upon
you. Whenever I met a good-looking kid, I would tremble
at the thought that he might be high-minded, though I
tolerated the idea that a petty, despicable mind might
inhabit a puny body. Since rectitude was your domain, I
would have none of it, though I often recognized its
nostalgic appeal. I had to fight against its charms. Criminals and the police are the most virile emanation of this
world. You cast a veil over them. They are your shameful
parts, which, however, I call, as you do, noble parts. The
insults exchanged by enemies bespeak a feigned hatred.
They seem to me charged rather with tenderness.

Sometimes I would meet him in the bar. I would walk
with him in the street. I could then imagine myself as a
kind of machiavellian thief playing at being "on the up

and up" with a cop, flirting with him, delicately flouting him while waiting to be nabbed. Never was there any exchange of impertinent remarks between us, or of cockiness or ironic threat, except once: suddenly grabbing my arm, he said, with determination in his voice:

"Come along, you're going with me . . ."

And in a gentle tone trailing off into a smile, he added, ". . . for a drink."

Detectives employ a number of such facetious remarks. Bernardini was indulging himself with me. As I left him, I said:

"I'm beating it."

Though the joke might have been mechanical in his case, it disturbed me. I felt as if I were penetrating to the very heart of the police. I must have wandered deep into it for a detective to be ironical with me about his function. However, it seems to me that this joke revealed to us the absurdity of our reciprocal situations. We were escaping from it so that we might meet smilingly in friendship only. Invective was banished from our relationship. I was his friend, would have liked to be his dearest friend, and though I felt that we did not love each other in our two chief qualities, as policeman and thief (it was by these that we were bound), we knew that they were only a means, something comparable to the nature of opposite electric poles whose meeting produces the incomparable spark. No doubt I could have loved a man equal to Bernard in charm, but, having to choose him, I would have preferred a cop to a hoodlum. In his presence I was subjugated chiefly by his splendid bearing, the play of his muscles which I sensed under his clothes, his gaze, in short, his particular qualities, but when I was alone and thought of our love, it was by the nocturnal power of the entire police force that I was dominated. (We feel impelled to use the words "Nocturnal" or "Sinister" when speaking of it. Like anyone else, detectives wear clothes of various colors; however, when fancying them, I see, as it were, a shadow over their faces and dress.)

He once asked me to "squeal" on some friends. By agreeing to do so, I could have deepened my love for him, but there is no need for you to know any more about this particular matter.

It is commonly said of a judge that he is lofty. In the symbolism of the Byzantine Empire, which copies the heavenly order, Eunuchs are said to represent Angels. Judges owe to their robes an ambiguity which is the sign of orthodox angelism. I have spoken elsewhere of the uneasiness which the idea of those celestial beings causes me. In like manner, judges. Their garments are droll, their behavior comical. If I consider them, I judge them and am disturbed by their intelligence. At a court hearing, when I was brought up on charges of theft, I said to Judge Rey:

"Will you allow me to clarify (it was a matter of establishing the fact that there had been certain provocations by paid police informers) something which one is forbidden to mention in a courtroom, and first of all to question you?"

"Eh? By no means. The statutes . . ."

He had sensed the danger of too human a relationship. His integrity might have been attacked. I burst out laughing, for I saw the judge retreating into his robe. You can twit them, but not cops, who have arms to grab criminals and thighs to bestride and dominate powerful motorcycles. I respected the police. They can kill. Not at a distance and by proxy, but with their hands. Their murders, though ordered, derive none the less from a particular, individual will implying, along with its decision, the responsibility of the murderer. The policeman is taught to kill. I like those sinister though smiling machines which are intended for the most difficult act of all: murder. That was how Java was trained in the Waffen S.S. In order to be a good bodyguard—he was the bodyguard of a German general—he was taught the swift use of a dagger, of certain judo holds, of a fine lasso and of his bare hands. The police come from a similar school, just as the young heroes of Dickens come from a school for pickpockets. As a result of frequenting the quarters of the vice squad and highway police, I am familiar with the stupidity of inspectors: it doesn't bother me. Nor does the scrubby ugliness of most of them. They aren't detectives, not yet, but rather the clumsy attempt toward the perfect insect. These ridiculous, puny existences are perhaps the many stages leading to a more finished form which is attained by only a few rare specimens. However, it was not in their heroic function that I cherished detectives: the dangerous pursuit of criminals, the self-sacrifice, a certain attitude which makes them popular, but rather in their offices, consulting records and files. The search bulletins posted on the walls, the photos and descriptions of wanted criminals, the contents of the registers, the objects under seal, create an atmosphere of sullen rancor, of foul infamy, and it gives me pleasure to know that these big strapping fellows are breathing it in and that it is corrupting them, that it is evilly corroding their minds. It was this police—note that I also require handsome representatives of it—to which I was devoted. Their broad, thick hands, extensions of their strong, lithe bodies which were used to physical struggle, could upset—with brutal and touching awkwardness—files which were charged with subtle questions. It is not the more dazzling crimes they contain that I would like to know about, but rather the more dismal, those which are called sordid and whose heroes are gloomy. As a result of the emotional shufflings they cause, crimes bring about enchanting situations: those twins, one of whom was a murderer, the other dying when his brother was beheaded; the babies choked by hot bread; a wonderful device in a macabre setting to delay the discovery of a murder; the stupor of the criminal who gets lost, turns about, goes back, and is caught in the neighborhood of the crime; the clemency of a snowfall which protects a thief's flight; the wind which throws the hounds off the track; the grandiose chance discoveries which culminate in the beheading of a man; the hostility of objects; your ingenuity in conquering them; secrets which prisons contain, though here they were torn from the bosom, slowly exhaled, shred by shred, by means of threat and fear. I envied Inspector Bernardini. He could take a murder or rape from the records, swell up with it, feast on it and return home. I do not mean that he was able to amuse himself with it as with a detective story. Not amuse himself; quite the contrary. To draw to himself the most unexpected, the most unhappy situations, to take upon himself the most humiliating confessions, which are the richest. Never to smile over them: it is these that are most able to elicit the marvels of pride. The vastest intelligence could be attributed to the lucid and sympathetic witness of so many wretched confessions. Perhaps it was also the quest of this intelligence that led me to those incredible adventures of the heart. What did the police of Marseille not contain? Yet never did I dare ask Bernard to take me back there with him, or to let me read his reports.

I knew that he associated with some gangsters in the neighborhood of the Opera, those who hung around the bars on the Rue Saint-Saëns. As he was not too sure about me, he did not introduce me to any of them. Since he granted me the favor of sucking his prick occasionally, I felt deeply grateful to him for allowing me to be his slave, but I never worried about whether it was wrong to love a cop.

In a friend's room, looking at his bed and all the bourgeois furnishings:

"I could never make love here." That kind of place freezes me. To have chosen it I would have had to make use of qualities and have preoccupations so remote from love that my life would have grown disenchanted with it. To love a man is not only to let myself be excited by some of the details which I call nocturnal because they create within me a darkness wherein I tremble (the hair, the eyes, a smile, the thumb, the thigh, the bush, etc.), but also to make these details render as shadow everything possible, to develop the shadow of the shadow, hence to thicken it, to extend its realm and throng it with darkness. It is not only the body with its adornments that excites me, nor the play of love alone, but also the prolongation of each of its erotic qualities. But these qualities can only be what they have been made to be by the actual experience of the one who bears their sign, whose bearing involves certain details wherein I think I find the seeds of such experiences. Thus, from every area of shadow, from every boy, I drew the most disturbing image so that my excitement might increase, and from all the areas of shadow I drew a nocturnal universe into which my lover plunged. Obviously, one who has a great many details attracts me more than others. And as I draw from them what they can give me, I extend them by bold adventures which are proof of their amorous potency. Every one of my lovers elicits a sinister story. The dangerous nocturnal adventures into which I let myself be drawn by my somber heroes are thus the elaboration of an erotic ceremonial, of a mating which is sometimes quite long.

Bernardini had many such details, the blossoming of

which no doubt accounted for his amazing career in the
police, which itself gave meaning to and justified such
details. I left Marseille at the end of a few weeks. Many
of my victims were complaining and threatening me. I
was in danger.

"If you were ordered to arrest me, would you do it?"
I asked Bernard.

He didn't seem troubled for more than ten seconds.
Puckering an eyebrow, he replied:

"I'd arrange not to have to do it myself. I'd ask a
friend."

Instead of revolting me, such baseness heightens my
love. Nevertheless, I left him and went to Paris. I felt
calmer. This brief encounter with a detective, the love
I bore him, the love I received from him and the amorous
blend of our two conflicting destinies had purified me.
Rested, rid for a while of all the slag that desire deposits,
I felt washed, purged, ready for a lighter leap. About
fifteen years later, when I had a crush on a cop's son, I
tried to transform him into a hoodlum.

(*The boy is twenty years old. His name is Pierre
Fièvres. He wrote to me asking me to buy him a motorcycle. I shall speak of his role a little later.*)

As I was now helping Armand, he gave me half of our
profits. He insisted that I assume a certain independence,
and he wanted me to have a room of my own. For the
sake of prudence, perhaps, for though he was protecting
me, the danger was growing. He chose one in another
hotel, on another street. Around noon, I would go to his
room, and we would plan our evening's program. We
would then go out for lunch. He also continued with his
opium traffic, in which Stilitano had a hand.

I would have been happy were it not that my love
for Armand had taken on such importance that I wonder

whether he never noticed it. His presence drove me wild. His absence worried me. After robbing a victim, we would spend an hour together in a bar, but what then? I knew nothing about his nights. I grew jealous of all the young bums who hung around the waterfront. Finally, my anguish reached a climax when one day, in my presence, Robert got uppity with him, though jokingly.

"And what about me? You think I don't know all about you?"

"What do you know?"

"Don't worry, I've got certain rights over you."

"You? You little bitch."

Robert burst out laughing.

"That's just it. It's because I am a little bitch. I'm your gal, see."

He said it coolly, without bluster, and with a wink at me. I thought Armand would strike him, or that his reply would be so sharp that Robert would keep still, but he smiled. He seemed to despise neither the boy's familiarity nor his passiveness. Had I displayed either of those two attitudes, he would have sailed into me. That was the way I learned how things stood between them. I was perhaps the friend whom Armand esteemed. Alas, I would have preferred to be chosen as his beloved mistress.

One evening Armand was waiting for me, leaning against the doorframe, in the posture of a Janizary guarding a park. I was an hour late and was sure he would bawl me out, perhaps even hit me; I was afraid. From the last or next-to-last step of the stairway I saw him stripped to the waist; his wide, blue denim trousers falling over his feet served as a base not for his bust but for his crossed arms. Perhaps his head dominated them; I don't know; only his arms existed, solid and muscular, forming a heavy coil of dark flesh, one of them adorned with a delicate tattoo representing a mosque with minaret and dome and a palm tree bent by a sandstorm. A long beige muslin scarf, the kind that legionnaires and colonials wrap about their heads for protection against the sand, hung from his neck and fell in a heap on his arms, the muscles of which bulged as they squeezed against his chest. The arms existed by themselves, that is, they were there, placed before him, his escutcheon and, in relief, his weapons.

No meditation, whether rapt or casual, on the planetary systems, the suns, nebulae and galaxies will ever enable me to contain, will ever console me for not containing, the world: confronted with the universe I am lost, but the simple attribute of a potent virility reassures me. Disturbing thoughts and anxiety cease. My tenderness—the finest gold or marble figure is inferior to a model in the flesh—arrays this power with bracelets of wild oats. The fear—because of my lateness—which made me almost shudder probably facilitated my emotion and revealed its meaning to me. The strange coronet of those knotted arms was the sufficient weapon of a naked warrior, though they also bore the memory of African campaigns. The tattoo—minaret and dome—disturbed me, reminding me of Stilitano's desertion when the vision of Cadiz in the sea lay beneath my eyes. I walked past him. Armand did not move.

"I'm late."

I dared not look at his arms. They were so strong that I feared I had hitherto been mistaken in concerning myself with his eyes and mouth. The latter, or what they expressed, had no other reality than that which had suddenly just been created by the interlacing of those arms on a wrestler's torso. Were they to unwind, Armand's most acute and exact reality would dissolve.

I realize now that had I stared at this knot of muscles I would have blushed, because they revealed to me what

Armand really was. If the king's banner, borne by a galloping horseman, appears alone, we may be moved, may bare our heads; if the king were to carry it himself, we would be crushed. The foreshortening proffered by the symbol when borne by what it is meant to signify gives and destroys the signification and the thing signified. (And everything was aggravated by the way his braided arms covered his torso!)

"I did the best I could to get here on time, but I'm late. It's not my fault."

Armand made no reply. Still leaning, he pivoted on his axis as a single block. Like the gates of a temple.

(The aim of this account is to embellish my earlier adventures, in other words, to extract beauty from them, to find in them the element which today will elicit song, the only proof of this beauty.)

His arms remained twisted. Armand stood there, the statue of Indifference.

His arms were also signs of a lordly penis which did not deign to grow erect beneath the blue cloth of the trousers. They suggested night—their amber color, their fur, their erotic mass (one evening, as he lay in bed, I ran my prick—without his daring to get angry—along his crossed arms, the way a blind man recognizes a face with his finger), and particularly the blue tattoo which made the first star appear in the sky. At the foot of the walls of the mosque, a legionnaire, leaning against the bent palm tree, had often waited for me at twilight in that same indifferent and sovereign posture. He seemed to be guarding an invisible treasure, and it now occurs to me that, despite our love, he was protecting his intact virginity. He was older than I. He was always first at our appointments in the parks of Meknes. With a vague look in his eyes—or was he turned inward on some clear vision? —he would stand there smoking a cigarette. Without his

moving an inch (he would just about mumble hello; he
never offered to shake hands), I would give him the
pleasure he desired and then adjust his clothes and leave
him. I would have loved him to squeeze me in his arms.
He was good looking, and though I have forgotten his
name, I remember that he claimed to be the son of La
Goulue.

The contemplation of Armand's arms that evening was,
I think, the one answer to all metaphysical anxieties.
Behind them Armand disappeared, destroyed, yet more
present and effective than his person could be, for he was
the animator of the blazon.

As for what actually happened, I don't quite remember,
except that he gave me two or three slaps, which it would
be impolite not to mention to you. He would not tolerate
my making him wait a second. Perhaps he feared that I
might completely disappear. For a few days I pretended
to look indulgently upon his quarrels with Robert, but I
suffered, out of love, resentment and rage. At present, I
would, perhaps, have resolved such anguish by an effort
to couple the two men I loved, one for his strength, the
other for his grace. A possible charity, now familiar to my
heart, might have made me try to achieve the happiness
not of two men, but of those more perfect qualities which
they betoken: strength and beauty. If they cannot be
united within me, may my kindness, by itself, achieve,
outside me, a knot of perfection—of love. I had some
savings. Without letting anyone know, neither Stilitano,
Armand, Sylvia nor Robert, I took the train and went
back to France.

In the Maubeuge forests, I realized that the country
which was so hard for me to leave, the enveloping region
for which I felt a sudden nostalgia as I crossed the last
frontier, was Armand's radiant kindness, and that it was

made up of all the elements, seen inside out, which composed his cruelty.

Unless there should occur an event of such gravity that my literary art, in the face of it, would be imbecilic and I should need a new language to master this new misfortune, this is my last book. I am waiting for heaven to fall across the corner of my face. Saintliness means turning pain to good account. It means forcing the devil to be God. It means obtaining the recognition of evil. For five years I have been writing books: I can say that I have done so with pleasure, but I have finished. Through writing I have attained what I was seeking. What will guide me, as something learned, is not what I have lived, but the tone in which I tell of it. Not the anecdotes, but the work of art. Not my life, but the interpretation of it. It is what language offers me to evoke it, to talk about it, render it. To achieve my legend. I know what I want. I know where I'm going. As for the chapters which follow (I have already said that a great number of them have been lost), I am delivering them in bulk.

(By legend I do not mean the more or less decorative notion which the public that knows my name will have of me, but rather the identity of my future life with the most audacious notion which I and others, after this account, may form of it. It remains to specify whether the fulfillment of my legend consists of the boldest possible criminal existence.)

In the street—I'm so afraid of being recognized by a policeman—I know how to withdraw into myself. Since my quintessence has taken refuge in the deepest, most secret retreat (a place in the depths of my body where I stay awake, or keep watch in the form of a tiny flame), I no longer fear anything. I am rash enough to think that

my body is free of all distinguishing signs, that it looks
empty, impossible to identify, since everything about me
has quite abandoned my image, my gaze, my fingers,
whose nervous tics vanish into thin air, and that the
inspectors also see that what is walking beside them on
the sidewalk is a mere shell, emptied of its man. But if I
walk along a quiet street, the flame grows, spreads to my
limbs, rises to my image and colors it with my likeness.

I accumulate rash acts: getting into stolen cars, walking
in front of stores where I have operated, showing obviously fake papers. I have the feeling that in a short time
everything is bound to break wide open. My rash acts are
serious matters and I know that airy-winged catastrophe
will emerge from a very, very slight mistake.[1] But while
I hope for misfortune as an act of grace, it is well for me
to plunge fully into the usual ways of the world. I want
to fulfill myself in the rarest of destinies. I have only a
dim notion of what it will be. I want it to have not a
graceful curve, slightly bent toward evening, but a hitherto unseen beauty, beautiful because of the danger which
works away at it, overwhelms it, undermines it. Oh let
me be only utter beauty! I shall go quickly or slowly, but
I shall dare what must be dared. I shall destroy appearances, the casings will burn away and one evening I shall
appear there, in the palm of your hand, quiet and pure,

---

[1] But what will prevent my destruction? Speaking of catastrophe,
I cannot help recalling a dream: a locomotive was pursuing me. I
was running along the tracks. I heard the machine puffing at my
heels. I left the rails and ran into the countryside. The locomotive
cruelly pursued me, but gently and politely it stopped in front of a
small, fragile wooden fence which I recognized as one of the fences
which closed off a meadow belonging to my foster parents and
where, as a child, I used to lead the cows to pasture. In telling a
friend about this dream, I said, ". . . the train stopped at the fence
of my childhood. . . ."

like a glass statuette. You will see me. Round about me
there will be nothing left.

By the gravity of the means and the splendor of the
materials which the poet used to draw near to men, I
measure the distance that separated him from them. The
depth of my abjection forced him to perform this convict's labor. But my abjection was his despair. And despair
was strength itself—and at the same time the matter for
putting an end to it. But if the work is of great beauty,
requiring the vigor of the deepest despair, the poet had
to love men to undertake such an effort. And he had to
succeed. It is right for men to shun a profound work if it
is the cry of a man monstrously engulfed within himself.

By the gravity of the means I require to thrust you
from me, measure the tenderness I feel for you. Judge
to what degree I love you from the barricades I erect in
my life and work (since the work of art should be only
the proof of my saintliness, not only must this saintliness
be real so that it may fecundate the work, but also that
I may brace myself, on a work already strong with saintliness, for a greater effort toward an unknown destina-
tion) so that your breath—I am corruptible to an extreme
—may not rot me. My tenderness is of fragile stuff. And
the breath of men would disturb the methods for seeking
a new paradise. I shall impose a candid vision of evil,
even though I lose my life, my honor and my glory in
this quest.

Creating is not a somewhat frivolous game. The creator
has committed himself to the fearful adventure of taking
upon himself, to the very end, the perils risked by his
creatures. We cannot suppose a creation that does not
spring from love. How can a man place before himself

something as strong as himself which he will have to
scorn or hate? But the creator will then charge himself
with the weight of his characters' sins. Jesus became man.
He expiated. Later, like God, after creating men, He
delivered them from their sins: He was whipped, spat
upon, mocked, nailed. That is the meaning of the expression: "He suffers in his flesh." Let us ignore the theologians. "Taking upon Himself the sins of the world" means
exactly this: experiencing potentially and in their effects
all sins; it means having subscribed to evil. Every creator
must thus shoulder—the expression seems feeble—must
make his own, to the point of knowing it to be his substance, circulating in his arteries, the evil given by him,
which his heroes choose freely. We wish to regard this as
one of the many uses of the generous myth of Creation
and Redemption. Though the creator grants his characters free will, self-determination, he hopes, deep down in
his heart, that they will choose Good. Every lover does
likewise, hoping to be loved for his own sake.

I wish for a moment to focus attention on the reality
of supreme happiness in despair: when one is suddenly
alone, confronting one's sudden ruin, when one witnesses
the irremediable destruction of one's work and self. I
would give all the wealth of this world—indeed it must
be given—to experience the desperate—and secret—state
which no one knows I know. Hitler, alone, in the cellar
of his palace, during the last minutes of the defeat of
Germany, surely experienced that moment of pure light—
fragile and solid lucidity—the awareness of his fall.

My pride has been colored with the crimson of my
shame.

Though saintliness is my goal, I cannot tell what it is.
My point of departure is the word itself, which indicates

the state closest to moral perfection. Of which I know nothing, save that without it my life would be vain. Unable to give a definition of saintliness—no more than I can of beauty—I want at every moment to create it, that is, to act so that everything I do may lead me to it, though it is unknown to me, so that at every moment I may be guided by a will to saintliness until I am so luminous that people will say, "He is a saint," or, more likely, "He was a saint." I am being led to it by a constant groping. No method exists. It is only obscurely and with no other proofs than the certainty of achieving saintliness that I make the gestures leading me to it. Possibly it may be won by a mathematical discipline, but I fear it would be a facile, well-mannered saintliness, with familiar features, in short, academic. But this is to achieve a mere semblance. Starting from the elementary principles of morality and religion, the saint arrives at his goal if he sheds them. Like beauty—and poetry, with which I merge it—saintliness is individual. Its expression is original. However, it seems to me that its sole basis is renunciation. I therefore also associate it with freedom. But I wish to be a saint chiefly because the word indicates the loftiest human attitude, and I shall do everything to succeed. I shall use my pride and sacrifice it therein.

Tragedy is a joyous moment. Feelings of joy will be conveyed by smiles, by a lightness of the whole body, and of the face. The hero is unaware of the seriousness of a tragic theme. Though he may catch a glimpse of it, he must not see it. Indifference is native to him. In popular dance halls there are sober young men, indifferent to the music which they seem to be leading rather than following. Others joyously strew among prostitutes the syphilis which they have reaped from one of them. With the decaying of their splendid bodies, foretold by wax figures

in fair booths, they go off calmly, with a smile on their
lips. If it be to death that he goes—a necessary end—
unless it be to happiness—he does so as if to the most
perfect, therefore most happy, self-fulfillment. He goes
off with joyous heart. The hero cannot sulk at a heroic
death. He is a hero only because of that death. It is the
condition so bitterly sought by creatures without glory;
itself is glory; it is (this death and the accumulation of
the apparent misfortunes leading to it) the crowning of
a predisposed life, but, above all, the gaze of our own
image in an ideal mirror which shows us as eternally
resplendent (until the dying away of the light which will
bear our name).

His temple bled. Two soldiers had just fought for some
long forgotten reason, and it was the younger who fell,
his temple smashed by the iron fist of the other, who
watched the blood flow and become a tuft of primroses.
The flowering spread rapidly. It reached the face, which
was soon covered with thousands of those compact flowers, sweet and violet as the wine vomited by soldiers.
Finally, the entire body of the young man lying in the
dust was a bank of flowers whose primroses grew big
enough to be daisies through which the wind blew. Only
one arm remained visible and moved, but the wind stirred
all the grasses. Soon all the victor could see was a single
hand making a clumsy sign of farewell and hopeless
friendship. Eventually the hand disappeared, caught in
the flowering compost. The wind died down slowly, regretfully. The sky grew dark after having first lit up the
eye of the brutal, murderous young soldier. He did not
weep. He sat down on the flower bed that his friend had
become. The wind stirred a bit, but a bit less. The soldier
brushed his hair from his eyes and rested. He fell asleep.

The smile of tragedy is also governed by a kind of humor with respect to the Gods. The tragic hero delicately flouts his destiny. He fulfills it so nicely that this time the object is not man but the Gods.

Having already been convicted of theft, I can be convicted again without proof, merely upon a casual accusation, just on suspicion. The law then says that I am capable of the deed. I am in danger not only when I steal, but every moment of my life, because I have stolen. My life is clouded by a vague anxiety which both weighs upon it and lightens it. To preserve the limpidity and keenness of my gaze, my consciousness must be sensitive to every act so that I can quickly correct it and change its meaning. This anxiety keeps me on the alert. It gives me the surprised attitude of a deer caught in the clearing. But the anxiety, which is a kind of dizziness, also sweeps me along, makes my head buzz and lets me trip and fall in an element of darkness where I lie low if I hear the ground beneath the leaves resounding with a hoof.

I have been told that among the ancients Mercury was the god of thieves, who thus knew which power to invoke. But we have no one. It would seem logical to pray to the devil, but no thief would dare do so seriously. To make a compact with him would be to commit oneself too deeply. He is too opposed to God, Who, we know, is the final victor. A murderer himself would not dare pray to the devil.

In order to desert Lucien I shall organize an avalanche of catastrophes around the desertion so that he will seem to be swept away by them. He will be a straw in the midst of the tornado. Even if he learns that I have willed his misfortune and hates me, his hatred will not affect me. Remorse, or the expression of reproach in his lovely eyes, will have no power to move me, since I shall be in the center of a hopeless sadness. I shall lose things which are dearer to me than Lucien, and which are less dear than my scruples. Thus, I would readily kill Lucien to engulf my shame in great pomp. Alas, a religious fear turns me from murder and draws me to it. Murder might very well transform me into a priest, and the victim into God. In order to destroy the efficacy of murder, perhaps I need only reduce it to the extreme by the practical necessity of a criminal act. I can kill a man for a few million francs. The glamor of gold can combat that of murder.

Was the former boxer Ledoux dimly aware of this by any chance? He killed an accomplice in order to take revenge. He created a disorder in the dead man's room to make it seem like theft and, seeing a five-franc note lying on the table, Ledoux took it and explained to his astonished girl friend:

"I'm keeping it for luck. Nobody'll say I committed murder without getting something out of it."

I shall fortify my mind rather quickly. When you think about murder, the important thing is not to let your eyelids droop or your nostrils dilate tragically, but to examine the idea very leisurely, with your eyes staring wide open, drawn up by the wrinkling of your forehead as if in naïve astonishment, in wonder. No remorse, no prospective sorrow can then appear at the corner of your eyes, nor can precipices hollow out under your feet. A bantering smile, a pleasant tune whistled between my teeth, a bit of irony in the fingers curled around the cigarette would be enough to renew my contact with desolation in satanic solitude (unless I should be very fond of some murderer of whom that gesture, smile and pleasant tune are characteristic). After stealing B.R.'s ring:

"What if he learns about it?" I asked myself. "I sold it to someone he knows!"

I imagine, for he likes me, his grief and my shame. So I envisage the worst: death. His.

On the Boulevard Haussmann I saw the spot where certain burglars had been arrested. To flee from the store, one of them had tried to break through the glass. By accumulating damage around his arrest, he thought he was giving it an importance that would detract from the fact preceding it: the burglary. He was already trying to surround his person with a bloody, astonishing, intimidating pomp, in the midst of which he himself remained pitiful. The criminal magnifies his exploit. He wants to disappear amid great display, in an enormous setting brought on by destiny. At the same time, he decomposes his deed into rigid moments, he dismembers it.

"What care I for men's contempt when my blood . . ."

Could I, unblushingly, still admire handsome criminals if I did not know their nature? If they have had the misfortune to serve the beauty of many poems, I wish to help them. The utilization of crime by an artist is impious. Someone risks his life, his glory, only to be used as ornament for a dilettante. Even though the hero be imaginary, a living creature inspired him. I refuse to take delight in his sufferings if I have not yet shared them. I shall first incur the scorn of men, their judgment. I distrust the saintliness of Vincent de Paul. He should have been willing to commit the galley slave's crime instead of merely taking his place in irons.

The tone of this book is likely to scandalize the best spirits and not the worst. I am not trying to be scandalous. I am assembling these notes for a few young men. I should like them to consider these remarks as the recording of a highly delicate ascesis. The experience is painful and I have not yet completed it. That its point of departure may be a romantic reverie matters little if I work at it rigorously, as at a mathematical problem, if I derive from it materials useful for the elaboration of a work of art, or for the achievement of a moral perfection (for the destruction, perhaps, of these very materials, for their dissolution) approaching that saintliness which to me is still only the most beautiful word in human language.

Limited by the world, which I oppose, jagged by it, I shall be all the more handsome and sparkling as the angles which wound me and give me shape are more acute and the jagging more cruel.

Acts must be carried through to their completion. Whatever their point of departure, the end will be beautiful. It is because an action has not been completed that it is vile.

When I turned my head, my eyes were dazzled by the gray triangle formed by the two legs of the murderer, one of whose feet was resting on the low ledge of the wall while the other stood motionless in the dust of the yard. The two legs were clothed in rough, stiff, dreary homespun. I was dazzled a second time for, having taken from between my teeth the white rose whose stem I had been chewing, I carelessly tossed it away (in the face, perhaps, of a hoodlum) and it caught, with sly cunning, in the fly forming the severe angle of gray cloth. This simple gesture escaped the guard. It even escaped the other prisoners and the murderer, who felt only a very slight shock.

When he looked at his trousers, he blushed with shame. Did he think it was a gob of spit or the sign of a pleasure granted him by the mere fact of being for a moment beneath the brightest sky in France? In short, his face turned crimson and, with a casual gesture, trying to conceal the act, he plucked out the absurd rose, which was stealthily clinging by the tip of a thorn, and stuffed it into his pocket.

I call saintliness not a state, but the moral procedure that leads me to it. It is the ideal point of a morality which I cannot talk about since I do not see it. It withdraws when I approach it. I desire it and fear it. This procedure may appear stupid. Yet, though painful, it is joyful. It's a gay girl. It foolishly assumes the figure of a Carolina carried off in her skirts and screaming with happiness.

I make of sacrifice, rather than of solitude, the highest virtue. It is the creative virtue par excellence. There must be damnation in it. Will anyone be surprised when I claim that crime can help me ensure my moral vigor?

When might I finally leap into the heart of the image, be myself the light which carries it to your eyes? When might I be in the heart of poetry?

I run the risk of going astray by confounding saintliness with solitude. But am I not, by this sentence, running the risk of restoring to saintliness the Christian meaning which I want to remove from it?

This quest for transparency may be vain. If attained, it would be repose. Ceasing to be "I," ceasing to be "you," the subsisting smile is a uniform smile cast upon all things.

The very day of my arrival at the Santé Prison—for one of my many stays there—I was brought up before the warden: I had babbled at the reception desk about a friend I had recognized going by. I was given two weeks of solitary confinement and was taken away at once. Three days later an assistant slipped me some butts. They had been sent to me by the prisoners in the cell to which I had been assigned, though I hadn't yet set foot in it. When I got out of the hole, I thanked them. Guy said to me:

"We saw there was someone new. It was written on the door. Genet. We didn't know who Genet was. We didn't see you come. We realized you were in solitary, so we slipped you the butts."

Because my name was down in the register for that cell, its occupants already knew that they were involved in an unknown penalty incurred for an offense in which they had no part. Guy was the soul of the cell. This curly-headed and fair-skinned, buttery adolescent was its inflexible conscience, its rigor. Every time he addressed me I felt the meaning of that strange expression:

"A load in the loins from a tommy gun."

He was arrested by the police. The following dialogue took place in my presence:

"You're the one who did the job on the Rue de Flandre."

"No, it wasn't me."

"It was you. The concierge recognizes you."

"It's someone who looks like me."

"She says his name is Guy."

"It's someone who looks like me and has the same name."

"She recognizes your clothes."

"He looks like me, has the same name and the same clothes."

"He's got the same hair."

"He looks like me, has the same name, the same clothes and the same hair."

"They found your fingerprints."

"He looks like me, has the same name, the same clothes, the same hair and the same fingerprints."

"That can keep on."

"To the very end."

"It was you who did the job."

"No, it wasn't me."

A letter from him contained the following passage (I had just been locked up again in the Santé): "Dear Jean, I'm too broke to send you a package. I don't have any dough, but I'd like to tell you something that I hope you'll be glad to hear. For the first time I felt like jerking off while thinking about you and I came. At least you can be sure you've got a pal outside who's thinking about you. . . ."

I sometimes reproach him for his familiarity with Inspector Richardeau. I try to explain to him that a detective is even lower than a stool pigeon. Guy hardly listens to me. He takes short steps when he walks. He is aware, around his neck, of the loose collar of his very soft silk shirt and, on his shoulders, of his well-cut jacket. He holds his head high and looks straight ahead, in front of him, severely, at the sad, gray, gloomy Rue de Barbès, though a pimp, behind the curtains in a rooming house, can see him pass by.

"You're really right," he says. "They're all bastards."

A moment later, when I thought he was no longer thinking about what I had been saying (a certain time elapsed without his thinking, so that he might thereby better feel a silver chain weighing at his wrist, or his mind empty in order to make room for this idea) he muttered:

"Yes, but a cop's not the same thing."

"Oh? You think so?"

Despite my arguments, which aimed at merging the cop and the stool pigeon, and at proving the former

more blameworthy, I felt as Guy did, though I did not
admit it to him, that it wasn't the same thing. I secretly
love, yes, I love the police. I wouldn't tell him how excited I used to be in Marseille whenever I walked by
the policemen's canteen on Belzunce Square. The interior
was full of Marseille cops, in uniform and in plainclothes.
The canteen fascinated me. They were snakes coiled up
and rubbing against each other in a familiarity untrou-
bled—and perhaps furthered—by abjectness.

Guy walked along impassively. Did he know that the
pattern of his mouth was too flabby? It gave his face a
childlike prettiness. Though naturally blond, his hair was
dyed dark. He wanted to pass as a Corsican—after a
while he started believing he really was one—and I suspected that he liked make-up.

"They're after me," he said.

A thief's activity is a succession of cramped though
blazing gestures. Coming from a scorched interior, each
gesture is painful and pitiful. It is only after a theft, and
thanks to literature, that the thief chants his gesture. His
success chants within his body a hymn which his mouth
later repeats. His failure enchants his distress. To my
smile and my shrug, Guy replied:

"I look too young. You have to look like a man with
the other guys."

I admired his utterly unbending will. He told me that
one of his bursts of laughter would betray him. I felt the
same pity for him as I would for a lion that was made
by its trainer to walk a tight rope.

Concerning Armand, of whom I speak little (modesty
prevents me, as does perhaps the difficulty of telling who
he was and what he meant to me, from giving an exact
notion of the value of his moral authority), his kindness
was, I think, a sort of element in which my secret (un-
avowable) qualities found their justification.

It was after I had left him, after I had put the frontier between him and me, that I felt this. He seemed to me intelligent. That is, he had dared, not unconsciously, to depart from moral rules, with the deceptive ease of men who are unaware of them. In fact, he had done so at the cost of a mighty effort, with the certainty of losing a priceless treasure, though with the further certainty of creating another, more precious than the one he had lost.

One evening, in a bar, we learned that a gang of international crooks had surrendered to the police—"like cowards, without a fight," as the Belgian papers put it—and everyone was commenting upon their behavior.

"They didn't have guts," said Robert. "Don't you agree?"

Stilitano didn't answer. He was afraid of discussing fear or boldness in my presence.

"You're not answering. Don't you agree? They claim they pulled off big jobs, bank robberies, train robberies, and then they give themselves up to the cops like good little boys. They could have defended themselves to the last bullet. At any rate, they're done for, since they're going to be extradited. France wants them. They'll get theirs. I'd have . . ."

"Stop shooting your mouth off!"

Armand's anger was sudden. He was glaring indignantly.

Robert replied, more humbly:

"Why, don't you agree with me?"

"When I was your age, I'd done more jobs than you and still I never talked about men, especially those who'd been nabbed. All that's left for them now is the trial. You're not big enough to judge."

This explanatory tone made Robert a bit bolder. He dared answer:

"Still and all, they got cold feet. If they did all they're said to have done. . . ."

"You lousy little bastard, it's just because they did all they're said to have done that they got cold feet, as you say. Do you know what they wanted? Eh, do you? Well, I'll tell you. The moment they saw it was all up, they wanted to give themselves a treat that they never in their lives had time for: getting cold feet. You get it? It was a treat for them to be able to surrender to the police. It gave them a rest."

Stilitano didn't bat an eyelash. I thought I could tell by his wry smile that he was familiar with the meaning of Armand's answer. Not in that assertive, heroic, insolent form, but in a more diffuse style. Robert didn't answer. He didn't understand the explanation at all, except that it had just placed him slightly outside the circle of the three of us.

I would have discovered this justification by myself, though later on. Armand's kindness consisted of allowing me to feel at ease in it. He understood everything. (I mean that he had solved my problems.) Not that I am suggesting that the explanation he dared give of the gangsters' surrender was valid in their case, but it was so for me—had it been a question of justifying my surrender in such circumstances. His kindness also consisted of his transforming into a revel, into a solemn and ridiculous display, a contemptible desertion of duty. Armand's concern was rehabilitation. Not of others or of himself, but of moral wretchedness. He conferred upon it the attributes which are the expression of the pleasures of the official world.

I am far from having his stature, his muscles and their fur, but there are days when I look at myself in a mirror and seem to see in my face something of his severe kindness. Then I feel proud of myself and of my ponderous, pushed-in mug. I don't know in what pauper's grave he lies buried, or whether he's still up and about, strolling around with his strong, supple body. He is the only one whose real name I want to transcribe. To betray him even so little would be too much. When he got up from his chair, he reigned over the world. Had he been slapped, physically insulted, he would not have flinched. He would have remained intact, just as great. He filled out all the space in our bed with his legs open in a wide, obtuse angle, where I would find only a small space to curl up. I slept in the shadow of his meat, which would sometimes fall over my eyes, and, upon awakening, I would sometimes find my forehead adorned with a massive and curious brown horn. When he awoke, his foot would push me out of bed, not brutally but with an imperious pressure. He wouldn't speak. He smoked while I prepared the coffee and toast of this Tabernacle where knowledge rested —and where it was distilled.

One evening, we learned in the course of a distasteful conversation that Armand used to go from Marseille to Brussels, from town to town, from café to café, making lace-paper cutouts in front of the customers in order to earn money enough to eat. The docker who told us that didn't joke about it. He spoke very simply and straightforwardly about the doilies and fancy handkerchiefs, the delicate linen work produced with a pair of scissors and folded paper.

"I've seen Armand at it. I've seen him do his act," he said.

The idea of my calm, hulking master doing woman's work moved me. No ridicule could touch him. I don't know which prison he had been in, whether he had been released or had escaped, but what I did learn about him pointed to that school of all delicacies: the shores of the Maroni River in Guiana or the penitentiaries of France.

As he listened to the docker, Stilitano smiled maliciously. I feared lest he try to wound Armand: I was right. The machine-made lace which he palmed off on pious ladies was a sign of nobility. It indicated Stilitano's

superiority over Armand. Yet I dared not beg him not to
mention the matter. To show such moral elegance toward
a crony would have revealed within me, in my heart,
weird landscapes, so softly lighted that a flick of the
thumb would have ruffled them. I pretended to be indifferent.

"You learn something new every day," said Stilitano.
"There's nothing wrong with that."

"That's what I say. One gets along however one can."

No doubt, to reassure myself, to bolster my insecurity,
I had to assume that my lovers were wrought of tough
matter. Here I was learning that the one who impressed
me most was composed of human woes. Today the memory which recurs to me most often is that of Armand,
whom I never saw in that occupation, approaching tables
in restaurants and cutting out—in Venetian point—his
paper lace. Perhaps it was then that he discovered, without anyone's help, the elegance, not of what is called
manners, but of the *manifold* play of attitudes. Whether
out of laziness, or because he wanted to humble me, or
because he felt a need for a ceremonial to enhance his
person, he required that I light his cigarette in my mouth
and then put it into his. I wasn't even supposed to wait
for his desire to manifest itself, but to anticipate it. I did
this in the beginning, but, being a smoker myself, in
order to do things more quickly and not make any waste
motions, I put two cigarettes into my mouth, lit them,
and then handed one to Armand. He brutally forbade this
procedure, which he considered inelegant. As before, I
had to take one cigarette from the pack, light it, put it
into his mouth and then take another for myself.

Since going into mourning means first submitting to a
sorrow from which I shall escape, for I transform it into
the strength necessary for departing from conventional
morality, I cannot steal flowers and lay them on the

grave of someone who was dear to me. Stealing defines a moral attitude which cannot be achieved without effort; it is a heroic act. Sorrow at the loss of a beloved person reveals to us our bonds with mankind. It requires of the survivor that he observe, above all, a strict dignity. So much so that our concern about this dignity will make us steal flowers if we cannot buy them. This act was the result of desperation at being unable to carry out the customary formality of farewell to the dead. Guy came to see me to tell me how Maurice B. had just been shot down.

"We need some wreaths."

"Why?"

"For the funeral."

His speech was clipped. He was afraid that if he lengthened the syllables his whole soul might droop. And perhaps he thought it was not a time for tears and wailing. What wreaths was he talking about, what funeral, what ceremony?

"The burial. We need flowers."

"Do you have any dough?"

"Not a penny. We'll take up a collection."

"Where?"

"Not in church, of course. Among our pals. In the bars."

"Everyone's broke."

It was not a burial for a dead man that Guy was demanding, but, more important, that the pomp of the world be accorded his hoodlum friend who had been shot down by a cop. He wished to weave for the humblest the richest of floral mantles. To honor the friend, but above all to glorify those who are the most wretched by employing the means used by those who regard them as such and are even responsible for their being so.

"Doesn't it make you sore to know that cops who get killed get first-class funerals?"

"Does that bother you?"

"Doesn't it you? And when they bury judges, the whole court walks behind."

Guy was excited. He was lit up with indignation. He was generous and without restraint.

"Nobody's got any dough."

"Got to find some."

"Go swipe some flowers with his pals."

"You're crazy!"

He spoke in a hollow voice, ashamedly, perhaps regretfully. A madman can pay homage to his dead with astonishing funerals. He can and must invent rites. Guy already had the pathetic attitude of a dog shitting. It squeezes, its gaze is fixed, its four paws are close together beneath its arched body; and it trembles, from head to reeking turd. I remember my shame, in addition to my surprise at witnessing so useless a gesture, when one Sunday, at the cemetery, my foster mother, after looking about her, tore a clump of marigolds from an unknown and quite fresh grave and replanted them on the grave of her daughter. Stealing flowers anywhere to cover the coffin of a loved one is a gesture—Guy was aware of this—which does not gratify the thief. No humor is tolerated in such a situation.

"Well, what are you going to do?"

"I'm going to rob, but fast. A stick-up."

"Have anything in mind?"

"No."

"Well?"

At night, with two friends, he pilfered some flowers from the Montparnasse Cemetery. They went over the wall on the Rue Froidevaux, near the urinal. It was, so Guy told me later, a lark. Perhaps, as always when he committed a burglary, he took a crap. At night, if it's dark, he lets down his pants, usually behind the main entrance, or at the bottom of the stairway, in the yard.

This familiar act restores his assurance. He knows that in French slang a turd is known as a "watchman."

"I'm going to post a watchman," he says. We then go up more calmly. The place is less strange to us.

They went looking for roses with a flashlight. It seems they were hardly able to distinguish them from the foliage. A joyous intoxication made them steal, run and joke among the monuments. "You can't imagine what it was like," he said to me. The women were given the job of weaving the wreaths and making the bouquets. It was their men who made the nicest ones.

In the morning everything was wilted. They threw the flowers into the garbage, and the concierge must have wondered what kind of orgy had taken place that night in rooms where no bouquet ever entered, except, occasionally, an orchid. Most of the pimps did not dare attend so poor a funeral. Their dignity, their insolence, required worldly solemnity. They sent their women. Guy went. When he came back, he told me how sad it had been.

"We looked ratty! It's too bad you didn't come. There were only whores and tramps."

"Oh! you know, I see them every day."

"It's not that, Jean. It was so that someone would answer when the mutes asked for the family. I felt ashamed."

(When I was in the Mettray Reformatory, I was ordered to attend the burial of a youngster who had died in the infirmary. We accompanied him to the little cemetery of the reformatory. The grave diggers were children. After they lowered the coffin, I swear that, if anyone had asked, as they do in the city, for "the family," I would have stepped forward, tiny in my mourning.)

Guy stretched a bit; then he smiled.

"Why were you ashamed?"

"It was too crummy. A pauper's funeral."

"We sure got tight. We drank all night long. I'm glad to be back. At least I'll be able to take off my shoes."

When I was young, I wanted to rob churches. Later on, I experienced the joy of removing rugs, vases and sometimes paintings. In M . . ., G . . . didn't notice the beauty of the laces. When I told him that the surplices and altar cloths were very valuable, his broad forehead wrinkled. He wanted a figure. In the sacristy I muttered, "I don't know."

"How much, fifty?"

I didn't answer. I was in a hurry to get out of that room where priests get dressed, undressed, button their cassocks and knot their albs.

"Well, how much? Fifty?"

His impatience got the better of me and I answered, "More, a hundred thousand."

G . . .'s fingers trembled, they got heavy. They were damaging the cloths and the angular laces. As for his face, which was in a bad light and was excited with greed, I don't know whether to call it hideous or splendid. We calmed down along the banks of the Loire. We sat down in the grass while waiting for the first freight train.

"You're lucky to know about those things. I'd have left the lace behind."

It was then that Guy suggested that he and I work more closely together. "All you'll have to do is let me know about the jobs and I'll do them," he said. I refused. In burglary, you cannot carry out what someone else has conceived. The one who does a job must be clever enough to allow for the unforeseen in a given project. All Guy saw in a thief's life was the splendid and brilliant, the scarlet and golden. To me, it is somber and subterranean. I see it as hazardous and perilous, just as he does, but with a peril different from breaking one's bones by falling from a roof or being pursued in a car and smashing up against a wall or being killed by a 6/35 bullet. I'm not cut out for those lordly spectacles in which you disguise yourself as a cardinal in order to steal the relics of a basilica, in which you take an airplane to outwit a rival gang. I don't care for such luxurious games.

When he stole a car, Guy would manage to drive off just when the owner appeared. He got a kick out of seeing the face of the man watching his car docilely going off with the thief. It was a treat for him. He would burst into an enormous, metallic laugh, a bit forced and artificial, and would drive off like the wind. It was rare for me not to suffer at the sight of the victim and his stupefaction, at his rage and shame.

When I got out of prison we met at a pimps' bar. At *La Villa*. The walls were covered with autographed photos, pictures of dance-hall hostesses, but chiefly of boxers and dancers. He had no money. He himself had just escaped.

"Don't you know of something to do?"

"I do."

I told him in a low voice that I intended to rob a friend who owned some *objets d'art* that could be sold abroad. (I had just written a novel entitled *Our Lady of the Flowers*, and its publication had won me some wealthy connections.)

"Do we have to beat the guy up?"

"No need. Listen."

I took a deep breath, I leaned over to him. I changed the position of my hands on the rail of the bar. I shifted my leg. In short, I was getting ready to jump.

"Listen. We could send the guy to jail for a week."

I can't exactly say that Guy's features moved, yet his whole physiognomy was transformed. Perhaps his face hardened and grew motionless. I was suddenly frightened

by the harshness of his blue stare. Guy bent his head over
a little to the side, without ceasing to look me in the face,
or, more exactly, to stare at me, to hold me fast. I suddenly realized the meaning of the expression: "I'm going
to pin you down!" His voice, when it answered, was low
and even, but leveled at my stomach. It shot from his
mouth with the rigidity of a column, of a ram. Its con-
strained monotone made it seem compressed, compact.

"What? Are *you* saying that, Jean? Are *you* telling me
to send a guy to the jug?"

My face remained as motionless as his, just as hard,
though more deliberately tense. To the gathering clouds
in his stormy face I opposed mine of stone, to his thunder
and lightning, my angles and points. Knowing that his
rigor would burst and give way to contempt, I faced it,
for a moment. I quickly thought of how I could save
myself without his suspecting that I had planned a vile
act. I had to have time on my side. I said nothing. I was
letting his amazement and contempt pour over me.

"I can bump a guy off. I'll beat your guy up and rob
him, if you want me to. All you've got to do is say so.
Well, tell me, Jean, you want me to bump him off?"

I stared at him and still said nothing. I assumed that
my face was impenetrable. Guy must have seen how tense
I was, must have thought I was at the point of an extremely dramatic moment, in fact, of checked will, of a
decision which astonished him enough to move him. But
I feared his severity, the more so since never had he
seemed to me more virile than that evening. As he sat
on the high stool, his strong, thick, rough hand rested on
his muscular thighs which bulged beneath the smooth
cloth of his trousers. In some indefinable element of
meanness, stupidity, virility, elegance, pomp and viscosity
which he had in common with them, he was the equal of

the pimps around us, and their friend. He dwarfed me. "They" dwarfed me.

"You realize what it is to send a guy there? We've both had it. Go on, we can't do that."

Had he himself betrayed and ratted on his friends? His intimacy with a police inspector had made me fear—and hope—that he was a squealer. Made me fear, for I was running the risk of being reported, made me fear further, for he would be preceding me in betrayal. Made me hope, for I would have a companion and support in vileness. I understood the loneliness and despair of the traveler who has lost his shadow. I remained silent and stared at him. My face was motionless. The time was not ripe for me to change tactics. "Let him flounder about in astonishment until he loses footing." However, I still could not help seeing his contempt, for he said, "But Jean, I regard you as my brother. Do you realize? If any guy, a guy from here, wanted to have you thrown in, I'd attend to him. And you, you tell me . . ."

He lowered his voice, for some of the pimps had drawn near. (Some of the whores too might have overheard us. The bar was packed.) My stare tried to get harder. My eyebrows knitted. I was chewing away at the inside of my lips and was still saying nothing.

"You know, if it had been anyone else but you who suggested that . . ."

In spite of the shell of will with which I was protecting myself, I was humiliated by the brotherly gentleness of his contempt. His words and the tone of his voice left me undecided. Was he or was he not a stool pigeon? I'll never know for sure. If he was, he might just as well have been despising me for an act that he himself would have been ready to commit. It was also possible that it repelled him to have me as a companion in vileness because I was less glamorous to him, less sparkling, than some other thief whom he would have accepted, I was aware of his contempt. He could easily have dissolved me, like rock-candy. Nevertheless, I had to preserve my rigidity without being too dead-set.

"But Jean, if it had been somebody else, I'd have knocked hell out of him. I don't know why I let you say it. No, I don't know why."

"All right, that'll do."

He lifted his head. His jaw dropped. My tone had surprised him.

"Huh?"

"I said that'll do."

I bent over closer and put my hand on his shoulder.

"Guy, my boy, you're all right. I was worried when I saw you so chummy with R. (the detective). I'm letting you know it. I had the jitters. I was scared you might have become a squealer."

"You're crazy. I was in cahoots with him, first because he's as crooked as they come, and then so that he'd get me some papers. He's a guy whose palm you can grease."

"All right, now I feel sure, but yesterday, when I saw you having a drink together, I swear it didn't look so good. Because I've never been able to stomach squealers. Do you realize that suspecting you was like being hit on the head? Thinking that you might've turned stool pigeon?"

I wasn't as careful as he had been when reproaching me, and I raised my voice a bit. The relief of no longer being despised restored my breath, made me bounce too high and too fast. I was carried away by the joy of emerging from contempt, also of being saved from a brawl which would have set all the pimps in the bar against me, and of dominating Guy in turn with an authority conferred upon me by my mastery of language.

A kind of self-pity enabled me to speak effortlessly with inflections that moved me, for I had lost, though I landed on my feet. My toughness and intransigence had shown a crack, and the matter of the burglary (which neither of us dared bring up again) was definitely out of the question. We were surrounded by very precious pimps. They were speaking loudly, though very politely. Guy talked to me about his woman. I answered as best I could. I was veiled in a great sadness which was pierced at times by the lightning of my rage. Loneliness (whose image might be a kind of fog or vapor emanating from me), torn apart for a moment by hope, closed over me again. I might have had a comrade in freedom (for I'm quite sure that Guy is an informer); he was denied me. I would have loved to betray with him. For I want to be able to love my accomplices. This extraordinarily lonely situation (of being a thief) must not leave me walled in with a graceless boy. During the act, fear, which is the matter (or rather the light) of which I am almost completely composed, may cause me to collapse in the arms of my accomplice. I do not think that I choose him to be big and strong so as to be protected in case of failure, but rather that an overpowering fear may throw me into the hollow of his arms, or thighs, those havens of delight. This choice, which often enables fear to give way so completely and turn to tenderness, is a dangerous one. I abandon myself too readily to those beautiful shoulders, to that back, those hips. Guy was tempting when we worked.

Guy came to see me in a state of terror. It was impossible to tell whether his panic was real. His face was pitiful that morning. He was more at ease in the corridors and on the stairways of the Santé with pimps whose prestige lay in the dressing gowns they put on to visit their lawyers. Did the security of prison give him a lighter bearing?

"I'm in the shit and I've got to get out of it. Show me a job to do so I can beat it to the sticks."

He persisted in living among pimps, and I recognized in his nervousness and in the fatal movement of his head the tragic tone of faggots and actresses. "Is it possible," I wondered, "that the 'men' in Montmartre are fooled by him?"

"You come blowing in without notice. I don't have jobs on tap."

"Anything, Jean. I'll bump someone off if I have to. I'm ready to drill a guy for just a little loose cash. Yesterday I nearly landed myself in the jug."

"That doesn't get me anywhere," I said smilingly.

"You don't realize. You live in a swell hotel."

He irritated me. What have I to fear of smart hotels, chandeliers, reception rooms, the friendship of men? Comfort may give me a certain boldness of spirit. And with my spirit already far off, I am sure that my body will follow.

Suddenly he looked at me and smiled.

"The gentleman receives me downstairs. Can't we go to your room? Is your kid there?"

"He is."

"Is he nice? Who is he?"

"You'll see."

When he had left us, I asked Lucien what he thought of Guy. Secretly I would have been happy had they loved each other.

"He's a queer-looking bird, with his hat. Gets himself up like a scarecrow."

And he immediately spoke of something else. Neither Guy's tattoos, nor his adventures, nor his boldness would have interested Lucien. All he saw was how ridiculously he was dressed. The elegance of hoodlums may be questioned by a man of taste. But they deck themselves out during the day, and especially at night, with as much care as a tart, and there is something touching about their seriousness. They want to shine. Egoism reduces their personalities to their bodies alone (the poverty of the home of a pimp who is better dressed than a prince). But what did this quest for elegance, almost always achieved, reveal about Guy? What does it mean when the details are that ridiculous little hat, that tight jacket, the pocket handkerchief? Nevertheless, though he lacked Lucien's childlike grace and discreet manner, his passionate temperament, warmer heart and more ardent, burning life still made him dear to me. He was capable, as he said, of committing murder, of ruining himself in an evening for a friend or for himself alone. He had guts. And perhaps all of Lucien's qualities do not have, in my eyes, the value of a single virtue of this ridiculous hoodlum.

My love for Lucien and my happiness in this love are beginning to induce me to recognize a morality more in conformity with your world. Not that I am more generous (I have always been that), but the rigid goal toward which I am moving, fierce as the iron shaft at the top of a glacier, so desirable, so dear to my pride and my despair, seems to me too great a threat to my love. Lucien is not aware that I am headed for infernal regions. I still like to go where he takes me. How much more intoxicating, to the point of dizziness, falling and vomiting, would be the love I bear him if Lucien were a thief and a traitor. But would he love me then? Do I not owe his tenderness and his delicate merging within me to his submission to the moral order? Yet I would like to bind myself to some iron monster, smiling though icy, who kills, steals, and delivers father and mother to the judges. I also desire this so as to be myself the monstrous exception which a monster, delegate of God, allows himself to be, and which satisfies my pride as well as my taste for moral solitude. Lucien's love fills me with joy, but if I go to Montmartre, where I lived for a long time, what I see there, and the squalor I sense, quicken my heartbeat, strain my body and soul. I know, better than anyone else, that there is nothing in disreputable neighborhoods; they are without mystery; yet they remain mysterious to me. To live again in such places so as to be in harmony with the underworld would require an impossible return to the past, for the pale-faced corner hoodlums have pale souls, and the most dreadful pimps are distressingly stupid. But at night, when Lucien has gone back to his room, I curl up fearfully under the sheets and want to feel against me the tougher, more dangerous and more tender body of a thief. I am planning for the near future a perilous outlaw's life in the most dissolute quarters of the most dissolute of ports. I shall abandon Lucien. Let him become whatever he can. I shall go away. I shall go to Barcelona, to Rio or elsewhere, but first to prison. I shall find Sek Gorgui there. The big negro will stretch out gently on my back. Gently, but with sure precision, his tool will enter me. It will not tremble. It will not jerk hastily like mine. That presence within me will so fill me that I shall forget to come. The negro, vaster than night, will cover me over. All his muscles will be conscious, however, of being the tributaries of a virility converging at that hard and violently charged point, his whole body quivering with goodness and self-interest, which exist only for my happiness. We shall be motionless. He will drive deeper. A kind of sleep will lay the negro out on my shoulders; I shall be crushed by his darkness, which will gradually dilute me. With my mouth open, I shall know he is in a torpor, held in that dark axis by his steel pivot. I shall be giddy. I shall have no further responsi-

bility. I shall gaze over the world with the clear gaze that
the eagle imparted to Ganymede.

The more I love Lucien, the more I lose my taste for
theft and thieves. I am glad that I love him, but a great
sadness, fragile as a shadow and heavy as the negro,
spreads over my entire life, just barely rests upon it,
grazes it and crushes it, enters my open mouth: it is
regret for my legend. My love for Lucien acquaints me
with the loathsome sweetness of nostalgia. I can abandon
him by leaving France. I would then have to merge him
in my hatred of my country. But the charming child has
the eyes, hair, chest and legs of the ideal hoodlums whom
I adore and whom I would feel I was abandoning in
abandoning him. His charm saves him.

This evening, as I was running my fingers through his
curls, he said to me dreamily:

"I'd really like to see my kid."

Instead of making him seem hard, these words softened
him. (Once when his ship put ashore, he made a girl
pregnant.) My eyes rest upon him more gravely, more
tenderly too. I gaze at this proud-faced, smiling youngster with his keen, gentle, roguish eyes as if he were a
young wife. The wound I inflict upon this male compels
me to a sudden respect, to new delicacies, and the dull,
remote and almost narrow wound makes him languid,
like the memory of the pains of childbirth. He smiles at
me. More happiness fills me. I feel that my responsibility
has become greater, as if—literally—heaven had just
blessed our union. But will he, later on, with his girl
friends, be able to forget what he was for me? What will
it do to his soul? What ache never to be cured? Will
he have, in this respect, the indifference of Guy, the same
smile accompanying the shrug with which he shakes off,
letting it drift in the wake of his swift walk, that dull and

heavy pain, the melancholy of the wounded male? Will a certain casualness toward all things be born of it?

Roger had often instructed me not to let him stay too long with the queers he had just picked up. We took the following precautions: as soon as he left the can or clump of bushes where he had just been accosted by a queer, Stilitano or I would follow him at a distance to his room— generally in a small hotel run by a former whore in a filthy, smelly street. I (or Stilitano) would wait a few minutes and then go up.

"But not too late, you understand, Jean? Not too late."

"He's got to have time at least to undress."

"Naturally. But make it fast. I'll always drop a little paper ball in front of the door."

He repeated this instruction so often and so urgently that I finally asked him:

"But why do you want me to be so quick? All you have to do is wait for me."

"You're crazy. I'm scared."

"Scared of what?"

"Don't you understand? I'll tell you. I get hot pants right away. If the guy has time just to grope me, I'm a goner. I can't be sure I won't let him."

"Well, let him."

"Don't be dumb. If I get hot pants I might let him stick me. And I mustn't. But don't tell Stil."

Lost in the forest, led by the ogre, Roger would drop little white pebbles; locked in by a wicked jailer, he signaled his presence by a message left in front of the door. One evening I foolishly amused myself with his fear. Stilitano and I waited a long time before going up. When we found the door, we opened it with infinite caution. A tiny entrance, narrow as an alcove, separated us from the room. With a red carnation between his toes, Roger, naked on the bed, was charming an old gentleman who was undressing slowly in front of the mirror. In the same mirror we saw the following spectacle: Roger skillfully raised his foot to his mouth and snatched the flower. After sniffing at it for a few seconds, he ran it over his armpit. The old man was all excited. He was getting mixed up in his buttons and suspenders, lusting after the splendid body so cleverly covered with flowers. Roger was smiling.

"You're my rambling rosebush," said the old man.

Just at that moment, Roger, wriggling under the rough sheets, turned on his belly and, planting the flower in his behind and crushing his cheek on the pillow, laughed out:

"And you're going to ramble over this one!"

"Here I come," said Stilitano who started moving.

He was calm. His modesty: I have already told how it adorned his occasionally almost bestial violence; however, realizing as I do now that this modesty is not an object, a kind of violet on his brow and hands (it did not give color to Stilitano), not a feeling but a constraint, the friction preventing the supple and noble play of the different parts of an inner mechanism, the refusal of an organism to participate in another's joy, the opposite of freedom, realizing that perhaps what elicited it was asinine cowardice, I hesitate to call it an adornment, not that I mean that foolishness cannot at times lend to gestures—whether through hesitation or brusqueness—a gracefulness which they would not otherwise have nor that this gracefulness is not an embellishment, but rather that Stilitano's modesty was a paleness; what brought it on was not the rush of blurred ideas, of mysterious waves; it was not a confusion carrying him off to new realms, unknown and yet foreshadowed; I would have thought him charming were he hesitating at the threshold of a world, the revelation of which made his cheeks quiver;

it was not love but the ebbing of life itself, leaving room only for the frightful void of imbecility. I am expressing as best I can, from the mere coloring of his epidermis, the attitude of Stilitano. This doesn't tell very much. But perhaps in this way I do manage to sketch the withered character contained in my memory. This time his modesty hampered neither his voice nor his walk. He strode to the bed threateningly. Prompter than prompt, Roger jumped up and made a dash for his clothes.

"You bitch!"

"What right have you . . ."

The old gentleman was trembling. He was like a figure in a cartoon showing an adulterer caught in the act. His back was turned to the mirror which reflected his narrow shoulders and yellowish bald head. The scene was lit up by a pink light.

"You shut up. And you," he said to Roger, "hurry up and get dressed."

Standing near his pile of clothes, the innocent Roger was still holding the flower. With the same innocence, he was still erect. His penis finally softened and gradually drooped, though he kept smiling. While Roger was putting on his clothes, Stilitano ordered the old man to hand over his valuables.

"You son of a bitch. You think you're going to screw my brother?"

"But I didn't . . ."

"Shut up. Hand over your dough."

"How much do you want?"

"All of it."

Stilitano spoke so coldly that the old man stopped insisting.

"Your watch."

"But . . ."

"I'll count to ten."

This remark, reminiscent of my childhood games, made Stilitano seem to me even more cruel. I felt as if he were playing, and that he might go very far since it was only a game. The old man undid his chain, from which the watch was hanging, and went forward to hand it to Stilitano, who took it.

"Your rings."

"My rings . . ."

The old fellow was now stammering. Stilitano, standing motionless in the middle of the room, pointed sharply to the objects he wanted. I was a little behind him, to his left, with my hands in my pockets, and I watched him in the mirror. I was sure that he would thus be, as he faced the trembling old queer, unnaturally cruel. In fact, when the old man told him that his knotted joints prevented him from removing the rings, he ordered me to turn on the water.

"Soap your fingers."

Very conscientiously the old man soaped his hands. He tried to take off his two gold signet rings, but without success. Desperate, and fearing that his fingers might be cut off, he gave his hand to Stilitano with the timid anxiety of a bride at the foot of the altar. Was I about to witness the hulking Stilitano's marriage (at a later time my emotion was almost visible when Monsieur B. took me through his park and stopped before a bed of carnations: "It's one of my finest flower beds," he said) to a trembling old man with wet hands? With a delicacy and precision that I thought contained a strange irony, Stilitano tried to pull the rings off. With one hand the old man held up the other which was being worked on. Perhaps he felt a secret joy in being stripped by a handsome male. (I note the exclamation of a poor hunchback from whom René had just snatched his last thousand-franc note without letting him have a moment's pleasure:

"It's too bad I haven't received my paycheck. I'd have given you all of it!" And René's answer: "Don't be shy about sending it to me.") As one does with babies, or as I myself would soap his one hand, Stilitano carefully soaped the old man's. Both of them were now calm. They were collaborating in a simple, matter-of-fact operation. Stilitano was taking it easy; he was being patient. I was sure that his rubbing would wear the finger down to the desired thinness. Finally he stepped back and, without losing his temper, slapped the old man twice. He gave it up as a bad job.

I've drawn out this account for two reasons. First, it enables me to relive a scene of inexhaustible charm. To Roger's immodesty in offering himself to old men are added some of the elements which are at the source of my lyricism. First, the flowers accompanying the robustness of a twenty-year-old boy. Without ceasing to smile, the boy exposed his manly valor—and submitted it—to the trembling desire of an old man. Stilitano's brutality in destroying this encounter and his cruelty in carrying out his destruction to the very end. Lastly, in that room, in front of a mirror, where all that youthfulness, despite appearances, was in league and in love—it seemed to me —with itself; and the presence of a half-dressed, ridiculous, *pitiful* old man, whose stricken self, just because I happen to call it *pitiful,* symbolized me.

The second reason: I think that all is not lost for me since Stilitano thus admitted that he loved Roger, and Roger, that he loved the other. They had recognized each other in shame.

Whether Lucien enters my room on tiptoe or comes rushing in, I always feel the same emotion. The imaginary tortures I invented for him cause me sharper pain than if he had suffered them. Am I to believe that my idea of him is dearer to me than the child who is its pretext and support? Nor can I bear to see his physical person in pain either. At times, in certain moments of tenderness, his gaze is slightly veiled; his lashes come together; a kind of mist clouds his eyes. His mouth then takes on a poignant smile. The horror of this face, for it does fill me with horror, means a plunge into my love for the child. I drown in it as in water. I see myself drowning. Death thrusts me into it. When he is asleep, I must not gaze down on it too often; I would lose my strength. And the strength I draw from it is meant only to ruin me and save him. The love I bear him is composed of a thousand signs of a deep tenderness which comes from him, from the depths of his heart, signs which, seemingly emitted by chance, are caught only by me.

At times I say to myself that if we stole together he might love me more. He would accept his lover's caprices.

"Anguish would shatter his shame," I tell myself, "the crust of shame."

I then reply to myself that his love, addressed to an equal, would have more violence, our life would be more tumultuous, but his love would be none the stronger thereby. In order to spare him any pain of which I am the cause, I would rather kill him. Lucien, whom I have called elsewhere my ambassador on earth, binds me to mortals. My industry consists of serving—for him and by him—the order which denies the one to which I would devote all my care. I shall, however, strive to make of him a visible and mobile masterpiece. The danger lies in the elements he offers me: naïveté, insouciance, laziness, the artlessness of his mind, his human respect. So I shall have to make use of what I am unaccustomed to, but with it I want to arrive at a happy solution.

Had he offered me the contrary qualities, I would have worked on them with the same zeal toward an opposite though equally uncommon solution.

I said earlier that the only criterion of an act is its elegance. I am not contradicting myself in asserting my choice of betrayal. Betrayal may be a handsome, elegant gesture, compounded of nervous force and grace. I definitely reject the notion of nobility which favors a harmonious form and ignores a more hidden, almost invisible beauty, a beauty which would have to be revealed elsewhere than in objectionable acts and things. No one will misunderstand me if I write: "Betrayal is beautiful," or will be so cowardly as to think—to pretend to think—that I am talking about cases in which it is necessary and noble, when it makes for the realization of Good. I was talking of low betrayal. The kind that cannot be justified by any heroic excuse. The sneaky, cringing kind, elicited by the least noble of sentiments: envy, hatred (though a certain ethic dares class hatred among the noble sentiments), greed. It is enough that the betrayer be aware of his betrayal, that he will it, that he be able to break the bonds of love uniting him with mankind. Indispensable for achieving beauty: love. And cruelty shattering that love.

If he has courage—please understand—the guilty man decides to be what crime has made him. Finding a justification is easy; otherwise, how would he live? He draws it from his pride. (Note the extraordinary power of verbal creation that springs from pride, as from anger.) He wraps himself up in his shame out of pride, a word which designates the manifestation of the boldest freedom. Within his shame, in his own spittle, he envelops himself; he spins a silk which is his pride. This is not a natural garment. The guilty man has woven it to protect himself, woven it crimson to embellish himself. No pride without guilt. If pride is the boldest freedom—Lucifer crossing swords with God—if pride is the wondrous cloak wherein my guilt, of which it is woven, stands erect, I want to be guilty. Guilt makes for singularity (destroys confusion); and if the culprit has a hard heart (for it is not enough to have committed a crime; one must deserve it and deserve having committed it), he raises it upon a pedestal of solitude. Solitude is not given to me; I earn it. I am led to it by a concern for beauty. I want to define myself in it, delimit my contours, emerge from confusion, set myself in order.

My being a foundling entailed a lonely youth and childhood. Being a thief led me to believe in the singularity of thievery. I told myself that I was a monstrous exception. In fact, my taste and my activity as a thief were related to my homosexuality, emerged from what had already set me apart in an exceptional solitude. I was utterly astounded when I saw how prevalent theft was. I was deep in the very heart of banality. To emerge from it, I had only to glorify myself with my thief's destiny and to will it. This once provoked a flash of wit which amused some fools. Was I called a bad thief? As if it mattered! The word thief determines the man whose chief activity is theft. Specifies him by eliminating—while he is so named—everything else he is other than a thief. Simplifies him. The poetry lies in his full awareness of being a thief. It may be that the awareness of any other quality capable of becoming so essential as to name you is likewise poetry. Yet it is well that the awareness of my singularity be named by an asocial activity: theft.

No doubt, the culprit who is proud of what he is owes his singularity to society but he must already have had it for society to recognize it and make him guilty of it. I wanted to oppose society, but it had already condemned

me, punishing not so much the actual thief as the in-
domitable enemy whose lonely spirit it feared. But it contained the singularity which was to fight against it, which
was to be a thorn in its flesh, a remorse—an anxiety—a
wound from which flowed its blood, which it dared not
shed itself. If I cannot have the most brilliant destiny, I
want the most wretched, not for the purpose of a sterile
solitude, but in order to achieve something new with such
rare matter.

I ran into Guy one day, not in Montmartre nor on the
Champs-Elysées, but at the Saint-Ouen flea-market. He
was dirty, ragged, covered with filth. And alone, in a
group of purchasers poorer and dirtier than the trades-
men. He was trying to sell a pair of sheets, probably
stolen from a hotel room. (I have often burdened myself
with things that made my figure and gait look absurd:
books under my armpits which prevented my arms from
moving, sheets or blankets rolled around my waist which
made me seem stout, umbrellas against my legs, medals
in a sleeve.) He was a sorry sight. Java was with me. We
recognized each other at once.

"Is that you, Guy?"

I don't know what he read on my face; his became
frightful.

"All right, let me alone."

"Listen . . ."

The sheets were draped on his forearms, in the noble
manner in which dummies display cloth in store windows.
Bending his head slightly to the side as if to emphasize
his words, he said:

"Forget me."

"But . . ."

"Pal, forget me."

Shame and humiliation must have denied him the saliva for a longer sentence. Java and I continued on our way.

In order to discover within himself—by means of gestures which reject them or aim to destroy them—the charming burglars whose occupations, whose craft, delight me, Maurice B. invents, and applies, gadgets to foil them. His ingenuity proves his idiosyncrasy, and that secretly (perhaps unconsciously) he is pursuing within himself the quest for evil. His house bristles with cunning devices: a high-tension current runs through a sheet of metal on his window rail; he has installed an alarm system; there are complicated locks on his doors, and so on. He does not have much to protect, but in this way he remains in contact with the agile and crafty spirit of evildoers.

God: my inner tribunal.

Saintliness: union with God.

Saintliness will be when the tribunal ceases, that is, when the judge and judged merge.

A tribunal decides between good and evil. It pronounces sentence, it imposes punishment.

I shall cease to be the judge and the accused.

Young people in love exhaust themselves in the quest for erotic situations. The poorer the imagination that discovers them and the deeper the love that produces them, the more *curious* they seem to be. Roger used to crush grapes in his girl's cunt, and then they would divide them and eat them. Occasionally he would offer some to his friends, who were astonished at being offered such a strange preserve. He also smeared his prick with chocolate cream.

"My girl's got a sweet tooth," he used to say.

One of my other lovers adorns his bush with ribbons. Another once wove a tiny wreath of daisies for the tip of his friend's prick. A phallic cult is fervently celebrated in private, behind the curtain of buttoned flies. If a rich imagination, availing itself of the disturbance, should turn it to account, just imagine the revels—to which plants and animals will be invited—that will ensue and the spirituality that will emanate from them and hover about them! I arrange in Java's bush the feathers that escape at night from the crushed pillow. The word balls is a roundness in my mouth. I am aware that my gravity, when I invent this part of the body, becomes my most essential virtue. Just as the magician draws countless wonders from his hat, I can draw from them all the other virtues.

René asked me whether I knew any queers he could rob.

"Not your pals, naturally. Your pals are out."

I thought for a few minutes and finally hit upon Pierre W., at whose home Java had stayed for a few days.

Pierre W., an old queer (of fifty), bald and affected, who wore steel-rimmed glasses. Java, who had met him on the Riviera, said to me:

"He puts them on the dresser when he makes love." One day, just for the fun of it, I asked him whether he was fond of Pierre W.

"You love him, admit it."

"You're crazy. I don't love him. But he's a good pal."

"Do you admire him?"

"Well, yes. He fed me. He even sent me some dough."

He had told me this six months before.

I asked him:

"Isn't there anything to swipe at Pierre's?"

"Not much, you know. He's got a gold watch."

"Is that all?"

"He may have some money, but you'd have to look for it."

René wanted exact details. He got them from Java who even agreed to make an appointment with his former lover and lead him into a trap where René would rob him. When he left us, René said to me:

"Java's pretty lousy. You've got to be a real heel to do what he's doing. You know, I wouldn't dare."

A curious atmosphere, of mourning and storm, darkened the world: I loved Java, who loved me, and hatred set us against each other. We couldn't stand it any more, we hated each other. When this raging hatred appeared, I felt myself disappearing, I saw him disappearing.

"You're a son of a bitch!"

"And you're a little skunk!"

For the first time, he was resolute; he was in a rage; he wanted to kill me; he was hard with anger. Ceasing to be an appearance, he was an apparition. What I had been for him ceased to be, while there remained, in both of us, waiting and watching over our delirium, the certainty of a reconciliation, a certainty so deep that we wept when it took place.

Java's cowardice, slackness, vulgarity of manner and feeling, and his stupidity, do not prevent me from loving him. I add his pleasant disposition. Either the confrontation or the mixture of these elements, or their interpenetration, makes for a new quality—a kind of alloy—which has no name. I add his physical person, his bulky and somber body. To render this new quality, I must use the image of a crystalloid, of which each of the forementioned elements would be a facet. Java sparkles. His water—and his fires—are precisely the peculiar virtue which I call Java and which I love. To sum up: I love neither cowardice nor stupidity; I do not love Java *for* one or *for* the other of these qualities; but their meeting within him fascinates me.

It may surprise the reader that the union of such flabby qualities should produce the sharp edges of rock crystal; it may surprise him that I compare, not acts, but the moral expression of acts to attributes of the measurable world. I have said that I was fascinated. This word contains the idea of a sheaf—or rather of a luminous sheaf of beams,[1] like the sparkling of crystal. These sparkles are the result of a certain arrangement of surfaces. It is to these sparkles that I am comparing the new quality—virtue—achieved by slackness, cowardice, etc.

This virtue has no name, unless it be that of the one from whom it emanates. Having found an inflammable substance, these fires which issue from him set me ablaze. That is what love is. Having applied myself to the quest of what I compare within me to this substance, I achieve, by reflection, the absence of such qualities. Encountering them in Java dazzles me. He sparkles. I burn, for he burns me. As I hold up my pen for a brief meditation, the words which crowd into my mind suggest light and heat, by means of which we usually speak of love: dazzlement, rays, fire, beams, fascination, burning. However, Java's qualities—those which make up his fires—are icy. Each of them separately suggests an absence of temperament, of temperature.[2]

---

[1] Sheaf: *faisceau*; fascinated: *fasciné*.—Translator's note.

[2] Java's dream. Upon entering my room—for if he sleeps with his girl he comes to see me during the day—Java related his dream. But first, that the night before he had met a sailor in the subway.

"It's the first time I've ever turned around to look at a handsome guy," he said.

"Didn't you try to grope him?"

What I have just written does not, I know, render Java but gives the idea of a moment which he was in my presence. It is now, when he is abandoning me, that I explain, by means of an image, why I suffer. We have just had a brutal split which has been very painful to me. Java avoids me. His silence, his rapid kisses, his rapid visits—he comes on a bicycle—are a flight. Beneath the chestnut trees on the Champs-Elysées I told him how passionately I loved him. I have a good chance. What attaches me to him even more just when I am about to leave him is his emotion, his bewilderment in the face of my resolution, the brutality of this sudden break. He is overwhelmed. What I tell him—about us, and chiefly about him—makes both of us such poignant creatures that his eyes grow dim. He is sad. He grieves in silence and this grief haloes him with a poetry which makes him more attractive, for he is now gleaming in the mist. I grow more attached to him when I have to leave him.

His hand, which grabbed the cigarette I offered him, is too weak, too fine for his heavily muscled body. I stand up and kiss him and tell him that this kiss is the last.

"No, Jean, there'll be others," he says.

A few minutes later, thinking about this scene, I sud-

"You're crazy. But I got onto his train. If he'd suggested it, I think I'd have gone to bed with him."

Then he complacently described the sailor. Finally he related the dream he had had the night following this encounter. In the dream, he was a cabin boy on a sailing ship. Another sailor was pursuing him with a knife and finally caught him aloft, in the ropes. Java then fell on his knees before the raised knife and said:

"I'll count to three. If you're not a coward, kill me."

Hardly had he uttered the last word, when the entire scene vanished.

"Afterward," he said, "I saw an ass."

"And then?"

"I woke up."

denly felt certain that, without my having been clearly
aware of it at first, the fragility of his hand had just made
my decision final and irrevocable.

His fingers sticky with balls of mistletoe crushed on
New Year's Day. His hands full of sperm.

Our room is darkened by wet clothes drying on ropes
which zigzag from wall to wall. This washing—shirts,
underpants, handkerchiefs, socks, towels—softens the
bodies and souls of the two fellows who share the room.
We go to sleep fraternally. Though his palms, which have
been soaking a long time in soapy water, are softer, he
compensates by more violence in our love-making.

After our quarrel, in which I insulted him with a
cruelty that proved my tenderness, I accused him of being cowardly and letting himself be had out of weakness
and for too little money (he once assured me that he had
protected his ass with his spread fingers. "The old guy
thought he was screwing me, but it was only my hand.
I made believe I was sleeping. He shot into my fingers.")
We were in the same room, bumping into the hanging
laundry which was still damp. Suddenly I took his head
into my hands and smiled at him. Hope returned to him,
mounted from his heart to his mouth, which smiled. His
eyes filled with tears. Inside my fly my prick was present.
Presiding over this intimate reconciliation, it swelled up
with joyous blood. It wanted to be in on the festivity. I
tenderly laid Java's docile hand on the bump. He lowered
his head gently.

In every important city in France I know at least one
thief with whom I have worked—or, having known him
in prison, with whom I have made plans and preparations
for various jobs. I can count on their help if I am ever
alone in their cities. These fellows, scattered all over
France, and sometimes in foreign countries, are a comfort

to me, even though I may not see them often. I makes
me feel calm and glad to know they are alive, active and
handsome, lurking in the shadow. My little pocket
address book in which their names are scrawled is endowed with a comforting power. It has the same authority
as a prick. It is my treasure. I transcribe: Jean B. in Nice.
Met him one night in Albert Premier Park. He didn't
have the heart to knock me out and steal my money, but
he let me know about the Mont-Boron affair. René D.
in Orléans. Jacques L. and Martino, sailors who stayed in
Brest. I met them in the Bougen jail. We did some deals
together, peddling dope. Dédé in Cannes, a pimp. In
Lyons, some crooks, a negro and a fellow who runs a
brothel. In Marseille I know a good twenty. Gabriel B.
in Pau. And so on. I've said they were handsome. Not
with regular good looks, but with something else, made
up of power, despair and many other qualities, the mention of which involves comment: shame, shrewdness, laziness, resignation, contempt, boredom, courage, cowardice,
fear . . . It would mean a long list. These qualities are
inscribed on my friends' faces or bodies, where they overlap, jostle and oppose one another. That is why I say
that these men have souls. Added to the complicity which
unites us is a secret understanding, a kind of tenuous pact
which seems as though it could be easily broken, but which
I know how to protect, to handle with nimble fingers:
it is the memory of our nights of love, or sometimes of a
brief amorous conversation, or of groping each other with
the restrained smile and sigh of an anticipation of pleasure. They all kindly allowed me to recharge myself at
each of their asperities, as at terminals where a current
was polarized. I think they were all dimly aware that they
were thus heightening my courage, inflaming me, giving
me a will to work and enabling me to gather enough force
—emanating from them—to protect them. Nevertheless,

I am alone. The address book in my pocket is the written proof that I had such friends; but their lives are apparently as incoherent as mine, and I really know nothing about them. Perhaps most of them are in prison. Where are the others? If they are wandering about, by what chance shall I meet them, and what will each of us be? However, even were the antithesis of vile and noble to remain, I would be able to discern among them moments of pride and rigor, and to recognize them as the scattered elements of a severity which I wish to assemble within me so as to make of them a deliberate masterpiece.

Armand's physical appearance—seaman's build, bulky and weary, dull eyes, close-cropped hair, nose broken not by a man's fist but by having crashed against the glass walls which cut us off from your world—evokes for me now, though it might not have done so in the past, the prison of which he seems to me the most significant, the most illustrious representative. I was summoned to him, hastened toward him, and it is now, in my desperation, that I dare be engulfed within him. The maternal element I perceived in him was not feminine. Men sometimes hail each other as follows:

"Well, Old Gal?"

"Hi, you Hen!"

"Is that you, Wench?"

This usage belongs to the world of poverty and crime. Of punished crime, which bears upon itself—or within itself—the mark of a faded brand. (I speak of it as of a flower, preferably as of a lily, when the brand was the *fleur de lis.*) These salutations indicate the downfall of men who once were strong. Having been wounded, they can now bear the equivocal. They even desire it. The tenderness that makes them unbend is not femininity but the discovery of ambiguity. I think they are prepared to impregnate themselves, to lay and hatch their eggs, but without any blunting of their cruel male sting.

The humblest beggars say among themselves:

"How's *la Grinche* going?" or "How's *la Chine?*"[1] *La Guyane* (Guiana) is a feminine noun. Guiana contains all those males who are called tough. In addition, it is a tropical region, at the world's waistband, the most feverish of all—with gold fever—where fierce tribes are still hidden in the swamps of the jungle. Thither I go—for though it has disappeared, it is now the ideal region of misfortune and penitence toward which proceeds, not my physical person, but the person that watches over it—with mingled fear and sweet exhiliration. Each of the toughs who haunt it has remained virile—like those of *la Chine* and *la Grinche*—but his downfall teaches him the uselessness of proving that he has. Armand was a man, wearily so. He slept on his muscles, like heroes on their laurels. He rested in his strength, and on it. If, with his fist placed on the delicate nape of a boy's neck, he brutally rammed the head down on his prick, he did it with indifference, or because he had not forgotten the careless methods and ways of a world where he must have lived a long time, from which I thought he had returned. If he was kind, as I have said he was, it was that he might offer me a hospitality which was to fulfill utterly my most secret desires—those which I discover with the greatest pain, in both senses of the term—but which are the only ones that can make of me the finest of characters, that is, the one most identical with myself. I aspire to Guiana. No longer to that geographical place now depopulated and emasculated, but to the proximity, the promiscuity, not in space but in con-

---

[1] *La Grinche* (panhandling) and *la Chine* (ragpicking) are beggars' slang. The significance of the feminine gender of these nouns is developed in the course of the paragraph.—Translator's note.

sciousness, of the sublime models, of the great archetypes of misfortune. Guiana is kindly. The respiratory movement which makes it rise and fall in a slow, though heavy and regular rhythm, is governed by an atmosphere of kindness. The place seems to be most cruelly dry and arid, and yet here am I expressing it by a theme of kindness: it suggests and imposes the image of a maternal breast, charged, in like manner, with a reassuring power, from which rises a slightly nauseating odor, offering me a shameful peace. I call the Virgin Mother and Guiana the Comforters of the Afflicted.

Armand seemed to have the same evil characteristics. Yet when I think of him, no cruel images rise up, but rather very tender ones, precisely such as would express my love not for him but for you. When, as I have already mentioned, I left Belgium, hounded by a kind of remorse or shame, I kept thinking of him in the train, and, having no hope of ever seeing him again, I went in strange pursuit of his ghost: as the train increased the distance between us, I had to force myself to reduce the space and time separating us, to rush backward in thought more and more swiftly, while the idea of his kindness—the only thing able to console me for his loss—forced itself upon me, grew more precise, to such a point that when the train (it first went through a forest of firs, and perhaps the sudden discovery of a clear landscape, as a result of its brutal break with the kindly shade of the firs, prepared the idea of catastrophe), near Maubeuge, roared over a bridge, I felt that, were the bridge to give way and the train to be cut in two, just about to drop into the sudden precipice, this kindness alone, which already filled me to the point of governing my acts, would have been enough to join the broken sections, restore the bridge and save the train from catastrophe. When we had crossed the viaduct, I even wondered whether everything I have just mentioned had not actually occurred. The train continued along the tracks. The landscape of France put Belgium behind me.

Armand's kindness did not consist of doing good: the idea of Armand, as it sped away from its bony and muscular pretext, became a kind of vaporous element in which I took refuge, and so sweet was this refuge that from within it I addressed to the world messages of gratitude. I would have found there the justification of my love for Lucien, which Armand would have approved. Unlike Stilitano, he would have contained me with my charge of love and of everything which is to come of it. Armand absorbed me. His kindness, thus, was not one of the qualities recognized by ordinary morality, but rather something which, as I think about it, still stirs within me emotions from which issue images of peace. It is by means of language that I experience it.

Even when they are completely relaxed, Stilitano, Pilorge, Michaelis and all the pimps and hoodlums I have ever met stand erect, not severely but calmly, without any tenderness; even in voluptuousness, or when dancing, they remain alone, reflected within themselves, delicately mirrored in their virility and strength, which polish and limit them as meticulously as an oil bath, and their buxom girl friends, unperturbed by their ardent presence, are, at the same time, reflected within themselves, and remain themselves, isolated by their beauty alone. I would like to make a bouquet of those handsome boys, to enclose them in a sealed glass vase. Perhaps an irritation would then melt the invisible matter which isolates them; in the shadow of Armand, who contains them all, they might flower, bloom and offer me the revels which are the pride of my ideal Guiana.

Amazed that all but one of the Church sacraments (the very word is sumptuous) suggest solemnity, I shall give the sacrament of penitence its rightful place in the liturgical ceremonial. In my childhood, it was reduced to a shamefaced and shifty mumbling, carried on with a shadow behind the shutter of the confessional, to a few prayers quickly recited as I knelt on a chair; but today it unfolds in full earthly pomp: when it is not the brief walk to the scaffold, it is the elaboration of that expedition which takes to the sea and continues throughout life in a fabulous region. I do not dwell on Guiana's special characteristics, which make it appear, ultimately, somber and splendid; its nights, palms, suns and gold are to be found in abundance on altars. If I had to live—perhaps I shall, though the idea is untenable—in your world, which, nevertheless, does welcome me, it would be the death of me. At the present time, when, having won by sheer force, I have signed an apparent truce with you, I find myself in exile. I do not care to know whether I desire prison so as to expiate a crime of which I am unaware. My nostalgia is so great that I shall have to be taken to it. I feel sure that only in prison shall I be able to continue a life which was cut off when I entered it. Rid of preoccupations with glory and wealth, I shall perform with slow, scrupulous patience the painful gestures of the punished. Every day I shall do a job governed by a rule which has no other authority than that of emanating from an order which presents the penitentiary and creates it. I shall wear myself out. The men I find there will help me. I shall become as polished as they, as pumiced.

But I am speaking of a penal colony which has been abolished. Let me therefore restore it in secret and live there in spirit, as in spirit Christians suffer the Passion. The only passable road to it must go through Armand and continue through the Spain of beggars, of shameful and humiliated poverty.

As I write these notes, I am thirty-five years old. I want to spend my remaining years in glory's opposite.

Stilitano had more integrity than Armand. If I think of them, I compare Armand to the expanding universe (as I understand it). Instead of being defined and reduced to observable limits, Armand constantly changes form as I pursue him. On the other hand, Stilitano is already encircled. The differences in the nature of the lace in which they dealt is also significant. When Stilitano dared laugh at Armand's talent, the latter did not lose his temper. I believe he controlled his anger. I do not think that Silitano's remark wounded him. He calmly went on smoking his cigarette and then said:

"Maybe you think I'm a dope?"

"I didn't say that."

"I know."

He kept smoking, with an absent-minded look. I had just been made aware of one of the mortifications—no doubt there were many—which Armand had suffered. This mass of pride was not composed of only bold, or even honorable elements. His beauty, vigor, voice and guts had not always assured his triumph, since he had had to submit, like a poor wretch, to an apprenticeship in lace making, to what is ordinarily expected of children who are allowed no other material than paper.

"You wouldn't think it," said Robert who had both elbows on the table and was resting his head in his hands.

"Wouldn't think what?"

"Why, that you know how to do that."

His usual unmannerliness dared not directly confront the man with his poverty. Robert spoke hesitantly. Stilitano was smiling. He, more than anyone, must have been aware of Armand's pain. Like me, he feared and hoped for the question—which Robert, moreover, dared not formulate:

"Where did you learn how to do it?"

The approach of a docker left it hanging. He merely mentioned a time as he passed Armand: eleven o'clock.

The tunes of a player piano lightened the thick smoke in the bar. Armand answered:

"All right."

His face remained just as sad. Since there were few whores around, the general tone was cordial and simple. If a man got up from his chair, he did so in all simplicity.

It was later on, when I thought of his thick palms and fingers, that it occurred. to me that the lace paper they made must have been ugly. Armand was too clumsy for such work. Unless he learned it in prison. Convicts are amazingly skillful. Their criminal fingers sometimes create delicate and fragile masterpieces with matches, cardboard, bits of string, with anything on hand. The pride they feel has the quality of the material and of the masterpiece: it is fragile and humble. Visitors occasionally congratulate prisoners on an inkwell carved from a nutshell, the way one praises a monkey or a dog: with amazement at their clever tricks.

When the docker had gone off, Armand's face remained unchanged.

"If you think a guy can know how to do everything, it's because you're just a little dope!"

I am inventing the words he used, but I have not forgotten the tone of the voice which uttered them. That illustrious voice was growling between his teeth. The thunder roared as it struck, with a light finger, the most precious vocal cords in the world. Armand stood up, still smoking.

"Let's get going," he said.

"O.K. Let's go."

With these words he decided that we would all go home to sleep. Stilitano paid. Armand walked out with his favorite display of elegance, his hurried gait. He strode down the street with his usual ease. Though that evening he uttered none of the words, none of his usual expressions which made people think he was coarse. I think he was swallowing his vexation. He was walking swiftly with his head high. At his side was Stilitano, with his sleek irony. And Robert, with his young insolence. I, close by, was their meditating consciousness, containing them, containing the idea of them. It was cold. My burly friends felt chilly. Their hands, deep in their pockets, meeting at the downiest spot of the body, were tugging at their duck trousers which outlined their buttocks. No one spoke. As we approached the Rue du Sac, Stilitano shook hands with Robert and Armand and said:

"I'm going to check on Sylvia before I go home. Want to come along, Jean?"

I went with him. We stumbled along the cobblestones for a while without talking. Stilitano was smiling. Without looking at me, Stilitano said:

"You've become pretty chummy with Armand."

"That's right. Why?"

"Oh, nothing . . ."

"Why do you mention it?"

"No reason."

We continued walking, though away from the spot where Sylvia worked.

"Tell me . . ."

"What?"

"If I had dough, would you have guts enough to rob me?"

Out of swagger—knowing that my boldness was just a stock attitude—I answered yes.

"I would. Why not? If you had a big pile."

He laughed.

"What about Armand? Would you dare?"

"Why do you ask me that?"

"Answer me."

"What about you?"

"Me? Why not? If he's got a big pile. I rob a lot of
other people. There's no reason not to. What about you?
Answer me."

By the change of tense, a sudden present in place of a
dubitative conditional, I realized that we had just agreed
to rob Armand. And I knew that as a result of calculation
and modesty I had been acting cynical in telling Stilitano
that I would rob him. Such cruelty in our relations was
bound to blot out the cruelty of acts aimed at a friend
of ours. In fact, we had realized that something united
us. Our complicity was not due to self-interest. It was
born of friendship.

"It's dangerous," I answered.

"Not very."

I was staggered at the thought that Stilitano must have
set aside his friendship with Robert to suggest such a
thing to me. I would have kissed him with gratitude had
he not been screened by his smile. Then I wondered
whether he had asked Robert the same thing and whether
Robert had refused. Perhaps at that very moment Robert
was trying to establish between Armand and himself the
same intimate relationship that bound me to Stilitano.
But I felt certain that I had chosen my partner in this
dance.

Stilitano explained what he expected of me: that I was
to steal, before Armand had time to smuggle it into Holland and France, the stock of opium which he was to
receive from the sailors and machinists of a tramp steamer
flying the Brazilian flag, the *Aruntai*.

"Why the hell worry about Armand? You and I were
in Spain together."

Stilitano spoke of Spain as of a heroic theater. We
walked along in the freezing dampness.

"Don't kid yourself about Armand. When he can rob
a guy . . ."

I realized that I was not to protest. Since I did not have enough power to decree moral laws (of my own making) which I could impose, I had to use the customary pretense, to be willing to act as a lover of justice in order to excuse my crimes.

". . . he's not shy about it. You ought to hear the stories about him. Just ask some of the guys who used to know him."

"If he knows that I'm the one . . ."

"He won't know. You'll just have to tell me where he hid it. I'll go up to his room when he's out."

I attempted to save Armand and added:

"I can't imagine that he'll leave it in the room. He must have a bunk somewhere."

"Then you've got to find it. You're smart enough to manage."

Before Armand had granted me the esteem of which I have already spoken, I probably would not have betrayed him. The mere thought of it would have horrified me. So long as he had not given me his confidence, betraying him had no meaning: it meant simply obeying the basic rule which governed my life. But now I loved him. I recognized his omnipotence. And though he might not love me, he contained me. His moral authority was so absolute, so generous, that it made intellectual rebellion within him impossible. The only way I could prove my independence was by acting on the emotional level. The idea of betraying Armand set me aglow. I feared and loved him too much not to want to deceive and betray and rob him. I sensed the anxious pleasure that goes with sacrilege. If he were God (he had known pity), and had he been well pleased with me, it were sweet to deny him. And better still was the fact that Stilitano, who did not love me and whom I would never have betrayed, should be helping me. His sharp personality aptly suggested the image of a dagger piercing the heart. The strength of the devil and his power over us lie in his irony. His seductiveness may be only his detachment. The force with which Armand denied the rules proved his own power—and the power of the rules over him. Stilitano smiled at them. His smile dissolved me. It was bold enough to express itself on a face of great beauty.

We entered a bar, and Stilitano explained what I would have to do.

"Did you tell Robert about it?"

"You're crazy. It's just between us."

"And you think there'll be a lot of dough in it?"

"I'll say! He's a miser. He made a terrific pile in France."

Stilitano seemed to have been thinking the matter over for a long time. I could see him rising up from a nocturnal life that had been lived before my eyes but had remained secret. Behind his smile he watched and spied. As we left the bar, a beggar came up to us; he asked for a handout. Stilitano looked at him rather contemptuously.

"Do what we do, pal. If you want dough, take it."

"Tell me where to find it."

"There's some in my pocket, and if you want it, go look for it."

"That's what you say, but if you were . . ."

Stilitano refused to enter into a conversation which might have gone on and in which he himself might have weakened. He very cleverly knew how to cut it short so as to sharpen his rigor, to give the appearance of being divided in clear-cut sections.

"When we want it, we take it where it is," he said to me. "We're not getting into trouble for bums."

Was he aware that it was the right moment to give me a lesson in severity, or did he himself feel a need to take deeper root in selfishness? Stilitano said this in such a way—with a knowing casualness—that the advice took on, in the night and fog, the proportions of a slightly arrogant philosophical truth agreeable to my natural bent, which was inclined toward pity. I could recognize in this unnatural truth the value of an attitude capable of protecting me from myself.

"You're right," I said. "If we get nabbed, he won't be the one who goes to jail. Let him shift for himself, if he's got the guts to."

By this remark I was not only wounding the most precious—though concealed—period of my life; I was establishing myself in my diamond-like wealth, in the city of diamond cutters and in that night of self-centered solitude whose facets sparkled. We approached the place where Sylvia worked, but it was late; she had gone home.[1] (I noted that when it came to his girl, his irony disappeared. He spoke of her without tenderness but without a smile.) Since prostitution was not regulated in Belgium as it was in France, a pimp could live with his girl without any danger. Stilitano and I headed for his hotel. He stopped talking about our plans but, cleverly, recalled our life in Spain.

"You had a big crush on me at the time."

"What about now?"

"Now? Do you still have it?"

I think he wanted to be assured of my love and that I would desert Armand for him. It was three or four in the morning. We had come from a country where the light and noise are violent.

"Not like before."

---

[1] We left quickly, for it is a well-known sign that when the whores aren't on their beat the police are nearby. "When the whores aren't around, the cops are" is an underworld proverb.

"No kidding?"

We were still walking. He smiled and glanced at me sideways.

"What's the matter?"

His smile was frightful. My effort—as often, and especially since that time—to be stronger than I was, to overcome my natural disposition, to lie about it, had made me utter a remark which, though spoken calmly, was a provocation. I had to explain, in detail, this first proposition, which was laid down like the premises of a theorem. My new attitude had to follow from the explanation and not vice versa.

"Nothing's the matter."

"Well? You don't like me as much?"

"I don't love you."

I felt my pants getting hot. At that moment we were passing under one of the arches of the bridge over which the railroad goes. It was darker than elsewhere. Stilitano had stopped and had turned to look at me. He took a step forward. I held my ground. With his mouth almost on mine, he muttered:

"Jean, I'm glad you've got nerve."

There were a few seconds of silence. I was afraid he might draw his knife to kill me, and I don't think I would have defended myself. But he smiled.

"Light me a cigarette," he said.

I took one from his pocket, lit it, took a long drag, and put it between his lips, in the middle. With a neat flick of his tongue, Stilitano moved it to the right corner of his mouth and, still smiling, took a step forward, threatening to burn my face if I didn't back up. My hand, which was hanging in front of me, went right to his basket. It was hard. Stilitano smiled and looked me in the eyes. He must have easily been storing the smoke in his chest. He opened his mouth without even a whiff escaping. All that was visible was the element of cruelty in himself and his accessories. The tender and hazy were banished. Yet I had seen him, not long before, in a humiliating situation. The fairground attraction known as the Palace of Mirrors is a labyrinth partitioned with plates of glass, some silvered and some transparent. You pay and enter; the problem is to get out. You move about desperately, bumping into your own image or into a visitor cut off from you by a glass. The onlookers witness from the street the search for the invisible path. (The scene I am about to describe gave me the idea for a ballet called *'Adame Miroir*.) As I approached the booth, the only one on the fairground, there was such a big crowd watching it that I knew something unusual was going on. The people were laughing. I recognized Roger in the crowd. He was staring at the involved mirror system; his face was tragically tense. Before seeing him I knew that Stilitano, and he alone, was trapped, *visibly* at a loss, in the glass corridors. No one could hear him, but by his gestures and his mouth one could tell he was screaming with anger. He was looking at the crowd in a rage, and they were looking at him and laughing. The manager of the booth was indifferent. Situations of that kind are quite common. Stilitano was alone. Everyone had found the way out, except him. The universe became strangely overcast. The shadow which suddenly covered things and people was the shadow of my solitude in the face of this despair, for Stilitano, exhausted with yelling and bumping into the plate glass, had resigned himself to being the laughing-stock of the onlookers and simply squatted on the floor, indicating thereby that he refused to go on. I hesitated, not knowing whether to leave or to fight for him and demolish his crystal prison. I looked at Roger, without his seeing me. He was still staring at Stilitano. I approached him. His straight but soft hair, parted in the middle, fell down to the side of his cheeks and met at his mouth. His head resembled certain palm trees. His eyes were wet with tears.

If I am accused of using such theatrical props as fun fairs, prisons, flowers, sacrilegious pickings, stations, frontiers, opium, sailors, harbors, urinals, funerals, cheap hotel rooms, of creating mediocre melodramas and confusing poetry with cheap local color, what can I answer? I have said that I love outlaws who have no other beauty than that of their bodies. The aforementioned props are steeped in the violence of men, in their brutality. Women are not involved in them. They are animated by male gestures. The traveling fairs in the North are dedicated to big blond fellows. They alone haunt them. Their girls cling with difficulty to their arms. It was the girls who were laughing at Stilitano's mishap.

Roger made up his mind and went in. We thought he'd get lost in the mirrors. We saw his abrupt, slow twists and turns, his sure-footedness. He lowered his eyes in order to get his bearings by the floor, which was less hypocritical than the glass. Guided by his certainty, he reached Stilitano. We saw his lips muttering. Stilitano stood up and, gradually regaining his poise, emerged with Roger in a kind of apotheosis. They had not seen me. Laughing and free, they continued around the fairground. As for me, I went home, alone. Was it the image of the wounded Stilitano that was exciting me so? I knew he could hold in the smoke of an entire cigarette, the consuming of which was manifested only by the glowing embers. At each inhalation, his face would light up. I felt his penis beneath my lightly groping fingers.

"You like it?"

I didn't answer. What was the use? He knew that my swagger had just gone dead. He took his left hand from his pocket and, putting his arm around my shoulders, squeezed me against him while the cigarette guarded his mouth, protecting it from a kiss. Someone was coming along. I muttered very quickly:

"I love you."

We pulled apart. When I left him at the door of his hotel, he was sure I would give him full information about Armand.

I returned to my room and went to bed. Even when my lovers deceived or hated me, I was never able to hate them. Separated by a thin wall from Armand, who was jazzing Robert, I suffered at not being in the place of either one of them or at not being with them or at not being one of them. I envied them, but I felt no hatred. I went up the wooden staircase very carefully, for it was squeaky and rickety and almost all the partitions were wooden. I imagine that when Armand took off his belt that evening, he did not crack it like a whip. He must have been aware of his strong, manly sadness and probably intimated to Robert with silent gestures that he was to obey his pleasure. In my eyes, Armand further justified his power, which also issued from happiness, from abjection. The lace paper had the same fragile structure—hardly meant for your morality—as the gimmicks of beggars. It belonged to the realm of artifice. It was as fake as their wounds, stumps and blindness.

This book does not aim to be a work of art, an object detached from an author and from the world, pursuing in the sky its lonely flight. I could have told of my past life in another tone, in other words. I have made it sound heroic because I have within me what is needed to do so, lyricism. My concern for coherence makes it my duty to carry on my adventure in the *tone* of my book. It will have served to define the indications which my *past presents*; I have laid my finger, heavily and many times, on poverty and punished crime. It is toward these that I shall go. Not with the premeditated intention of finding them, in the manner of Catholic saints, but slowly, without trying to evade the fatigues and horrors of the venture.

But am I being clear? It is not a matter of applying a philosophy of unhappiness. Quite the contrary. The prison —let us name that place in both the world and the mind— toward which I go offers me more joys than your honors and festivals. Nevertheless, it is these which I shall seek. I aspire to your recognition, your consecration.

Heroized, my book, which has become my Genesis, contains—should contain—the commandments which I cannot transgress. If I am worthy of it, it will reserve for me the infamous glory of which it is the great master, for to what shall I refer if not to it? And, purely from the viewpoint of a more commonplace morality, would it not be logical for this book to draw my body on and lure me to prison? Not, may I point out, through some swift procedure governed by your principles, but by means of a fatality contained within it, which I have put there, and which, as I have intended, keeps me as witness, field of experimentation and living proof of its virtue and my responsibility.

I wish to speak of these prison festivals. The surrounding presence of wounded males is already a blessing that is granted me. However, I mention this in passing; other situations (the army, sport, etc.) can offer me a similar one. In the second volume of this *Journal*, which will be called *Morals Charge*, I intend to report, describe and comment upon the festivals of an inner prison that I discover within me after going through the region of myself which I have called Spain.